THE PLATED SPOON

AND OTHER TALES OF

SHERLOCK HOLMES

Edited by
LOREN D. ESTLEMAN

TYRUS
BOOKS

Published by TYRUS BOOKS
an imprint of F+W Media, Inc.
10151 Carver Road, Suite 200
Blue Ash, OH 45242. U.S.A.
www.tyrusbooks.com

ISBN 10: 1-4405-7450-2
ISBN 13: 978-1-4405-7450-4
eISBN 10: 1-4405-7451-0
eISBN 13: 978-1-4405-7451-1

Printed in the United States of America.

10 9 8 7 6 5 4 3 2 1

Cover design by Sylvia McArdle.
Cover images © sdmix/123RF; old-maps.co.uk.
Interior spot art © Archim Prill/123RF.

This book is available at quantity discounts for bulk purchases.
For information, please call 1-800-289-0963.

As always, this book is dedicated to the memory of Sir Arthur Conan Doyle; with additional thanks to Ormond G. Smith and John Russell Coryell, creators of Nick Carter, the American Sherlock Holmes, and to Frederick Van Rensselaer Dey, who wrote more Carter stories than any other author.

ALWAYS HOLMES

We seek him here, we seek him there,
Those Frenchies seek him everywhere.
Is he in heaven?—Is he in hell?
That demmed, elusive Pimpernel.

Thus, in the Baroness Orczy's timeless *The Scarlet Pimpernel*, does the foppish Percy Blakeney—altogether a more entertaining character than his alter ego, the swashbuckling Pimpernel—sum up the spectral character of the enemy of Republican France under the Terror. He is, it seems, ubiquitous, yet invisible.

The first adjective sums up another great figure of literature, while the second most certainly does not. Sherlock Holmes is, indeed, everywhere, and as obvious to all as the most minute clues were to him.

I've said elsewhere that Holmes shares a special place in our language with Frankenstein and Dr. Jekyll and Mr. Hyde, as a shortcut to explanation. People who have never read the classic novels written by Mary Shelley and Robert Louis Stevenson, and who have managed to avoid their innumerable adaptations to film and radio, know what it means to "create a Frankenstein," and recognize "a Jekyll and Hyde character" when they see one; likewise, people ignorant of the novels and stories of Sir Arthur Conan Doyle—and their innumerable adaptations to film and radio—are aware of what's intended when one party calls another "Sherlock." Depending upon the context, the second party has either been complimented upon his perspicacity or made the butt of withering sarcasm.

Slow to catch on in the beginning, the world's first consulting detective and his amanuensis, Dr. John H. Watson, clicked with their third outing, "A Scandal in Bohemia," assuring that brand-new enterprise known as *The Strand Magazine* six decades in the stalls and immortality in legend. From the moment Holmes laid eyes upon the cunning Irene Adler in the July 1891 issue until thirty-six years later, when he reasoned out the eccentric behavior of Sir Robert Norberton and his sister, Lady Beatrice Falder, in "The Adventure of Shoscombe Old Place," the detecting partners were a public fixture, having made the leap meanwhile from printed page to early motion-picture screen—and from the shadowy fluff of imagination to the solid marble of myth.

I speak not of the connoisseurs: the variegated buffs, scholars, and debaters who have flayed and reassembled Holmes and Watson in learned papers and at lecterns in both hemispheres, written straight-faced "obituaries" of them both, and attempted, with all the grim reasoning of a historian determined to clear the name of Richard III, to expunge the mystery from the good doctor's peripatetic battle wound ("Leg? Shoulder? Which was it, man?"). I speak instead of the greater population who can't walk a hundred yards in any direction without tripping over some reference to Holmes and Watson.

In their own time, their distinctive profiles hung from staples outside public-houses, decorated snuff boxes, sold candy, crackers, cigarettes, men's hosiery, razors, and root beer. Nearly a century before "product placement," the culture we now call Madison Avenue had jumped the gun by exploiting fiction to sell widgets. (The practice continues to this day: although just what Mycroft's kid brother has to do with housing development in the American suburbs is one for "Sherlock *Homes*.")

Where fame leads, satire follows. Holmes and Watson were swiftly lampooned by Conan Doyle's (perhaps) jealous colleagues. Maurice

Leblanc's "Holmlock Shears" (who bungles an attempt to nab master criminal Arsene Lupin) may have been the first, appearing even as eager readers awaited the next Holmes story by Conan Doyle, but it was by no means the last. Since then, we've had Schlock Homes, Solar Pons, Basil of Baker Street (a mouse cohabiting at 221B), and hundreds of others, including a gaggle of Doorlocks, Hemlocks, Sheerlucks, Hardlucks, Dumblucks—and six delirious minutes with Daffy Duck, complete with deerstalker and curve-stemmed pipe (with Porky Pig's Watson at his side), hot on the trail of the "Shropshire Slasher" in the Looney Tunes classic, "Deduce, You Say!" (Daffy was a latecomer: In 1924's *Sherlock, Jr.*, Buster Keaton stepped literally from the audience up onto the silent screen to usurp the role of his hero—sixty years before Jeff Daniels escorted Mia Farrow into *The Purple Rose of Cairo*.)

Other imitations have been less than forthcoming about their source. As deep a footprint as Dame Agatha Christie made in the development of the detective story, her short fiction featuring Hercule Poirot relies suspiciously upon the Doylean template: a gifted amateur detective rejecting all but the most outré problems to challenge his intellect, while his retired British military housemate records the circumstances for the reading public. But then, I've written elsewhere about the debt Holmes owed to Edgar Allan Poe's C. Auguste Dupin, so I point the finger with mercy.

I've been unable to determine just how Conan Doyle felt about all this apery, but by the time it reached crisis point, he'd gone sour on Holmes and declined to discuss him even in private. (When he finally relented, in an interview filmed shortly before his death in 1930, he spent much of his time denigrating Watson's intelligence; writers are not immune to the influence of bastardizations of their own work. Poirot's Captain Hastings, for instance, makes the good doctor look like Stephen Hawking.)

To call the original "pervasive" would be to state what must be obvious even to the bumbling Watson of silver-screen slander. Try to think of another figure, fictional or actual, from the Victorian period whose very name is as cutting-edge as this week's hip-hop slang: When it looked as if my *Sherlock Holmes vs. Dracula* might be adapted to film (with Pierce Brosnan and Alexander Gudunov suggested as the leads), I had to plead with the screenwriter to strike "No shit, Sherlock!" from the Count's dialogue.

The creators of *Elementary* and *Sherlock*, two currently popular TV series that bring our favorite detecting duo into the present century, were faced not only with the challenge of familiarizing Holmes with cell phones and DNA, but also of overcoming audience disbelief when characters learn his name and act as if they'd never heard it before; really, it's like the entire case of a western saying, "Wyatt *who?*" A society with no awareness of Sherlock Holmes borders on *The Twilight Zone*. (*The Godfather III* suffered from the same dichotomy, with characters inhabiting an alternate 1970s in which "I'll make him an offer he can't refuse" has not been hardwired into the culture.)

In this climate, it's difficult to picture Conan Doyle's own failed experiments in christening his most famous creation. Not for him, he said later, to be so blatant as to resort to "Hawk" or "Sharps." If the writer's scrawl on a surviving scrap of paper is to be accepted as evidence, literature's favorite duo would have been known—or more likely unknown—by names that resound like plug nickels. Fortunately—citing Conan Doyle again—he fondly recalled drubbing an opponent named Sherlock at cricket sometime in his past. Would Scarlett O'Hara be the vixen we remember had Margaret Mitchell stuck with "Pansy," and *The Great Gatsby* as haunting had F. Scott Fitzgerald insisted upon *Tremalchio in East Egg*? Holmes said it best: "There is nothing so important as trifles."

Ironically, we need not hear or read the name to recognize the man. The aquiline profile, the (non-canonical) fore-and-aft cap and curved-stem pipe, the magnifying glass held close to the face are sufficient. As much as we owe this image to illustrators and actors, the relationship with the character in the stories is deeply rooted; those who approach them with preconceived notions are rarely shocked or disappointed. Sir Laurence Olivier's performance in the classic film notwithstanding, ten readers of Emily Brontë's *Wuthering Heights* will come away with ten different pictures of Heathcliff; and don't let's get started on whether Johnny Weissmuller or Buster Crabbe was the best Tarzan, or was Sean Connery or Daniel Craig the James Bond that Ian Fleming intended. Fists have flown over less. But surely everyone in the civilized world (and most in the undeveloped one) could pick Sherlock Holmes out of a police lineup. We can't escape him, although why we should try is a mystery only he could clear up.

With apologies to Baroness Orczy and Percy Blakeney (and to the skills of the authors whose work follows this preface), I offer the following doggerel:

> *We see him here, we see him there,*
> *Our world sees him everywhere.*
> *He's in our blood; he's in our bones,*
> *that grand illusive Sherlock Holmes.*
> —LOREN D. ESTLEMAN

CONTENTS

THE ADVENTURE OF THE TWO COLLABORATORS

J.M. BARRIE

Sir Arthur Conan Doyle's opinion of the rash of Holmes pastiches that appeared in his lifetime is largely unknown, but he singled out his friend J.M. Barrie's "The Adventure of the Two Collaborators" as "the best of all the numerous parodies." Barrie, of course, was the author of Peter Pan, *a play whose hero is every bit as durable and iconic as Holmes himself, thanks to generations of children (and their parents). Considering the common practise of casting women as Pan onstage, Irene Adler's talent for cross-dressing seems to have fascinated both authors.*

In bringing to a close the adventures of my friend Sherlock Holmes I am perforce reminded that he never, save on the occasion which, as you will now hear, brought his singular career to an end, consented to act in any mystery which was concerned with persons who made a livelihood by their pen.

"I am not particular about the people I mix among for business purposes," he would say, "but at literary characters I draw the line."

We were in our rooms in Baker Street one evening. I was (I remember) by the centre table writing out "The Adventure of the Man Without a Cork Leg" (which had so puzzled the Royal Society and all the other scientific bodies of Europe), and Holmes was amusing himself with a little revolver practise. It was his custom of a summer evening to fire round my head, just shaving my face, until he had made a photograph of me on the opposite wall, and it is a slight proof of his skill that many of these portraits in pistol shots are considered admirable likenesses.

I happened to look out of the window, and, perceiving two gentlemen advancing rapidly along Baker Street, asked him who they were. He immediately lit his pipe, and, twisting himself on a chair into the figure 8, replied:

"They are two collaborators in comic opera, and their play has not been a triumph."

I sprang from my chair to the ceiling in amazement, and he then explained:

"My dear Watson, they are obviously men who follow some low calling. That much even you should be able to read in their faces. Those little pieces of blue paper which they fling angrily from them are Durrant's Press Notices. Of these they have obviously hundreds about their person (see how their pockets bulge). They would not dance on them if they were pleasant reading."

I again sprang to the ceiling (which is much dented), and shouted: "Amazing! but they may be mere authors."

"No," said Holmes, "for mere authors only get one press notice a week. Only criminals, dramatists, and actors get them by the hundred."

"Then they may be actors."

"No, actors would come in a carriage."

"Can you tell me anything else about them?"

"A great deal. From the mud on the boots of the tall one I perceive that he comes from South Norwood. The other is as obviously a Scotch author."

"How can you tell that?"

"He is carrying in his pocket a book called (I clearly see) *Auld Licht Something*. Would anyone but the author be likely to carry about a book with such a title?"

I had to confess that this was improbable.

It was now evident that the two men (if such they can be called) were seeking our lodgings. I have said (often) that my friend Holmes seldom gave way to emotion of any kind, but he now turned livid with passion. Presently this gave place to a strange look of triumph.

"Watson," he said, "that big fellow has for years taken the credit for my most remarkable doings, but at last I have him—at last!"

Up I went to the ceiling, and when I returned the strangers were in the room.

"I perceive, gentlemen," said Mr. Sherlock Holmes, "that you are at present afflicted by an extraordinary novelty."

The handsomer of our visitors asked in amazement how he knew this, but the big one only scowled.

"You forget that you wear a ring on your fourth finger," replied Mr. Holmes calmly.

I was about to jump to the ceiling when the big brute interposed.

"That tommy-rot is all very well for the public, Holmes," said he, "but you can drop it before me. And, Watson, if you go up to the ceiling again I shall make you stay there."

Here I observed a curious phenomenon. My friend Sherlock Holmes *shrank*. He became small before my eyes. I looked longingly at the ceiling, but dared not.

"Let us cut the first four pages," said the big man, "and proceed to business. I want to know why—"

"Allow me," said Mr. Holmes, with some of his old courage. "You want to know why the public does not go to your opera."

"Exactly," said the other ironically, "as you perceive by my shirt stud." He added more gravely, "And as you can only find out in one way I must insist on your witnessing an entire performance of the piece."

It was an anxious moment for me. I shuddered, for I knew that if Holmes went I should have to go with him. But my friend had a heart of gold.

"Never," he cried fiercely, "I will do anything for you save that."

"Your continued existence depends on it," said the big man menacingly.

"I would rather melt into air," replied Holmes, proudly taking another chair. "But I can tell you why the public don't go to your piece without sitting the thing out myself."

"Why?"

"Because," replied Holmes calmly, "they prefer to stay away."

A dead silence followed that extraordinary remark. For a moment the two intruders gazed with awe upon the man who had unraveled their mystery so wonderfully. Then drawing their knives—

Holmes grew less and less, until nothing was left save a ring of smoke, which slowly circled to the ceiling.

The last words of great men are often noteworthy. These were the last words of Sherlock Holmes: "Fool, fool! I have kept you in luxury for years. By my help you have ridden extensively in cabs, where no author was ever seen before. *Henceforth you will ride in buses!*"

The brute sunk into a chair aghast.

The other author did not turn a hair.

To A. Conan Doyle, from his friend
—J.M. Barrie

THE SURGEON'S KIT

ELLERY QUEEN

he name Ellery Queen is nearly as well known—and fully synonymous with detective fiction—as is Sir Arthur Conan Doyle. "The Surgeon's Kit," excerpted from A Study in Terror, *pays fitting tribute to the deductive acrobatics and clever Holmes-Watson banter of the originals. The novel was adapted from the 1965 film of the same title, but for those familiar only with the movie, Queen provides a surprise: an alternative solution, uncovered by detective Ellery himself.*

"You are quite right, Watson. The Ripper may well be a woman." It was a crisp morning in the fall of the year 1888. I was no longer residing permanently at No. 221B Baker Street. Having married, and thus become weighted with the responsibility of providing for a wife—a most delightful responsibility—I had gone into practice. Thus, the intimate relationship with my friend Mr. Sherlock Holmes had dwindled to occasional encounters.

On Holmes's side, these consisted of what he mistakenly termed "impositions upon your hospitality" when he required my services as an assistant or a confidant. "You have such a patient ear, my dear fellow," he would say, a preamble that always brought me pleasure, because it meant that I might again be privileged to share in the danger and excitement of another chase. Thus, the thread of my friendship with the great detective remained intact.

My wife, the most understanding of women, accepted this situation like Griselda. Those who have been so constant to my inadequate accounts of Mr. Sherlock Holmes's cases of detection will remember her as Mary Morstan, whom I providentially met while I was involved, with Holmes, in the case I have entitled "The Sign of Four." As devoted a wife as any man could boast, she had patiently left me to my own devices on too many long evenings whilst I perused my notes on Holmes's old cases.

One morning at breakfast, Mary said, "This letter is from Aunt Agatha."

I laid down my newspaper. "From Cornwall?"

"Yes, the poor dear. Spinsterhood has made her life a lonely one. Now her doctor has ordered her to bed."

"Nothing serious, I trust."

"She gave no such indication. But she is in her late seventies, and one never knows."

"Is she completely alone?"

"No. She has Beth, my old nanny, with her, and a man to tend the premises."

"A visit from her favourite niece would certainly do her more good than all the medicine in the world."

"The letter does include an invitation—a plea, really—but I hesitated . . . ."

"I think you should go, Mary. A fortnight in Cornwall would benefit you also. You have been a little pale lately." This statement of mine was entirely sincere; but another thought, a far darker one, coloured it. I venture to say that, upon that morning in 1888, every responsible man in London would have sent his wife or sister or sweetheart away, had the opportunity presented itself. This, for a single, all-encompassing reason. Jack the Ripper prowled the night-streets and dark alleys of the city.

Although our quiet home in Paddington was distant in many ways from the Whitechapel haunts of the maniac, who could be certain? Logic went by the boards where the dreadful monster was concerned.

Mary was thoughtfully folding the envelope. "I don't like to leave you here alone, John."

"I assure you I'll be quite all right."

"But a change would do you good, too, and there seems to be a lull in your practise."

"Are you suggesting that I accompany you?"

Mary laughed. "Good heavens, no! Cornwall would bore you to tears. Rather that you pack a bag and visit your friend Sherlock Holmes. You have a standing invitation at Baker Street, as well I know." I am afraid my objections were feeble. Her suggestion was a most alluring one. So, with Mary off to Cornwall and arrangements relative to my practise quickly made, the transition was achieved; to Holmes's satisfaction, I flatter myself in saying, as well as to my own.

It was surprising how easily we fell into the well-remembered routine.

Even though I knew I could never again be satisfied with the old life, my renewed proximity to Holmes was delightful. Which brings me, in somewhat circuitous fashion, back to Holmes's remark out of the blue. He went on, "The possibility of a female monster cannot by any means be ignored."

It was the same old cryptic business, and I must confess that I was slightly annoyed. "Holmes! In the name of all that's holy, I gave no indication whatever that such a thought was passing through my mind."

Holmes smiled, enjoying the game. "Ah, but confess, Watson. It was."

"Very well. But—"

"And you are quite wrong in saying that you gave no indication of your trend of thought."

"But I was sitting here quietly—motionless, in fact!—reading my *Times*."

"Your eyes and your head were far from motionless, Watson. As you read, your eyes were trained on the extreme left-hand column of the newspaper, which contains an account of Jack the Ripper's latest atrocity. After a time you turned your gaze away from the story, frowning in anger. The thought that such a monster should be able to roam London's streets with impunity was clearly evident."

"That is quite true."

"Then, my dear fellow, your eyes, seeking a resting-place, fell upon that copy of *The Strand Magazine* lying beside your chair. It happens to be open to an advertisement in which Beldell's is offering ladies' evening gowns at what they purport to be a bargain price. One of the gowns in the advertisement is displayed upon a model. Instantly, your expression changed; it became reflective. An idea had dawned upon you. The expression persisted as you raised your head and redirected your gaze towards the portrait of Her Majesty, which hangs beside the fireplace. After a moment, your expression cleared, and you nodded to yourself. You had become satisfied with the idea that had come to you. At which point, I agreed. The Ripper could well be a female."

"But, Holmes—"

"Come, now, Watson. Your retirement from the lists has dulled your perceptions."

"But when I glanced at the *Strand* advertisement, I could have had any of a dozen thoughts!"

"I disagree. Your mind was totally occupied with the story of the Ripper, and surely the advertisement concerning ladies' evening gowns was too far afield from your ordinary interests to divert your thoughts. Therefore, the idea that came to you had to be adjunct to your ponderings upon the monster. You verified this by raising your eyes to the Queen's portrait upon the wall."

"May I ask how that indicated my thought?" asked I, tartly.

"Watson! You certainly saw neither the model nor our gracious Queen as suspects. Therefore, you were scrutinising them as women."

"Granted," I retorted, "but would I not have been more likely to regard them as victims?"

"In that case, your expression would have reflected compassion, rather than that of a bloodhound come suddenly upon the scent."

I was forced to confess defeat. "Holmes, again you destroy yourself by your own volubility."

Holmes's heavy brows drew together. "I do not follow."

"Imagine what an image you would create were you to refuse all explanation of your amazing deductions!"

"But at what expense," said he, drily, "to your melodramatic accounts of my trifling adventures."

I threw up my hands in surrender; and Holmes, who rarely indulged in more than a smile, on this occasion, echoed my hearty laughter.

"So long as the subject of Jack the Ripper has arisen," said I, "allow me a further question. Why have you not interested yourself in the grisly affair, Holmes? If for no other reason, it would be a signal service to the people of London."

Holmes's long, thin fingers made an impatient gesture. "I have been busy. As you know, I returned from the Continent only recently, where the mayor of a certain city retained me to solve a most curious riddle. Knowing your turn of mind, I presume you would call it 'The Case of the Legless Cyclist.' One day I shall give you the details for your files."

"I shall be delighted to get them! But you are back in London, Holmes, and this monster is terrorising the city. I should think you would feel obligated—"

Holmes scowled. "I am obligated to no one."

"Pray do not misunderstand me—"

"I'm sorry, my dear Watson, but you should know me well enough to assume my total indifference towards such a case."

"At the risk of appearing more dense than most of my neighbours—"

"Consider! When given a choice, have I not always sought out problems of an intellectual character? Have I not always been drawn to adversaries of stature? Jack the Ripper, indeed! What possible challenge could this demented oaf present? A slavering cretin roaming the streets after dark, striking at random."

"He has baffled the London Police."

"I venture to suggest that that may reflect the shortcomings of Scotland Yard rather than any particular cleverness on the part of the Ripper."

"But still—"

"The thing will end soon enough. I daresay that one of these nights Lestrade will trip over the Ripper while the maniac is in the process of committing a murder, and thus bring him triumphantly to book." Holmes was chronically annoyed with Scotland Yard for not measuring up to his own stern efficiency; for all his genius, he could be childishly obstinate on such occasions. But further comment from me was cut off by the ringing of the downstairs bell. There was a slight delay; then we heard Mrs. Hudson ascending, and it was with astonishment that I observed her entrance. She was carrying a brown parcel and a pail of water, and she wore an expression of sheer fright.

Holmes burst out laughing for the second time that morning. "It's quite all right, Mrs. Hudson. The package appears harmless enough. I'm sure we shall not need the water."

Mrs. Hudson breathed a sigh of relief. "If you say so, Mr. Holmes. But since that last experience, I was taking no chances."

"And your alertness is to be commended," said Holmes, as he took the parcel. After his long-suffering landlady left, he added, "Just recently, Mrs. Hudson brought me a parcel. It was in connection with an unpleasant little affair I brought to a satisfactory conclusion, and it was sent by a vengeful gentleman who underestimated the keenness of my hearing. The ticking of the mechanism was quite audible to me, and I called for a pail of water. The incident gave Mrs. Hudson a turn from which she has still not recovered."

"I don't wonder!"

"But what have we here? Hmmm. Approximately fifteen inches by six. Four inches thick. Neatly wrapped in ordinary brown paper. Postmark: Whitechapel. The name and address written by a woman, I should hazard, who seldom puts pen to paper."

"That seems quite likely, from the clumsy scrawl. And that is certainly done in a woman's hand."

"Then we agree, Watson. Excellent! Shall we delve deeper?"

"By all means!"

The arrival of the parcel had aroused his interest, not to mention mine; his deep-set grey eyes grew bright when he removed the wrappings and drew forth a flat leather case. He held it up for my inspection. "Well, now. What do you make of this, Watson?"

"It is a surgeon's instrument case."

"And who would be better qualified to know? Would you not say also that it is expensive?"

"Yes. The leather is of superb quality. And the workmanship is exquisite."

Holmes set the case upon the table. He opened it, and we fell silent. It was a standard set of instruments, each fitting snugly into its appropriate niche in the crimson velvet lining of the case. One niche was empty.

"Which instrument is missing, Watson?"

"The large scalpel."

"The postmortem knife," said Holmes, nodding and whipping out his lens. "And now, what does this case tell us?" As he examined the case and its contents closely, he went on. "To begin with the obvious, these instruments belonged to a medical man who came upon hard times." Obliged, as usual, to confess my blindness, I said, "I am afraid that is more obvious to you than to me."

Preoccupied with his inspection, Holmes replied absently, "If you should fall victim to misfortune, Watson, which would be the last of your possessions to reach the pawnbroker's shop?"

"My medical instruments, of course. But—"

"Precisely."

"Wherein do you perceive that this case was pledged?"

"There is double proof. Observe, just there, through my lens." I peered at the spot he indicated. "A white smudge."

"Silver polish. No surgeon would cleanse his instruments with such a substance. These have been treated like common cutlery by someone concerned only with their appearance."

"Now that you point it out, Holmes, I must agree. And what is your second proof?"

"These chalk marks along the spine of the case. They are almost worn away, but if you will examine them closely, you will see that they constitute a number. Such a number as a pawnbroker would chalk upon a pledged article. Obviously, the counterpart of the number upon the pawn-ticket."

I felt the choler rising to my face. It was all too evident to me now.

"Then the kit was stolen!" I exclaimed. "Stolen from some surgeon, and disposed of, for a pittance, in a pawnshop!" My readers will forgive my indignation, I am sure; it was difficult for me to accept the alternative—that the practitioner would have parted with the instruments of a noble calling under even the most grievous circumstances.

Holmes, however, soon disillusioned me. "I fear, my dear Watson," said he, quite cheerfully, "that you do not perceive the finer aspects of the evidence. Pawnbrokers are a canny breed. It is part of their stock-in-trade not only to appraise the articles brought to them for pledge, but the persons offering them as well. Had the broker who dispensed his largesse for this surgical case entertained the slightest suspicion that it had been stolen, he would not have displayed it in his shop window, as of course you observe he has done."

"As of course I do not!" said I, testily. "How can you possibly know that the case has been displayed in a window?"

"Look closely," said Holmes. "The case lay open in a place exposed to the sun; does not the faded velvet on the inner surface of the lid tell us that? Moreover, the pronounced character of the fading marks the time span as an appreciable one. Surely this adds up to a shop window?" I could only nod. As always, when Holmes explained his astonishing observations, they appeared child's play.

"It is a pity," said I, "that we do not know where the pawnshop lies. This curious gift might merit a visit to its source."

"Perhaps in good time, Watson," said Holmes, with a dry chuckle. "The pawnshop in question is well off the beaten track. It faces south, on a narrow street. The broker's business is not flourishing. Also, he is of foreign extraction. Surely you see that?"

"I see nothing of the sort!" said I, nettled again.

"To the contrary," said he, placing his fingertips together and regarding me kindly, "you see everything, my dear Watson; what you fail to do is to observe. Let us take my conclusions in order. These instruments were not snatched up by any of the numerous medical students in the City of London, which would assuredly have been the case had the shop lain on a well-travelled thoroughfare. Hence my remark that it lies off the beaten track."

"But must it lie on the south side of a narrow street?"

"Note the location of the bleached area. It runs neatly along the uppermost edge of the velvet lining, not elsewhere. Therefore, the sun touched the open case only at its zenith, when its rays were not obstructed by the buildings on the opposite side of the street. Thus the pawnshop stands on the south side of a narrow street."

"And your identification of the pawnbroker as of foreign extraction?"

"Observe the numeral seven in the chalked pledge-mark on the spine. There is a short cross-mark on the ascender. Only a foreigner crosses his sevens in such a fashion."

I felt, as usual, like the fifth-form schoolboy who had forgotten the words to the national anthem. "Holmes, Holmes," said I, shaking my head, "I shall never cease to marvel—"

But he was not listening. Again, he had stooped over the case, inserting his tweezers beneath the velvet lining. It gave way, and he peeled it off.

"Aha! What have we here? An attempt at concealment?"

"Concealment? Of what? Stains? Scratches?"

He pointed a long, thin finger. "That."

"Why, it's a coat of arms!"

"One with which I confess I am not familiar. Therefore, Watson, be kind enough to hand down my copy of Burke's *Peerage*." He continued to study the crest as I moved dutifully towards the bookshelves, murmuring to himself. "Stamped into the leather of the case. The surface is still in excellent condition." He came erect. "A clew to the character of the man who owned the case."

"He was careful with his possessions, perhaps?"

"Perhaps. But I was referring to—"

He broke off. I had handed him the Burke, and he leafed swiftly through the pages. "Aha, here we have it!" After a quick scrutiny, Holmes closed the book, laid it on the table, and dropped into a chair. He stared intently into space with his piercing eyes.

I could contain my patience no longer. "The crest, Holmes! Whose is it?"

"I beg your pardon, Watson," said Holmes, coming to with a start. "Shires. Kenneth Osbourne, the Duke of Shires."

The name was well known to me, as indeed to all England. "An illustrious line."

Holmes nodded absently. "The estates, unless I mistake, lie in Devonshire, hard by the moors, among hunting lands well regarded by noble sportsmen. The manor house—it is more of a feudal castle in appearance—is some four hundred years old, a classic example of Gothic architecture. I know little of the Shires history, beyond the patent fact that the name has never been connected with the world of crime."

"So, Holmes," said I, "we are back to the original question."

"Indeed we are."

"Which is: this surgeon's case—why was it sent to you?"

"A provocative question."

"Perhaps an explanatory letter was delayed."

"You may well have hit upon the answer, Watson," said Holmes. "Therefore, I suggest we give the sender a little time, let us say until—" he paused to reach for his well-worn *Bradshaw's*, that admirable guide to British rail movements "—until ten-thirty tomorrow morning. If an explanation is not then forthcoming, we shall repair to Paddington Station and board the Devonshire express."

"For what reason, Holmes?"

"For two reasons. A short journey across the English countryside, with its changing colours at this time of year, should greatly refresh two stodgy Londoners."

"And the other?"

The austere face broke into the most curious smile. "In all justice," said my friend Holmes, "the Duke of Shires should have his property returned to him, should he not?" And he sprang to his feet and seized his violin.

"Wait, Holmes!" said I. "There is something in this you have not told me."

"No, no, my dear Watson," said he, drawing his bow briskly across the strings. "It is simply a feeling I have, that we are about to embark upon deep waters."

THE ADVENTURE OF THE DYING SHIP

EDWARD D. HOCH

dward D. Hoch holds a unique distinction that I doubt will ever be equaled: a short story of his appeared in every issue of Ellery Queen's Mystery Magazine *for thirty-five years. Six years after his passing in 2008, "The Adventure of the Dying Ship," his last Holmes pastiche, appeared in the February 2014 issue, which traditionally celebrates Sherlock Holmes in complimentary copies handed out at the annual Baker Street Irregulars banquet in January (popularly considered the month of Holmes's birth). Holmes, Watson, and the* Titanic: Who could ask for more? Reprinted by permission of Patricia Hoch.*

I write of this late in life, because I feel some record must be left of the astounding events of April 1912. I am aware that prior attempts to record my adventures personally have suffered when compared to those of my old and good friend Watson, but following my retirement from active practice as a consulting detective late in 1904 I saw very little of him. There were occasional weekend visits when he was in the area of my little Sussex home overlooking the Channel, but for the most part we had retired to our separate lives. It was not until 1914, at the outbreak of the Great War, that we would come together for a final adventure.

But that was more than two years away when I decided, quite irrationally, to accept an invitation from the president of the White Star Line to be a guest on the maiden voyage of RMS *Titanic* across the Atlantic to New York. He was a man for whom I had performed a slight service some years back, not even worthy of mention in Watson's notes, and he hardly owed me compensation on such a grand scale. There were several reasons why I agreed to it, but perhaps the truth was that I had simply grown bored with retirement. Still in my mid-fifties and enjoying good health, I had quickly learned that even at the height of season, the physical demands of beekeeping were slight indeed. The winter months were spent in correspondence with fellow enthusiasts, and a review and classification of my past cases. What few needs I had were seen to by an elderly housekeeper.

My initial reaction upon receiving the invitation was to ignore it. I had never been much of a world traveler, except for my years in Tibet and the Middle East, but the offer to revisit America intrigued me for two reasons. It would enable me to visit places like the Great Alkali Plain of Utah and the coal-mining region of Pennsylvania, which had figured in some of my investigations. And I could meet with one or two American beekeepers with whom I'd struck up a correspondence. I agreed to the invitation on one condition—that I travel under an assumed name. For the voyage I became simply Mr. Smith, a name I shared with five other passengers and the ship's captain.

Early April had been a time of chilly temperatures and high winds. I was more than a little apprehensive as I departed from London on the first-class boat train to Southampton, arriving there at 11:30 A.M. on Wednesday the 10th. Happily, my seat companion on the boat train proved to be a young American writer and journalist named Jacques Futrelle. He was a stocky man with a round, boyish face and dark hair that dipped down over his forehead on the right side. He wore pince-nez glasses and flowing bow tie, with white gloves that seemed formal for the occasion. Because of his name I took him to be French at first, but he quickly corrected my misapprehension. "I am a Georgian, sir, by way of Boston," he told me, "which might explain my strange accent."

"But surely your name—"

"My family is of French Huguenot stock. And you are—?"

"Smith," I told him.

"Ah!" He indicated the attractive woman seated across the aisle from us. "This is my wife, May. She is also a writer."

"A journalist like your husband?" I asked.

She gave me a winning smile. "We both write fiction. My first story appeared in *The Saturday Evening Post* some years back." She added, "The maiden voyage of the *Titanic* might provide an article for your old employer, Jacques."

He laughed. "I'm certain the *Boston American* will have any number of Hearst writers covering the voyage. They hardly need me, though I do owe them a debt of gratitude for publishing my early short stories while I worked there."

"Might I be familiar with your books?" I asked. Retirement to Sussex had left me with a mixed blessing, time to read the sort of popular fiction which I'd always ignored in the past.

It was May Futrelle who answered for him. "His novel *The Diamond Master* was published three years ago. I think that is the best of his romances, though many people prefer his detective stories."

The words stirred my memory. "Of course! Futrelle! You are the author of 'The Problem of Cell 13.' I have read that gem of a story more than once."

Futrelle smiled slightly. "Thank you. It has proven to be quite popular. My newspaper published it over six days and offered prizes for the correct solution."

"Your detective is known as The Thinking Machine."

The smile widened a bit. "Professor Augustus S.F.X. Van Dusen. I have published nearly fifty stories about the character in the past seven years, and I have another seven with me that I wrote on our journey. None has equaled the popularity of the first, however."

Fifty stories! That was more than Watson had published about our exploits up to that time, but Futrelle was correct in saying the first of them had been the most popular. "Have you two ever collaborated?" I asked.

May Futrelle laughed. "We swore that we never would, but we did try it once, in a way. I wrote a story that seemed to be a fantasy, and Jacques wrote his own story in which The Thinking Machine provided a logical solution to mine."

The talk shifted from his writing to their travels and I found him a most pleasant conversationalist. The time on the boat train passed quickly, and before long we were at the docks in Southampton. We parted then, promising to see each other on the voyage.

I stood on the dock for a moment, staring up at the great ship before me. Then I boarded the *Titanic* and was escorted to my cabin. It was suite B-57 on the starboard side of Bridge Deck B, reached by the impressive Grand Staircase or by a small elevator. Once in the cabin I found a comfortable bed with a brass and enamel head- and footboard. There was a wardrobe room next to the bed and a luxurious sitting area opposite it. An electric space heater provided warmth if needed. The suite's two windows were framed in gleaming brass. In the bath and WC there was a marble-topped sink. For just a moment I wished that my old friend Watson was there to see it.

I had been on board barely a half-hour when the ship cast off, exactly at noon. As the tugs maneuvered it away from the dock and moved downstream into the River Test, I left my stateroom on the bridge deck and went out to the railing, lighting a cigarette as I watched our progress past banks lined with well-wishers. Then we stopped, narrowly avoiding a collision with another ship. It was almost an hour before we were under way again, and the next twenty-four hours were frustrating ones. We steamed downstream to the English Channel, and then across to Cherbourg where 274 additional passengers boarded by tender. Then it was a night crossing to Queenstown, Ireland, where we anchored about two miles offshore while more passengers were brought out by tender.

When at last the anchor was raised for the final time, Captain Smith posted a notice that there were some 2,227 passengers and crew aboard, the exact number uncertain. This was about two-thirds the maximum capacity of 3,360 passengers and crew.

As I watched us pull out at 1:30 P.M. on Thursday, April 11, I suddenly realized that an attractive red-haired young woman had joined me on deck.

"Is this your first trip across?" she asked.

"Across the Atlantic, yes," I said to discourage any discussion of my past.

"I'm Margo Collier. It's my first, too."

Women seldom have been an attraction to me, but there were exceptions. Looking into the deep, intelligent eyes of Margo Collier I knew she could have been one of them had I not been old enough to have sired her. "A pleasure to meet you," I replied. "I am Mr. Smith."

She blinked, or winked, at me. "Mr. John Smith, no doubt. Are you in first class?"

"I am. And you are an American, judging by the sound of your accent."

"I thought you could tell from my red hair."

I smiled. "Do all Americans have red hair?"

"The ones that are in trouble seem to. Sometimes I think it's my red hair that gets me into trouble."

"What sort of trouble could one so young have gotten into?"

Her expression changed, and in an instant she was coldly serious. "There's a man on board who's been following me, Mr. Holmes."

The sound of my own name startled me. "You know me, Miss Collier?"

"You were pointed out by one of the ship's officers. He was telling me about the famous people on board—John Jacob Astor, Benjamin Guggenheim, Sherlock Holmes, and many others."

I laughed. "My life's work has hardly been comparable to theirs. But pray tell me of this man who follows you. We are, after all, on shipboard. Perhaps he only strolls the deck as you do yourself."

She shook her head. "He was following me before I boarded the ship at Cherbourg." She grew suddenly nervous. "I can say no more now. Could you meet me in the first-class lounge on A deck? I'll try to be in the writing room tomorrow morning at eleven."

I bowed slightly. "I'll expect to see you then, Miss Collier."

There was a chill in the air on Friday morning, though the weather was calm and clear. Captain Smith reported that the *Titanic* had covered 386 miles since leaving Queenstown harbour. I ate an early breakfast in the first-class dining saloon, and, after a stroll around the deck, spent some time in the ship's gymnasium on the boat deck. The idea of using a rowing machine on this great ocean liner appealed to me, though I'm certain Watson would have groused about it, reminding me of my age. Finally, shortly before eleven, I went down one flight of stairs to the writing room.

Margo Collier was seated alone at one of the tables, sipping a cup of tea. The reading and writing room adjoined the first-class lounge. It was a spacious, inviting area with groups of upholstered chairs and tables placed at comfortable intervals. I smiled as I seated myself opposite her. "Good morning, Miss Collier. Did you have a good night's sleep?"

"As well as could be expected," she murmured, her voice barely carrying across the table. "The man who's been following me is in the lounge right now, standing by that leaded glass window."

I turned casually in my chair and realized that Jacques Futrelle and his wife were seated with an older man in a black suit. Seeing them gave me an excuse to walk into the lounge and get a better look at the man she'd indicated. I paused at their table with a few words of greeting, noting that the man with them was studying the tea leaves in one of the cups.

"Mr. Smith!" May Futrelle greeted me. "You must meet Franklin Baynes, the British spiritualist."

The man eyed me solemnly as he stood up to shake my hand. "Smith? What is your line of work?"

"I am retired from a research position. This voyage is strictly for pleasure. But I see you are at work, sir, attempting to divine the world in a teacup."

"The Futrelles asked for a demonstration."

"I will leave you to it," I said, continuing on my way into the wood-panelled lounge. The man Margo Collier had indicated now stood a few paces from the window. He was almost bald, with a growth of greying beard along his chin, and his left hand was clutched around the knob of a thick walking stick. As I approached, he turned on me with blazing eyes.

"Has she sent you to confront me, sir?"

"Miss Collier says you have been following her since Cherbourg. You are frightening the poor woman half to death. Would you care to identify yourself?"

The bearded man drew himself up until he was almost my height. "I am Pierre Glacet. Cherbourg is my home. I am like yourself."

"And why do you follow her?" I asked, not quite understanding his remark.

"Because she runs away from me. Margo Collier is my wife."

I cannot pretend that the news did not astound me. I had noticed the faint indentation on her ring finger, but I assumed it was only the sign of a broken engagement in one so young. Likewise, the manner in which she approached me had seemed quite sincere.

"I find that difficult to believe," I told Glacet.

"Ask her! We have been married for more than a year, though we are living apart at the moment."

"Under what circumstances?"

"That is a personal matter, sir."

"How were you able to obtain a booking on the voyage at the last minute in order to follow her?"

"The ship is not fully booked at these prices."

"Forgive me, sir, if I have done you an injustice." I retreated back to the writing room where Margo Collier was waiting.

"Did you confront him, Mr. Holmes?" she asked immediately.

"I did. The man claims to be your legal husband. Is that true?"

"We are separated. He has no business following me about!"

"I am sorry, Mrs. Glacet. I am, or was, a consulting detective. I have never been a marriage counsellor."

"Mr. Holmes—"

"Pardon me, madam. I can no longer help you." I turned and walked away.

For the rest of the day and the next, I managed to avoid both Margo Collier and Pierre Glacet. The *Titanic* covered 519 miles on its second day, though it received several warnings of heavy pack ice from other ships. Captain Smith assured us via his posted notices that ice warnings were not uncommon for April crossings.

On Saturday evening, I dined with the Futrelles and the spiritualist Franklin Baynes in the first-class dining saloon. He was an interesting gentleman, well steeped in occult lore. Futrelle seemed especially taken with him, and I could only assume that the author was researching a possible idea for one of his detective stories. It developed that the spiritualist was travelling to America for a series of lectures and demonstrations.

"You are a showman, then," I proposed, as much to bait him as anything else.

"No, no!" he insisted. "Spiritualism is as much a science as Madame Curie's radiology."

May Futrelle spoke. "Mr. Baynes has invited us to his cabin after dinner for a demonstration of some of his devices. Perhaps you could join us, Mr. Smith."

"By all means, do so!" Baynes urged.

I agreed with some reluctance, and, following dessert, we took the elevator up three floors to his stateroom on the promenade deck. It was even larger than my cabin, and I wondered if this, too, might be a reward from the White Star president. The spiritualist went directly to his steamer trunk and opened it. He removed a crystal ball some six inches in diameter, mounted on a wooden base with an electrical cord attached. Quickly unplugging the cabin's electric space heater by the bed, he plugged his device in its place. The crystal ball sprang to life with a bright intense light.

"Look in here, Mr. Smith, but not too long, or you will be blinded."

"What am I supposed to see?" I inquired.

"Perhaps those who have gone before you into the great beyond."

I glanced at the brightly glowing filament for an instant and then looked away, its image burnt into my retina. "I see nothing of the past," I told him, "though something of the future might be had in lights like this."

Franklin Baynes unplugged the crystal ball and brought out an oversized deck of cards. I began to suspect he was more magician than spiritualist. "You are not a believer in the hereafter, Mr. Smith, in that other world where our ancestors await us, where it is always spring and the fairies and elves flit across the meadow?"

I smiled slightly. "I have my own vision of the hereafter, Mr. Baynes. It is not the same as yours."

May Futrelle seemed to sense that the visit to his cabin had been a mistake. "We really should be going, Jacques," she told her husband.

The spiritualist shook their hands. "Thank you for dinner. It was most delightful. And you, Mr. Smith. I trust we can discuss our differing views before the ship docks in New York."

"Perhaps," I agreed.

I left the cabin in the company of the Futrelles and walked a few steps to the elevator. "Obviously the man is something of a charlatan," May said, "but Jacques thinks he might get a story idea out of this."

"It's always possible," I agreed.

The elevator arrived and I opened the folding gate for them. Jacques peered at me and asked, "If it's not too personal a question, Mr. Smith, are you a detective?"

"Why do you ask?"

"Our steward told us you were the famous Mr. Sherlock Holmes."

I laughed as I stepped into the elevator with them and closed the gate. "My secret seems to be a secret no longer. You're the second person who has confronted me about my identity."

"We won't tell anyone," May promised, "though Mr. Baynes has heard it, too. Certainly it's an honour to meet you. Jacques was inspired to write his stories after reading Dr. Watson's accounts of your cases."

"Watson glamourizes me, I fear."

"How is the old fellow?" Futrelle asked.

"Fine. He comes to see me on occasion, though it's been some time now since I've had the pleasure of his company." I got off one flight down on the bridge deck. "I'll see you tomorrow," I told them.

Futrelle grinned. "Good night, Mr. Smith."

Sunday, April 14—the longest day of my life—began with divine services held in the first-class dining saloon. I had overslept and when I went for breakfast at 10:30 I found the service in progress. That was how I happened upon Margo Collier again. She spotted me at once, standing in the back of the room, and pushed through the late arrivals to join me. "Hello, Mr. Holmes."

"Hello, Mrs. Glacet."

"Please don't call me that. If you would grant me time, I could explain the entire matter to you."

Something in her desperate tone made me regret the harshness of my earlier dismissal. "Very well," I said. "Join me at dinner tonight in the first-class saloon. I will be in the outer reception room at eight o'clock."

"I will be there," she promised, brightening at once.

During the day I continued to hear reports of ice sightings from the other passengers. In the twenty-four hours since noon Saturday, we had covered another 546 miles, and the map showed us approaching the Grand Banks of Newfoundland. The temperature had remained in the forties much of the afternoon, but after 5:30, as darkness descended it plunged quite quickly to 33 degrees. Captain Smith altered the ship's course slightly to the south and west, possibly as a precaution to avoid icebergs. Lookouts in the crow's nest would remain on duty all night watching for ice. Looking up at them from the top deck, I decided it must be the loneliest of shipboard tasks, even though there were two men up there.

Exactly at 8:00, Margo Collier met me in the reception room on the saloon deck. "My cabin is second class," she confided. "I feared they might put another woman in with me to occupy the other bunk, but happily, I'm alone."

"That is more pleasant," I agreed as were shown to our table.

"Did you know that the passengers' maids and valets eat in a separate dining room on Shelter Deck C? I saw it yesterday as I was touring the ship. They just have long communal tables, of course."

"Nothing about this ship would surprise me," I admitted. "It must be the grandest thing afloat." At the far end of the dining saloon an orchestra had begun to play.

The menu was a delight, as it had been each night of the voyage thus far. Margo Collier ordered the roast duckling with apple sauce. After some debate between the lamb and the filet mignon, I chose the latter with boiled new potatoes and creamed carrots, preceded by oysters and cream of barley soup.

"Now let us get down to business," I told the young woman. "Tell me about your marriage to Pierre Glacet."

She sighed and began her story. "As you can see, there is a great difference in our ages. I met him on a weekend holiday in Cherbourg last year, and he persuaded me to work for him."

"Work? What sort of work?"

"He is a consulting detective like yourself, Mr. Holmes."

At last I understood the meaning of the man's words, "I am like yourself." He, too, knew my identity, as most everyone on the ship seemed to. "Being in his employ hardly necessitated marriage, did it?" I asked.

"He specializes in cases involving family matters. Often his investigations involve checking into hotels to keep certain parties under surveillance. He needed me to pose as his wife, and since he is a moral man he felt we should be truly married if we were to share a hotel room."

"You agreed to this?" I asked with some astonishment.

"Not at first. The idea of being married to a man more than twice my age, who had a greying beard and walked with a cane, was more than I could imagine. I agreed to it only when he assured me it would be a marriage in name only, for business purposes. The pay he offered was quite good, and I agreed to try it for one year."

"What happened next?"

"We went through a brief civil ceremony, which he assured me could be easily annulled. I quickly found out, Mr. Holmes, that I had made a foolish mistake. The first time we shared a hotel room while shadowing someone, he was a perfect gentleman, sleeping on the sofa while I took the only bed. After that things began to change. He mentioned the troubles with his leg, and how uncomfortable hotel room sofas were. I allowed him to share the bed, but nothing more. Gradually he began taking liberties, and when I objected he reminded me that we were legally man and wife. After a few months of that, I left him."

"And he has been following you ever since?"

"No. Even though I remained in Cherbourg through the winter months, he made no effort to bother me. It was when I decided to go to America and purchased my ticket on the *Titanic* that I saw him again. He wanted me to stay in Cherbourg."

Over a dessert of Waldorf pudding I tried to learn more about the French detective's cases. "Were they all divorces?"

"No, no. Some involved confidence men trying to swindle wealthy widows. I remember a pair of them, Cozel and Sanbey, who operated as a team. We followed them to Paris once, and I kept Mr. Cozel occupied in a café while Pierre searched his room." She smiled at the memory. "We had some good times together."

"Then why did you seek my protection?"

"He wanted more than I was willing to give," she said with a sigh. "When I saw him on the ship, I feared I would end up having to fight him off."

"I will speak with him again before we dock in New York," I promised. "Perhaps I can persuade him to leave you alone."

We parted around eleven as the orchestra was playing *The Tales of Hoffmann*, and I decided to go up to the boat deck for a stroll. The temperature was just below freezing, with a mist that cut visibility sharply. I thought of the poor seamen in the crow's nest and shivered for them. Then I retreated inside to the first-class smoking room on A Deck. I could hear the orchestra still playing. May had already retired for the evening, but Futrelle was sitting alone enjoying a nightcap. I joined him and ordered one myself. We were having a lively conversation about detective stories when there was a faint grinding jar to the ship.

"Iceberg!" someone shouted. Several of us ran outside to look. We were in time to see a giant berg, almost as high as the boat deck, vanishing into the mist astern.

"That was a close call," Futrelle said. "I think we actually scraped it going past!"

We went back inside to finish our drinks. After about ten minutes I observed that the level of liquid in my glass was beginning to tilt a bit toward the bow of the ship. Before that fact could register in my mind, Margo Collier came running in. "What is it?" I asked, seeing her ashen face.

"I've been seeking you everywhere, Mr. Holmes. My husband has fallen down the elevator shaft! He's dead."

It was true. One of the first-class stewards had noticed the open gate on the top deck. Looking into the shaft, he'd been able to make out a body on top of the elevator car four floors below. Futrelle and I reached the scene just as the broken body of Pierre Glacet was being removed.

I stared hard at the body as it lay in the corridor, then said, "Let me through here, please."

A ship's officer blocked the way. "Sorry, sir. You're too near the shaft."

"I want to examine it."

"Nothing to see in there, sir. Just the elevator cables."

He was correct, of course. The top of the car had nothing on it. "Can you raise it up so I can see to the bottom of the shaft?" I asked.

Futrelle smiled at my request. "Are you searching for a murder weapon, Mr. Holmes?"

I did not answer, but merely stared at the bottom of the shaft as it came into view beneath the rising car. It was empty, as I suspected it would be. Some first-class passengers came in to use the elevator, but the officer directed them to the main staircase or the aft elevator. "Why is the ship listing?" one of the gentlemen asked.

"We're looking into it," the officer said. For the first time I was aware that we were tilting forward, and I remembered the liquid in my glass. From far off came the sudden sound of a lively ragtime tune being played by the orchestra.

Franklin Baynes, the spiritualist, was coming down the stairs from the boat deck. "What's going on?" he asked. "The crew is uncovering the lifeboats."

Captain Smith himself appeared on the stairs in time to hear the question. "It's just a precaution," he told them. "The ship is taking on water."

"From that iceberg?" Futrelle asked.

"Yes. Please gather your families and follow directions to your lifeboat stations."

Margo Collier seemed dazed. "This ship is unsinkable! There are waterproof compartments. I read all the literature."

"Please follow instructions," the captain said, a bit more sharply. "Leave that body where it is."

"I must get to May," Futrelle said. I hurried after him. There would be time for the rest later.

Within minutes we were on the deck with May. She was clinging to her husband, unwilling to let go. "Aren't there enough lifeboats for everyone?" she asked. The answer was already plain. The *Titanic* was sinking and there was room enough for only half the passengers in the lifeboats. It was 12:25 A.M. when the order came for women and children to abandon ship. We had scraped against the iceberg only forty-five minutes earlier.

"Jacques!" May Futrelle screamed, and he pushed her to safety in the nearest lifeboat. "Now what?" he asked me, as the half-full lifeboat was being lowered to the dark churning waters. "Do we go back for our murderer?"

"So you spotted it, too?" I asked, already leading the way.

"The missing cane. I only saw Glacet once, but he walked with the aid of a stout walking stick."

"Exactly," I agreed. "And I'm told he used it regularly. It wasn't on top of the elevator car and it hadn't slipped down to the bottom of the shaft. That meant he didn't step into that empty shaft accidentally. He had help." We were on the Grand Staircase now, and spotted our quarry. "Didn't he, Mr. Baynes?"

He turned at the sound of his name, and drew a revolver from under his coat. "Damn you, Holmes! You'll go down with the ship."

"We all will, Baynes. The women and children are leaving. The rest of us will stay. Glacet recognized you as a confidence man he'd once pursued, a man named Sanbey—a simple anagram for Baynes. Somehow you got him into your cabin tonight to stare at your electric crystal ball. When the bright light had temporarily blinded him, you helped him to the elevator, then sent the car down and pushed him after it. Only you forgot his walking stick. That probably went over the side when you discovered it."

The great ship listed suddenly, throwing us against the staircase railing. "I'm getting out of here, Holmes! I'll find room in a lifeboat if I have to don women's clothes!" He raised the revolver and fired.

And in that instant, before I could move, Futrelle jumped between us. He took the bullet meant for me and collided with Baynes, sending them both over the railing of the Grand Staircase.

Somehow I made my way into the night air. It was just after one o'clock, and the orchestra had moved to the boat deck to continue playing. The remaining passengers were beginning to panic. Suddenly someone grabbed me and shoved me toward a lifeboat. "Only twelve aboard Starboard Number One, sir. Plenty of room for you."

"I'll stay," I said, but it was not to be. I was pushed bodily into the boat as it was being lowered.

It was from there, an hour later, that I saw the last of the great *Titanic* vanish beneath the waves, carrying a victim, a murderer, and a mystery writer with it. Two hours after that, a ship called the *Carpathia* plucked us from the water, amidst floating ice and debris. Margo Collier was among the survivors, but I never saw her again.

A final note by Dr. Watson: It was not until 1918, at the close of the Great War, that my old friend Holmes entrusted this account to my care. By that time, my literary agent, Arthur Conan Doyle, had embraced spiritualism. He refused to handle a story in which a spiritualist was revealed to be a sham and a murderer. This most dramatic of adventures has remained unpublished.

EXCERPT FROM *THE INSIDIOUS DR. FU-MANCHU*

SAX ROHMER

*H*istory doesn't tell us what Conan Doyle thought of Sax Rohmer's series about Dr. Fu-Manchu, an international supercriminal bent on conquering the western world; but the similarities between the pipe-smoking, blunt-spoken Denis Nayland-Smith and his amanuensis, Dr. Petrie, and Holmes and Watson certainly suggest Rohmer was more than familiar with Conan Doyle's adventures. There is a school of thought, too, that maintains the very concept of the underworld mastermind was first introduced in "The Final Problem," in which Holmes did battle with Professor Moriarty. But just as Rohmer's predecessor built upon Poe's Dupin, this series brought intriguing twists to the fog-shrouded world known to Holmes and Watson. This excerpt is from* The Insidious Dr. Fu-Manchu *(published previously in England as* The Mystery of Dr. Fu-Manchu*), the first in the series, which stretched from 1913 to 1959 (with new material discovered and published in 1970 and 1973, decades after the author's death). It is reprinted by permission of the Sax Rohmer Estate.*

CHAPTER II

Sir Crichton Davey's study was a small one, and a glance sufficed to show that, as the secretary had said, it offered no hiding place. It was heavily carpeted, and overly full of Burmese and Chinese ornaments and curios, and upon the mantelpiece stood several framed photographs that showed this to be the sanctum of a wealthy bachelor who was no misogynist. A map of the Indian Empire occupied the larger part of one wall. The grate was empty, for the weather was extremely warm, and a green-shaded lamp on the littered writing-table afforded the only light. The air was stale, for both windows were closed and fastened.

Smith immediately pounced upon a large, square envelope that lay beside the blotting pad. Sir Crichton had not even troubled to open it, but my friend did so. It contained a blank sheet of paper!

"Smell!" he directed, handing the letter to me. I raised it to my nostrils. It was scented with some pungent perfume.

"What is it?" I asked.

"It is a rather rare essential oil," was the reply, "which I have met with before, though never in Europe. I begin to understand, Petrie."

He tilted the lampshade and made a close examination of the scraps of paper, matches, and other debris that lay in the grate and on the hearth. I took up a copper vase from the mantelpiece, and was examining it curiously when he turned, a strange expression upon his face.

"Put that back, old man," he said quietly.

Much surprised, I did as he directed.

"Don't touch anything in the room. It may be dangerous."

Something in the tone of his voice chilled me, and I hastily replaced the vase, and stood by the door of the study, watching him search, methodically, every inch of the room—behind the books, in all the ornaments, in table drawers, in cupboards, on shelves.

"That will do," he said at last. "There is nothing here and I have no time to search further."

We returned to the library.

"Inspector Weymouth," said my friend, "I have a particular reason for asking that Sir Crichton's body be removed from this room at once and the library locked. Let no one be admitted on any pretense whatever until you hear from me." It spoke volumes for the mysterious credentials borne by my friend that the man from Scotland Yard accepted his orders without demur, and, after a brief chat with Mr. Burboyne, Smith passed briskly downstairs. In the hall, a man who looked like a groom out of livery was waiting.

"Are you Wills?" asked Smith.

"Yes, sir."

"It was you who heard a cry of some kind at the rear of the house about the time of Sir Crichton's death?"

"Yes, sir. I was locking the garage door, and, happening to look up at the window of Sir Crichton's study, I saw him jump out of his chair. Where he used to sit at his writing, sir, you could see his shadow on the blind. Next minute I heard a call out in the lane."

"What kind of call?"

The man, whom the uncanny happening clearly had frightened, seemed puzzled for a suitable description.

"A sort of wail, sir," he said at last. "I never heard anything like it before, and don't want to again."

"Like this?" inquired Smith, and he uttered a low, wailing cry, impossible to describe. Wills perceptibly shuddered; and, indeed, it was an eerie sound.

"The same, sir, I think," he said, "but much louder."

"That will do," said Smith, and I thought I detected a note of triumph in his voice. "But stay! Take us through to the back of the house."

The man bowed and led the way, so that shortly we found ourselves in a small, paved courtyard. It was a perfect summer's night, and the deep blue vault above was jeweled with myriads of starry points. How impossible it seemed to reconcile that vast, eternal calm with the hideous passions and fiendish agencies, which that night had loosed a soul upon the infinite.

"Up yonder are the study windows, sir. Over that wall on your left is the back lane from which the cry came, and beyond is Regent's Park."

"Are the study windows visible from there?"

"Oh, yes, sir."

"Who occupies the adjoining house?"

"Major-General Platt-Houston, sir; but the family is out of town."

"Those iron stairs are a means of communication between the domestic offices and the servants' quarters, I take it?"

"Yes, sir."

"Then send someone to make my business known to the Major-General's housekeeper; I want to examine those stairs."

Singular though my friend's proceedings appeared to me, I had ceased to wonder at anything. Since Nayland Smith's arrival at my rooms, I seemed to have been moving through the fitful phases of a nightmare. My friend's account of how he came by the wound in his arm; the scene on our arrival at the house of Sir Crichton Davey; the secretary's story of the dying man's cry, "The red hand!"; the hidden perils of the study; the wail in the lane—all were fitter incidents of delirium than of sane reality. So, when a white-faced butler made us known to a nervous old lady who proved to be the housekeeper of the next-door residence, I was not surprised at Smith's saying:

"Lounge up and down outside, Petrie. Everyone has cleared off now. It is getting late. Keep your eyes open and be on your guard. I thought I had the start, but he is here before me, and, what is worse, he probably knows by now that I am here, too."

With which he entered the house and left me out in the square, with leisure to think, to try to understand.

The crowd that usually haunts the scene of a sensational crime had been cleared away, and it had been circulated that Sir Crichton had died from natural causes. The intense heat having driven most of the residents out of town, I practically had the square to myself, and I gave myself up to a brief consideration of the mystery in which I so suddenly had found myself involved.

By what agency had Sir Crichton met his death? Did Nayland Smith know? I rather suspected that he did. What was the hidden significance of the perfumed envelope? Who was that mysterious personage whom Smith so evidently dreaded, who had attempted to take his life, who—presumably—had murdered Sir Crichton? Sir Crichton Davey, during the time that he had held office in India, and during his long term of service at home, had earned the good will of all, British and native alike. Who was his secret enemy?

Something touched me lightly on the shoulder.

I turned, my heart fluttering like a child's. This night's work had imposed a severe strain even upon my callous nerves.

A girl wrapped in a hooded opera-cloak stood at my elbow, and, as she glanced up at me, I thought that I never had seen a face so seductively lovely nor of so unusual a type. With the skin of a perfect blonde, she had eyes and lashes as black as a Creole's, which, together with her full red lips, told me that this beautiful stranger, whose touch had so startled me, was not a child of our northern shores.

"Forgive me," she said, speaking with an odd, pretty accent, and laying a slim hand with jeweled fingers confidingly upon my arm, "if I startled you. But—is it true that Sir Crichton Davey has been—murdered?"

I looked into her big, questioning eyes, a harsh suspicion laboring in my mind, but could read nothing in their mysterious depths— only I wondered anew at my questioner's beauty. The grotesque idea momentarily possessed me that, were the bloom of her red lips due to art and not to nature, their kiss would leave—though not indelibly—just such a mark as I had seen upon the dead man's hand. But I dismissed the fantastic notion as bred of the night's horrors, and worthy only of a mediaeval legend. No doubt she was some friend or acquaintance of Sir Crichton who lived close by.

"I cannot say that he has been murdered," I replied, acting upon the latter supposition, and seeking to tell her what she asked as gently as possible.

"But he is—dead?"

I nodded.

She closed her eyes and uttered a low, moaning sound, swaying dizzily. Thinking she was about to swoon, I threw my arm round her shoulder to support her, but she smiled sadly, and pushed me gently away.

"I am quite well, thank you," she said.

"You are certain? Let me walk with you until you feel quite sure of yourself."

She shook her head, flashed a rapid glance at me with her beautiful eyes, and looked away in a sort of sorrowful embarrassment, for which I was entirely at a loss to account. Suddenly she resumed:

"I cannot let my name be mentioned in this dreadful matter, but—I think I have some information—for the police. Will you give this to—whomever you think proper?"

She handed me a sealed envelope, again met my eyes with one of her dazzling glances, and hurried away. She had gone no more than ten or twelve yards, and I still was standing bewildered, watching her graceful, retreating figure, when she turned abruptly and came back.

Without looking directly at me, but alternately glancing towards a distant corner of the square and towards the house of Major-General Platt-Houston, she made the following extraordinary request:

"If you would do me a very great service, for which I always would be grateful,"—she glanced at me with passionate intentness—"when you have given my message to the proper person, leave him and do not go near him any more tonight!"

Before I could find words to reply, she gathered up her cloak and ran. Before I could determine whether or not to follow her (for her words had aroused anew all my worst suspicions), she had disappeared! I heard the whirr of a restarted motor at no great distance, and, in the instant that Nayland Smith came running down the steps, I knew that I had nodded at my post.

"Smith!" I cried as he joined me, "tell me what we must do!" And rapidly I acquainted him with the incident.

My friend looked very grave; then a grim smile crept round his lips.

"She was a big card to play," he said; "but he did not know that I held one to beat it."

"What! You know this girl! Who is she?"

"She is one of the finest weapons in the enemy's armory, Petrie. But a woman is a two-edged sword, and treacherous. To our great good fortune, she has formed a sudden predilection, characteristically Oriental, for yourself. Oh, you may scoff, but it is evident. She was employed to get this letter placed in my hands. Give it to me."

I did so.

"She has succeeded. Smell."

He held the envelope under my nose, and, with a sudden sense of nausea, I recognized the strange perfume.

"You know what this presaged in Sir Crichton's case? Can you doubt any longer? She did not want you to share my fate, Petrie."

"Smith," I said unsteadily, "I have followed your lead blindly in this horrible business and have not pressed for an explanation, but I must insist before I go one step farther upon knowing what it all means."

"Just a few steps farther," he rejoined, "as far as a cab. We are hardly safe here. Oh, you need not fear shots or knives. The man whose servants are watching us now scorns to employ such clumsy, tell-tale weapons."

Only three cabs were on the rank, and, as we entered the first, something hissed past my ear, missed both Smith and me by a miracle, and, passing over the roof of the taxi, presumably fell in the enclosed garden occupying the center of the square.

"What was that?" I cried.

"Get in—quickly!" Smith rapped back. "It was attempt number one! More than that I cannot say. Don't let the man hear. He has noticed nothing. Pull up the window on your side, Petrie, and look out behind. Good! We've started."

The cab moved off with a metallic jerk, and I turned and looked back through the little window in the rear.

"Someone has got into another cab. It is following ours, I think."

Nayland Smith lay back and laughed unmirthfully.

"Petrie," he said, "if I escape alive from this business I shall know that I bear a charmed life."

I made no reply, as he pulled out the dilapidated pouch and filled his pipe.

"You have asked me to explain matters," he continued, "and I will do so to the best of my ability. You no doubt wonder why a servant of the British Government, lately stationed in Burma, suddenly appears in London, in the character of a detective. I am here, Petrie—and I bear credentials from the very highest sources—because, quite by accident, I came upon a clew. Following it up, in the ordinary course of routine, I obtained evidence of the existence and malignant activity of a certain man. At the present stage of the case I should not be justified in terming him the emissary of an Eastern Power, but I may say that representations are shortly to be made to that Power's ambassador in London."

He paused and glanced back towards the pursuing cab.

"There is little to fear until we arrive home," he said calmly. "Afterwards there is much. To continue: This man, whether a fanatic or a duly appointed agent, is, unquestionably, the most malign and formidable personality existing in the known world today. He is a linguist who speaks with almost equal facility in any of the civilized languages, and in most of the barbaric. He is an adept in all the arts and sciences that a great university could teach him. He also is an adept in certain obscure arts and sciences, which no university of today can teach. He has the brains of any three men of genius. Petrie, he is a mental giant."

"You amaze me!" I said.

"As to his mission among men: Why did M. Jules Furneaux fall dead in a Paris opera house? Because of heart failure? No! Because his last speech had shown that he held the key to the secret of Tongking. What became of the Grand Duke Stanislaus? Elopement? Suicide? Nothing of the kind. He alone was fully alive to Russia's growing peril. He alone knew the truth about Mongolia. Why was Sir Crichton Davey murdered? Because had the work he was engaged upon ever seen the light, it would have shown him to be the only living Englishman who understood the importance of the Tibetan frontiers. I say to you solemnly, Petrie, that these are but a few. Is there a man who would arouse the West to a sense of the awakening of the East, who would teach the deaf to hear, the blind to see, that the millions only await their leader? He will die. And this is only one phase of the devilish campaign. The others I can merely surmise."

"But, Smith, this is almost incredible! What perverted genius controls this awful secret movement?"

"Imagine a person, tall, lean and feline, high shouldered, with a brow like Shakespeare and a face like Satan, a close-shaven skull, and long, magnetic eyes of the true cat-green. Invest him with all the cruel cunning of an entire Eastern race, accumulated in one giant intellect, with all the resources of science past and present, with all the resources, if you will, of a wealthy government—which, however, has already denied all knowledge of his existence. Imagine that awful being, and you have a mental picture of Dr. Fu-Manchu, the yellow peril incarnate in one man."

HOW WATSON LEARNED THE TRICK

SIR ARTHUR CONAN DOYLE

"*How Watson Learned the Trick*" *has appeared rarely, if ever, in the same volume with the other Sherlock Holmes stories written by Sir Arthur Conan Doyle. He wrote this sketch in 1922 at the request of Queen Mary, consort to King George V, to be bound and included in the library of her opulent dollhouse alongside other miniature works by Rudyard Kipling, J.M. Barrie, Joseph Conrad, Somerset Maugham, and many other literati. The story's a bit hard on Watson's hubris, but bears fond echoes of his attempt to deduce the identity of the owner of the forgotten walking stick in* The Hound of the Baskervilles. *Reprinted here by permission of the Sir Arthur Conan Doyle Estate.*

Watson had been watching his companion intently ever since he had sat down to the breakfast table. Holmes happened to look up and catch his eye.

"Well, Watson, what are you thinking about?" he asked.

"About you."

"Me?"

"Yes, Holmes. I was thinking how superficial are these tricks of yours, and how wonderful it is that the public should continue to show interest in them."

"I quite agree," said Holmes. "In fact, I have a recollection that I have myself made a similar remark."

"Your methods," said Watson severely, "are really easily acquired."

"No doubt," Holmes answered with a smile. "Perhaps you will yourself give an example of this method of reasoning."

"With pleasure," said Watson. "I am able to say that you were greatly preoccupied when you got up this morning."

"Excellent!" said Holmes. "How could you possibly know that?"

"Because you are usually a very tidy man and yet you have forgotten to shave."

"Dear me! How very clever!" said Holmes. "I had no idea, Watson, that you were so apt a pupil. Has your eagle eye detected anything more?"

"Yes, Holmes. You have a client named Barlow, and you have not been successful with his case."

"Dear me, how could you know that?"

"I saw the name outside his envelope. When you opened it you gave a groan and thrust it into your pocket with a frown on your face."

"Admirable! You are indeed observant. Any other points?"

"I fear, Holmes, that you have taken to financial speculation."

"How *could* you tell that, Watson?"

"You opened the paper, turned to the financial page, and gave a loud exclamation of interest."

"Well, that is very clever of you, Watson. Any more?"

"Yes, Holmes, you have put on your black coat, instead of your dressing gown, which proves that you are expecting some important visitor at once."

"Anything more?"

"I have no doubt that I could find other points, Holmes, but I only give you these few, in order to show you that there are other people in the world who can be as clever as you."

"And some not so clever," said Holmes. "I admit that they are few, but I am afraid, my dear Watson, that I must count you among them."

"What do you mean, Holmes?"

"Well, my dear fellow, I fear your deductions have not been so happy as I should have wished."

"You mean that I was mistaken."

"Just a little that way, I fear. Let us take the points in their order: I did not shave because I have sent my razor to be sharpened. I put on my coat because I have, worse luck, an early meeting with my dentist. His name is Barlow, and the letter was to confirm the appointment. The cricket page is beside the financial one, and I turned to it to find if Surrey was holding its own against Kent. But go on, Watson, go on! It's a very superficial trick, and no doubt you will soon acquire it."

TWO SHABBY FIGURES

LAURIE R. KING

aurie R. King's novels about Mary Russell answer the question asked by many Sherlockians about Holmes's life in retirement, touched on but briefly in Conan Doyle's "The Lion's Mane" and "His Last Bow." They've been enormously successful, and add new layers to the detective partners we thought we knew everything about. This excerpt is from The Beekeeper's Apprentice, *the first in the series. It is reprinted by permission of the author.*

The discovery of a sign of true intellect outside ourselves procures us something of the emotion Robinson Crusoe felt when he saw the imprint of a human foot on the sandy beach of his island.

I was fifteen when I first met Sherlock Holmes, fifteen years old with my nose in a book as I walked the Sussex Downs, and nearly stepped on him. In my defence I must say it was an engrossing book, and it was very rare to come across another person in that particular part of the world in that war year of 1915. In my seven weeks of peripatetic reading amongst the sheep (which tended to move out of my way) and the gorse bushes (to which I had painfully developed an instinctive awareness) I had never before stepped on a person.

It was a cool, sunny day in early April, and the book was by Virgil. I had set out at dawn from the silent farmhouse, chosen a different direction from my usual—in this case southeasterly, towards the sea—and had spent the intervening hours wrestling with Latin verbs, climbing unconsciously over stone walls, and unthinkingly circling hedgerows, and would probably not have noticed the sea until I stepped off one of the chalk cliffs into it.

As it was, my first awareness that there was another soul in the universe was when a male throat cleared itself loudly not four feet from me. The Latin text flew into the air, followed closely by an Anglo-Saxon oath. Heart pounding, I hastily pulled together what dignity I could and glared down through my spectacles at this figure hunched up at my feet: a gaunt, greying man in his fifties wearing a cloth cap, ancient tweed greatcoat, and decent shoes, with a threadbare Army rucksack on the ground beside him. A tramp perhaps, who had left the rest of his possessions stashed beneath a bush. Or an Eccentric. Certainly no shepherd.

He said nothing. Very sarcastically. I snatched up my book and brushed it off.

"What on earth are you doing?" I demanded. "Lying in wait for someone?"

He raised one eyebrow at that, smiled in a singularly condescending and irritating manner, and opened his mouth to speak in that precise drawl which is the trademark of the overly educated upper-class English gentleman. A high voice; a biting one: definitely an Eccentric.

"I should think that I can hardly be accused of 'lying' anywhere," he said, "as I am seated openly on an uncluttered hillside, minding my own business. When, that is, I am not having to fend off those who propose to crush me underfoot." He rolled the penultimate *r* to put me in my place.

Had he said almost anything else, or even said the same words in another manner, I should merely have made a brusque apology and a purposeful exit, and my life would have been a very different thing. However, he had, all unknowing, hit squarely on a highly sensitive spot. My reason for leaving the house at first light had been to avoid my aunt, and the reason (the most recent of many reasons) for wishing to avoid my aunt was the violent row we'd had the night before, a row sparked by the undeniable fact that my feet had outgrown their shoes, for the second time since my arrival three months before. My aunt was small, neat, shrewish, sharp-tongued, quick-witted, and proud of her petite hands and feet. She invariably made me feel clumsy, uncouth, and unreasonably touchy about my height and the corresponding size of my feet. Worse, in the ensuing argument over finances, she had won.

His innocent words and his far-from-innocent manner hit my smouldering temper like a splash of petrol. My shoulders went back, my chin up, as I stiffened for combat.

I had no idea where I was, or who this man was, whether I was standing on his land or he on mine, if he was a dangerous lunatic or an escaped convict or the lord of the manor, and I did not care. I was furious.

"You have not answered my question, sir," I bit off.

He ignored my fury. Worse than that, he seemed unaware of it. He looked merely bored, as if he wished I might go away.

"What am I doing here, do you mean?"

"Exactly."

"I am watching bees," he said flatly, and turned back to his contemplation of the hillside.

Nothing in the man's manner showed a madness to correspond with his words. Nonetheless I kept a wary eye on him as I thrust my book into my coat pocket and dropped to the ground—a safe distance away from him—and studied the movement in the flowers before me.

There were indeed bees, industriously working at stuffing pollen into those leg sacs of theirs, moving from flower to flower. I watched, and was just thinking that there was nothing particularly noteworthy about these bees when my eyes were caught by the arrival of a peculiarly marked specimen. It seemed an ordinary honeybee but had a small red spot on its back. How odd—perhaps what he had been watching? I glanced at the Eccentric, who was now staring intently off into space, and then looked more closely at the bees, interested in spite of myself. I quickly concluded that the spot was no natural phenomenon, but rather paint, for there was another bee, its spot slightly lopsided, and another, and then another odd thing: a bee with a blue spot as well. As I watched, two red spots flew off in a northwesterly direction. I carefully observed the blue-and-red spot as it filled its pouches and saw it take off towards the northeast.

I thought for a minute, got up, and walked to the top of the hill, scattering ewes and lambs, and when I looked down at a village and river I knew instantly where I was. My house was less than two miles from here. I shook my head ruefully at my inattention, thought for a moment longer about this man and his red- and blue-spotted bees, and walked back down to take my leave of him. He did not look up, so I spoke to the back of his head.

"I'd say the blue spots are a better bet, if you're trying for another hive," I told him. "The ones you've only marked with red are probably from Mr. Warner's orchard. The blue spots are farther away, but they're almost sure to be wild ones." I dug the book from my pocket, and when I looked up to wish him a good day he was looking back at me, and the expression on his face took all words from my lips—no mean accomplishment. He was, as the writers say but people seldom actually are, openmouthed. He looked a bit like a fish, in fact, gaping at me as if I were growing another head. He slowly stood up, his mouth shutting as he rose, but still staring.

"What did you say?"

"I beg your pardon, are you hard of hearing?" I raised my voice somewhat and spoke slowly. "I said, if you want a new hive you'll have to follow the blue spots, because the reds are sure to be Tom Warner's."

"I am not hard of hearing, although I am short of credulity. How do you come to know of my interests?"

"I should have thought it obvious," I said impatiently, though even at that age I was aware that such things were not obvious to the majority of people. "I see paint on your pocket-handkerchief, and traces on your fingers where you wiped it away. The only reason to mark bees that I can think of is to enable one to follow them to their hive. You are either interested in gathering honey or in the bees themselves, and it is not the time of year to harvest honey. Three months ago we had an unusual cold spell that killed many hives. Therefore I assume that you are tracking these in order to replenish your own stock."

The face that looked down at me was no longer fishlike. In fact, it resembled amazingly a captive eagle I had once seen, perched in aloof splendour looking down the ridge of his nose at this lesser creature, cold disdain staring out from his hooded grey eyes.

"My God," he said in a voice of mock wonder, "it can think."

My anger had abated somewhat while watching the bees, but at this casual insult it erupted. Why was this tall, thin, infuriating old man so set on provoking an unoffending stranger? My chin went up again, only in part because he was taller than I, and I mocked him in return.

"My God, it can recognise another human being when it's hit over the head with one." For good measure I added, "And to think that I was raised to believe that old people had decent manners."

I stood back to watch my blows strike home, and as I faced him squarely my mind's eye finally linked him up with rumours I had heard and the reading I had done during my recent long convalescence, and I knew who he was, and I was appalled.

I had, I should mention, always assumed that a large part of Dr. Watson's adulatory stories were a product of that gentleman's inferior imagination. Certainly he always regarded the reader to be as slow as himself. Most irritating. Nonetheless, behind the stuff and nonsense of the biographer there towered a figure of pure genius, one of the great minds of his generation. A Legend.

And I was horrified: Here I was, standing before a Legend, flinging insults at him, yapping about his ankles like a small dog worrying a bear. I suppressed a cringe and braced myself for the casual swat that would send me flying.

To my amazement, however, and considerable dismay, instead of counterattacking he just smiled condescendingly and bent down to pick up his rucksack. I heard the faint rattle of the paint bottles within. He straightened, pushed his old-fashioned cap back on his greying hair, and looked at me with tired eyes.

"Young man, I—"

"*Young man!*" That did it. Rage swept into my veins, filling me with power. Granted I was far from voluptuous, granted I was dressed in practical, that is, male, clothing—this was not to be borne. Fear aside, Legend aside, the yapping lapdog attacked with all the utter contempt only an adolescent can muster. With a surge of glee I seized the weapon he had placed in my hands and drew back for the coup de grâce. "'Young man'?" I repeated. "It's a damned good thing that you did retire, if that's all that remains of the great detective's mind!" With that I reached for the brim of my oversized cap and my long blonde plaits slithered down over my shoulders.

A series of emotions crossed his face, rich reward for my victory. Simple surprise was followed by a rueful admission of defeat, and then, as he reviewed the entire discussion, he surprised me. His face relaxed, his thin lips twitched, his grey eyes crinkled into unexpected lines, and at last he threw back his head and gave a great shout of delighted laughter. That was the first time I heard Sherlock Holmes laugh, and although it was far from the last, it never ceased to surprise me, seeing that proud, ascetic face dissolve into helpless laughter. His amusement was always at least partially at himself, and this time was no exception. I was totally disarmed.

He wiped his eyes with the handkerchief I had seen poking from his coat pocket; a slight smear of blue paint was transferred to the bridge of his angular nose. He looked at me then, seeing me for the first time. After a minute he gestured at the flowers.

"You know something about bees, then?"

"Very little," I admitted.

"But they interest you?" he suggested.

"No."

This time both eyebrows raised.

"And, pray tell, why such a firm opinion?"

"From what I know of them they are mindless creatures, little more than a tool for putting fruit on trees. The females do all the work; the males do . . . well, they do little. And the queen, the only one who might amount to something, is condemned for the sake of the hive to spend her days as an egg machine. And," I said, warming to the topic, "what happens when her equal comes along, another queen with which she might have something in common? They are both forced—for the good of the hive—to fight to the death. Bees are great workers, it is true, but does not the production of each bee's total lifetime amount to a single dessertspoonful of honey? Each hive puts up with having hundreds of thousands of bee-hours stolen regularly, to be spread on toast and formed into candles, instead of declaring war or going on strike as any sensible, self-respecting race would do. A bit too close to the human race for my taste."

Mr. Holmes had sat down upon his heels during my tirade, watching a blue spot. When I had finished, he said nothing, but put out one long, thin finger and gently touched the fuzzy body, disturbing it not at all. There was silence for several minutes until the laden bee flew off—northeast, towards the copse two miles away, I was certain. He watched it disappear and murmured almost to himself, "Yes, they are very like *Homo sapiens*. Perhaps that is why they so interest me."

"I don't know how sapient you find most *Homines*, but I for one find the classification an optimistic misnomer." I was on familiar ground now, that of the mind and opinions, a beloved ground I had not trod for many months. That some of the opinions were those of an obnoxious teenager made them none the less comfortable or easy to defend. To my pleasure he responded.

"*Homo* in general, or simply *vir*?" he asked, with a solemnity that made me suspect that he was laughing at me. Well, at least I had taught him to be subtle with it.

"Oh, no. I am a feminist, but no man hater. A misanthrope in general, I suppose like yourself, sir. However, unlike you I find women to be the marginally more rational half of the race."

He laughed again, a gentler version of the earlier outburst, and I realised that I had been trying to provoke it this time.

"Young lady," he stressed the second word with gentle irony, "you have caused me amusement twice in one day, which is more than anyone else has done in some time. I have little humour to offer in return, but if you would care to accompany me home, I could at least give you a cup of tea."

"I should be very pleased to do so, Mr. Holmes."

"Ah, you have the advantage over me. You obviously know my name, yet there is no one present of whom I might beg an introduction to yourself." The formality of his speech was faintly ludicrous considering that we were two shabby figures facing each other on an otherwise deserted hillside.

"My name is Mary Russell." I held out my hand, which he took in his thin, dry one. We shook as if cementing a peace pact, which I suppose we were.

"Mary," he said, tasting it. He pronounced it in the Irish manner, his mouth caressing the long first syllable. "A suitably orthodox name for such a passive individual as yourself."

"I believe I was named after the Magdalene, rather than the Virgin."

"Ah, that explains it then. Shall we go, Miss Russell? My housekeeper ought to have something to put in front of us."

It was a lovely walk, that, nearly four miles over the downs. We thumbed over a variety of topics strung lightly on the common thread of apiculture. He gestured wildly atop a knoll when comparing the management of hives with Machiavellian theories of government, and cows ran snorting away. He paused in the middle of a stream to illustrate his theory juxtaposing the swarming of hives and the economic roots of war, using examples of the German invasion of France and the visceral patriotism of the English. Our boots squelched for the next mile. He reached the heights of his peroration at the top of a hill and launched himself down the other side at such a speed that he resembled some great flapping thing about to take off.

He stopped to look around for me, took in my stiffening gait and my inability to keep up with him, both literally and metaphorically, and shifted into a less manic mode. He did seem to have a good practical basis for his flights of fancy and, it turned out, had even written a book on the apiary arts entitled *A Practical Handbook of Bee Culture.* It had been well received, he said with pride (this from a man who, I remembered, had respectfully declined a knighthood from the late queen), particularly his experimental but highly successful placement within the hive of what he called the Royal Quarters, which had given the book its provocative subtitle: *With Some Observations upon the Segregation of the Queen.*

We walked, he talked, and under the sun and his soothing if occasionally incomprehensible monologue I began to feel something hard and tight within me relax slightly, and an urge I had thought killed began to make the first tentative stirrings towards life. When we arrived at his cottage we had known each other forever.

Other more immediate stirrings had begun to assert themselves as well, with increasing insistence. I had taught myself in recent months to ignore hunger, but a healthy young person after a long day in the open air with only a sandwich since morning is likely to find it difficult to concentrate on anything other than the thought of food. I prayed that the cup of tea would be a substantial one, and was considering the problem of how to suggest such a thing should it not be immediately offered, when we reached his house, and the housekeeper herself appeared at the door, and for a moment I forgot my preoccupation. It was none other than the long-suffering Mrs. Hudson, whom I had long considered the most underrated figure in all of Dr. Watson's stories. Yet another example of the man's obtuseness, this inability to know a gem unless it be set in gaudy gold.

Dear Mrs. Hudson, who was to become such a friend to me. At that first meeting she was, as always, imperturbable. She saw in an instant what her employer did not, that I was desperately hungry, and proceeded to empty her stores of food to feed a vigorous appetite. Mr. Holmes protested as she appeared with plate after platter of bread, cheese, relishes, and cakes, but watched thoughtfully as I put large dents in every selection. I was grateful that he did not embarrass me by commenting on my appetite, as my aunt was wont to do, but to the contrary he made an effort to keep up the appearance of eating with me. By the time I sat back with my third cup of tea, the inner woman satisfied as she had not been for many weeks, his manner was respectful, and that of Mrs. Hudson contented as she cleared away the débris.

"I thank you very much, Madam," I told her.

"I like to see my cooking appreciated, I do," she said, not looking at Mr. Holmes. "I rarely have the chance to fuss, unless Dr. Watson comes. This one," she inclined her head to the man opposite me, who had brought out a pipe from his coat pocket, "he doesn't eat enough to keep a cat from starving. Doesn't appreciate me at all, he doesn't."

"Now, Mrs. Hudson," he protested, but gently, as at an old argument, "I eat as I always have; it is you who will cook as if there were a household of ten."

"A cat would starve," she repeated firmly. "But you have eaten something today, I'm glad to see. If you've finished, Will wants a word with you before he goes, something about the far hedge."

"I care not a jot for the far hedge," he complained. "I pay him a great deal to fret about the hedges and the walls and the rest of it for me."

"He needs a word with you," she said again. Firm repetition seemed her preferred method of dealing with him, I noted.

"Oh, blast! Why did I ever leave London? I ought to have put my hives in an allotment and stayed in Baker Street. Help yourself to the bookshelves, Miss Russell. I'll be back in a few minutes." He snatched up his tobacco and matches and stalked out, Mrs. Hudson rolled her eyes and disappeared into the kitchen, and I found myself alone in the quiet room.

Sherlock Holmes's house was a typical ageless Sussex cottage, flint walls and red tile roof. This main room, on the ground floor, had once been two rooms, but was now a large square with a huge stone fireplace at one end, dark, high beams, an oak floor that gave way to slate through the kitchen door, and a surprising expanse of windows on the south side where the downs rolled on to the sea. A sofa, two wing chairs, and a frayed basket chair gathered around the fireplace, a round table and four chairs occupied the sunny south bay window (where I sat), and a work desk piled high with papers and objects stood beneath a leaded, diamond-paned window in the west: a room of many purposes. The walls were solid with bookshelves and cupboards.

Today I was more interested in my host than in his books, and I looked curiously at the titles (*Blood Flukes of Borneo* sat between *The Thought of Goethe* and *Crimes of Passion in Eighteenth-Century Italy*) with him in mind rather than with an eye to borrowing. I made a circuit of the room (tobacco still in a Persian slipper at the fireplace, I smiled to see; on one table a small crate stenciled LIMÓNES DE ESPAÑA and containing several disassembled revolvers; on another table three nearly identical pocket watches laid with great precision, chains and fobs stretched out in parallel lines, with a powerful magnifying glass, a set of calipers, and a paper and pad covered with figures to one side) before ending up in front of his desk.

I had no time for more than a cursory glance at his neat handwriting before his voice startled me from the door.

"Shall we sit out on the terrace?"

I quickly put down the sheet in my hand, which seemed to be a discourse on seven formulae for plaster and their relative effectiveness in recording tyre marks from different kinds of earth, and agreed that it would be pleasant in the garden. We took up our cups, but as I followed him across the room towards the French doors my attention was drawn by an odd object fixed to the room's south wall: a tall box, only a few inches wide but nearly three feet tall and protruding a good eighteen inches into the room. It appeared to be a solid block of wood but, pausing to examine it, I could see that both sides were sliding panels.

"My observation hive," Mr. Holmes said.

"Bees?" I exclaimed. "Inside the house?"

Instead of answering he reached past me and slid back one of the side panels, and revealed there a perfect, thin, glass-fronted beehive. I squatted before it, entranced. The comb was thick and even across the middle portion, trailed off at the edges, and was covered by a thick blanket of orange and black. The whole was vibrating with energy, though the individuals seemed to be simply milling about, without purpose.

I watched closely, trying to make sense of their apparently aimless motion. A tube led in at the bottom, with pollen-laden bees coming in and denuded bees going out; a smaller tube at the top, clouded with condensation, I assumed was for ventilation.

"Do you see the queen?" Mr. Holmes asked.

"She's here? Let me see if I can find her." I knew that the queen was the largest bee in the hive, and that wherever she went she had a fawning entourage, but it still took me an embarrassingly long time to pick her out from her two hundred or so daughters and sons. Finally I found her, and couldn't imagine why she had not appeared instantly. Twice the size of the others and imbued with dumb, bristling purpose, she seemed a creature of another race from her hive mates. I asked their keeper a few questions—did they object to the light, was the population as steady here as in a larger hive—and then he slid the cover over the living painting and we went outside. I remembered belatedly that I was not interested in bees.

Outside the French doors lay an expanse of flagstones, sheltered from the wind by a glass conservatory that grew off the kitchen wall and by an old stone wall with herbaceous border that curved around the remaining two sides. The terrace gathered in the heat until its air danced, and I was relieved when he continued down to a group of comfortable-looking wooden chairs in the shade of an enormous copper beech. I chose a chair that looked down towards the Channel, over the head of a small orchard that lay in a hollow below us. There were tidy hive boxes arranged among the trees and bees working the early flowers of the border. A bird sang. Two men's voices came and receded along the other side of the wall. Dishes rattled distantly from the kitchen. A small fishing boat appeared on the horizon and gradually worked its way towards us.

I suddenly came to myself with the realisation that I was neglecting my conversational responsibilities as a guest. I moved my cold tea from the arm of my chair to the table and turned to my host.

"Is this your handiwork?" I asked, indicating the garden.

He smiled ironically, though whether at the doubt in my voice or at the social impulse that drove me to break the silence, I was not certain.

"No, it is a collaboration on the part of Mrs. Hudson and old Will Thompson, who used to be head gardener at the manor. I took an interest in gardening when I first came here, but my work tends to distract me for days on end. I would reappear to find whole beds dead of drought or buried in bramble. But Mrs. Hudson enjoys it, and it gives her something to do other than pester me to eat her concoctions. I find it a pleasant spot to sit and think. It also feeds my bees—most of the flowers are chosen because of the quality of honey they produce."

"It is a very pleasant spot. It reminds me of a garden we once had when I was small."

"Tell me about yourself, Miss Russell."

I started to give him the obligatory response, first the demurral and then the reluctant flat autobiography, but some slight air of polite inattention in his manner stopped me. Instead, I found myself grinning at him.

"Why don't you tell me about myself, Mr. Holmes?"

"Aha, a challenge, eh?" There was a flare of interest in his eyes.

"Exactly."

"Very well, on two conditions. First, that you forgive my old and much-abused brain if it is slow and creaking, for such thought patterns as I once lived by are a habit and become rusty without continual use. Daily life here with Mrs. Hudson and Will is a poor whetting stone for sharp wit."

"I don't entirely believe that your brain is underused, but I grant the condition. And the other?"

"That you do the same for me when I have finished with you."

"Oh. All right. I shall try, even if I lay myself open to your ridicule." Perhaps I had not escaped the edge of his tongue after all.

"Good." He rubbed his thin dry hands together, and suddenly I was fixed with the probing eye of an entomologist. "I see before me one Mary Russell, named after her paternal grandmother."

I was taken aback for a moment, then reached up and fingered the antique locket, engraved MMR, that had slipped out from the buttons of my shirt. I nodded.

"She is, let us see, sixteen? fifteen, I think? Yes, fifteen years of age, and despite her youth and the fact that she is not at school she intends to pass the University entrance examinations." I touched the book in my pocket and nodded appreciatively. "She is obviously left-handed, one of her parents was Jewish—her mother, I think? Yes, definitely the mother—and she reads and writes Hebrew. She is at present four inches shorter than her American father—that was his suit? All right so far?" he asked complacently.

I thought furiously. "The Hebrew?" I asked.

"The ink marks on your fingers could only come with writing right to left."

"Of course." I looked at the accumulation of smears near my left thumbnail. "That is very impressive."

He waved it aside. "Parlour games. But the accents are not without interest." He eyed me again, then sat back with his elbows on the chair's armrests, steepled his fingers, rested them lightly on his lips for a moment, closed his eyes, and spoke.

"The accents. She has come recently from her father's home in the western United States, most likely northern California. Her mother was one generation away from Cockney Jew, and Miss Russell herself grew up in the southwestern edges of London. She moved, as I said, to California, within the last, oh, two years. Say the word 'martyr,' please." I did so. "Yes, two years. Sometime between then and December both parents died, very possibly in the same accident in which Miss Russell was involved last September or October, an accident which has left scar tissue on her throat, scalp, and right hand, a residual weakness in that same hand, and a slight stiffness in the left knee."

The game had suddenly stopped being entertaining. I sat frozen, my heart ceasing to beat while I listened to the cool, dry recitation of his voice.

"After her recovery she was sent back home to her mother's family, to a tight-fisted and unsympathetic relative who feeds her rather less than she needs. This last," he added parenthetically, "is I admit largely conjecture, but as a working hypothesis serves to explain her well-nourished frame poorly covered by flesh, and the reason why she appears at a stranger's table to consume somewhat more than she might if ruled strictly by her obvious good manners. I am willing to consider an alternative explanation," he offered, and opened his eyes, and saw my face.

"Oh, dear." His voice was an odd mixture of sympathy and irritation. "I have been warned about this tendency of mine. I do apologise for any distress I have caused you."

I shook my head and reached for the cold dregs in my teacup. It was difficult to speak through the lump in my throat.

Mr. Holmes stood up and went into the house, where I heard his voice and that of the housekeeper trading a few unintelligible phrases before he returned, carrying two delicate glasses and an open bottle of the palest of wines. He poured it into the glasses and handed me one, identifying it as honey wine—his own, of course. He sat down and we both sipped the fragrant liquor. In a few minutes the lump faded, and I heard the birds again. I took a deep breath and shot him a glance.

"Two hundred years ago you would have been burnt." I was trying for dry humour but was not entirely successful.

"I have been told that before today," he said, "though I cannot say I have ever fancied myself in the rôle of a witch, cackling over my pot."

"Actually, the book of Leviticus calls not for burning, but for the stoning of a man or a woman who speaks with the spirits—*ioob*, a necromancer or medium—or who is a *yidooni*, from the verb 'to know,' a person who achieves knowledge and power other than through the grace of the Lord God of Israel, er, well, a sorcerer." My voice trailed off as I realised that he was eyeing me with the apprehension normally reserved for mumbling strangers in one's railway compartment or acquaintances with incomprehensible and tiresome passions. My recitation had been an automatic response, triggered by the entry of a theological point into our discussion. I smiled a weak reassurance. He cleared his throat.

"Er, shall I finish?" he asked.

"As you wish," I said, with trepidation.

"This young lady's parents were relatively well-to-do, and their daughter inherited, which, combined with her daunting intelligence, makes it impossible for this penurious relative to bring her to heel. Hence, she wanders the downs without a chaperone and remains away until all hours."

He seemed to be drawing to a close, so I gathered my tattered thoughts.

"You are quite right, Mr. Holmes. I have inherited, and my aunt does find my actions contrary to her idea of how a young lady should act. And because she holds the keys to the pantry and tries to buy my obedience with food, I occasionally go with less than I would choose. Two minor flaws in your reasoning, however."

"Oh?"

"First, I did not come to Sussex to live with my aunt. The house and farm belonged to my mother. We used to spend summers here when I was small—some of the happiest times of my life—and when I was sent back to England I made it a condition of accepting her as guardian that we live here. She had no house, so she reluctantly agreed. Although she will control the finances for another six years, strictly speaking she lives with me, not I with her." Another might have missed the loathing in my voice, but not he. I dropped the subject quickly before I gave away any more of my life. "Second, I have been carefully judging the time by which I must depart in order to arrive home before dark, so the lateness of the hour does not really enter in. I shall have to take my leave soon, as it will be dark in slightly over two hours, and my home is two miles north of where we met."

"Miss Russell, you may take your time with your half of our agreement," he said calmly, allowing me to shelve the previous topic. "One of my neighbours subsidises his passion for automobiles by providing what he insists on calling a taxi service. Mrs. Hudson has gone to arrange for him to motor you home. You may rest for another hour and a quarter before he arrives to whisk you off to the arms of your dear aunt."

I looked down, discomfited. "Mr. Holmes, I'm afraid my allowance is not large enough to allow for such luxuries. In fact, I have already spent this week's monies on the Virgil."

"Miss Russell, I am a man with considerable funds and very little to spend them on. Please allow me to indulge in a whim."

"No, I cannot do that." He looked at my face and gave in.

"Very well, then, I propose a compromise. I shall pay for this and any subsequent expenses of the sort, but as a loan. I assume that your future inheritance will be sufficient to absorb such an accumulation of sums?"

"Oh, yes." I laughed as I recalled vividly the scene in the law office, my aunt's eyes turning dark with greed. "There would be no problem." He glanced at me sharply, hesitated, and spoke with some delicacy.

"Miss Russell, forgive my intrusion, but I tend towards a rather dim view of human nature. If I might enquire as to your will . . . ?" A mind reader, with a solid grasp of the basics of life. I smiled grimly.

"In the event of my death my aunt would get only an adequate yearly amount. Hardly more than she gets now."

He looked relieved. "I see. Now, about the loan. Your feet will suffer if you insist on walking the distance home in those shoes. At least for today, use the taxi. I am even willing to charge you interest if you like."

There was an odd air about his final, ironic offer that in another, less self-possessed person might have verged on a plea. We sat and studied each other, there in the quiet garden of early evening, and it occurred to me that he might have found this yapping dog an appealing companion. It could even be the beginnings of affection I saw in his face, and God knows that the joy of finding as quick and uncluttered a mind as his had begun to sing in me. We made an odd pair, a gangling, bespectacled girl and a tall, sardonic recluse, blessed or cursed with minds of hard brilliance that alienated all but the most tenacious. It never occurred to me that there might not be subsequent visits to this household. I spoke, and acknowledged his oblique offer of friendship.

"Spending three or four hours a day in travel does leave little time for other things. I accept your offer of a loan. Shall Mrs. Hudson keep the record?"

"She is scrupulously careful with figures, unlike myself. Come, have another glass of my wine, and tell Sherlock Holmes about himself."

"Are you finished, then?"

"Other than obvious things such as the shoes and reading late by inadequate light, that you have few bad habits, though your father smoked, and that unlike most Americans he preferred quality to fashion in his clothing—other than the obvious things, I will rest for the moment. It is your move. But mind you, I want to hear from you, not what you have picked up from my enthusiastic friend Watson."

"I shall try to avoid borrowing his incisive observations," I said drily, "though I have to wonder if using the stories to write your biography wouldn't prove to be a two-edged sword. The illustrations are certainly deceptive; they make you look considerably older. I'm not very good at guessing ages, but you don't look much more than, what, fifty? Oh, I'm sorry. Some people don't like to talk about their age."

"I am now fifty-four. Conan Doyle and his accomplices at *The Strand* thought to make me more dignified by exaggerating my age. Youth does not inspire confidence, in life or in stories, as I found to my annoyance when I set up residence in Baker Street. I was not yet twenty-one, and at first found the cases few and far between. Incidentally, I hope you do not make a habit of guessing. Guessing is a weakness brought on by indolence and should never be confused with intuition."

"I will keep that in mind," I said, and reached for my glass to take a swallow of wine while thinking about what I had seen in the room. I assembled my words with care. "To begin: You come from a moderately wealthy background, though your relationship with your parents was not entirely a happy one. To this day you wonder about them and try to come to grips with that part of your past." To his raised eyebrow I explained, "That is why you keep the much-handled formal photograph of your family on the shelf close to your chair, slightly obscured to other eyes by books, rather than openly mounting it on the wall and forgetting them." Ah, how sweet was the pleasure of seeing the look of appreciation spread over his face and hearing his murmured phrase, "Very good, very good indeed." It was like coming home.

"I could add that it explains why you never spoke to Dr. Watson about your childhood, as someone so solid and from such a blatantly

normal background as he is would doubtless have difficulty understanding the special burdens of a gifted mind. However, that would
be using his words, or rather lack of them, so it doesn't count. Without being too prying, I should venture to say that it contributed to
your early decision to distance yourself from women, for I suspect
that someone such as yourself would find it impossible to have an
other than all-inclusive relationship with a woman, one that totally
integrated all parts of your lives, unlike the unequal and somewhat
whimsical partnership you have had with Dr. Watson." The expression on his face was indescribable, wandering between amusement
and affrontery, with a touch each of anger and exasperation. It finally
settled on the quizzical. I felt considerably better about the casual hurt
he had done me, and plunged on.

"However, as I said, I don't mean to intrude on your privacy. It
was necessary to have the past as it contributes to the present. You
are here to escape the disagreeable sensation of being surrounded by
inferior minds, minds that can never understand because they are just
not built that way. You took a remarkably early retirement twelve years
ago, apparently in order to study the perfection and unity of bees and
to work on your magnum opus on detection. I see from the bookshelf
near your writing desk that you have completed seven volumes to date,
and I presume, from the boxes of notes under the completed books,
that there are at least an equal number yet to be written up." He nodded and poured us both more wine. The bottle was nearly empty.

"Between yourself and Dr. Watson, however, you have left me with
little to deduce. I could hardly assume that you would leave behind
your chemical experiments, for example, though the state of your cuffs
does indicate that you have been active recently—those acid burns are
too fresh to have frayed much in the wash. You no longer smoke cigarettes, your fingers show, though obviously your pipe is used often, and
the calluses on your fingertips indicate that you have kept up with the
violin. You seem to be as unconcerned about bee stings as you are about

finances and gardening, for your skin shows the marks of stings both old and new, and your suppleness indicates that the theories about bee stings as a therapy for rheumatism have some basis. Or is it arthritis?"

"Rheumatism, in my case."

"Also, I think it possible that you have not entirely given up your former life, or perhaps it has not entirely given you up. I see a vague area of pale skin on your chin, which shows that some time last summer you had a goatee, since shaven off. There hasn't been enough sun yet to erase the line completely. As you don't normally wear a beard, and would, in my opinion, look unpleasant with one, I can assume it was for the purpose of a disguise, in a rôle which lasted some months. Probably it had to do with the early stages of the war. Spying against the Kaiser, I should venture to say."

His face went blank, and he studied me without any trace of expression for a long minute. I squelched a self-conscious smile. At last he spoke.

"I did ask for it, did I not? Are you familiar with the work of Dr. Sigmund Freud?"

"Yes, although I find the work of the next, as it were, generation more helpful. Freud is overly obsessed with exceptional behavior: an aid to your line of work, perhaps, but not as useful for a generalist."

There was a sudden commotion in the flower bed. Two orange cats shot out and raced along the lawn and disappeared through the opening in the garden wall. His eyes followed them, and he sat squinting into the low sun.

"Twenty years ago," he murmured. "Even ten. But here? Now?" He shook his head and focused again on me.

"What will you read at University?"

I smiled. I couldn't help it; I knew just how he was going to react, and I smiled, anticipating his dismay.

"Theology."

His reaction was as violent as I had known it would be, but if I was sure of anything in my life, it was that. We took a walk through the gloaming to the cliffs, and I had my look at the sea while he wrestled with the idea, and by the time we returned he had decided that it was no worse than anything else, though he considered it a waste, and said so. I did not respond.

The automobile arrived shortly thereafter, and Mrs. Hudson came out to pay for it. Holmes explained our agreement, to her amusement, and she promised to make a note of it.

"I have an experiment to finish tonight, so you must pardon me," he said, though it did not take many visits before I knew that he disliked saying goodbye. I put out my hand and nearly snatched it back when he raised it to his lips rather than shaking it as he had before. He held on to it, brushed it with his cool lips, and let it go.

"Please come to see us anytime you wish. We are on the telephone, by the way. Ask the exchange for Mrs. Hudson, though; the good ladies sometimes decide to protect me by pretending ignorance, but they will usually permit calls to go through to her." With a nod he began to turn away, but I interrupted his exit.

"Mr. Holmes," I said, feeling myself go pink, "may I ask you a question?"

"Certainly, Miss Russell."

"How does *The Valley of Fear* end?" I blurted out.

"The what?" He sounded astonished.

"*Valley of Fear*. In *The Strand*. I hate these serials, and next month is the end of it, but I just wondered if you could tell me, well, how it turned out."

"This is one of Watson's tales, I take it?"

"Of course. It's the case of Birlstone and the Scowrers and John McMurdo and Professor Moriarty and—"

"Yes, I believe I can identify the case, although I have often wondered why, if Conan Doyle so likes pseudonyms, he couldn't have given them to Watson and myself as well."

"So how did it end?"

"I haven't the faintest notion. You would have to ask Watson."

"But surely you know how the case ended," I said, amazed.

"The case, certainly. But what Watson has made of it, I couldn't begin to guess, except that there is bound to be gore and passion and secret handshakes. Oh, and some sort of love interest. I deduce, Miss Russell; Watson transforms. Good day." He went back into the cottage.

Mrs. Hudson, who had stood listening to the exchange, did not comment, but pressed a package into my hands, "for the trip back," although from the weight of it the eating would take longer than the driving, even if I were to find the interior space for it. However, if I could get it past my aunt's eyes it would make a welcome supplement to my rations. I thanked her warmly.

"Thank you for coming here, dear child," she said. "There's more life in him than I've seen for a good many months. Please come again, and soon?"

I promised, and climbed into the car. The driver spun off in a rattle of gravel, and so began my long association with Mr. Sherlock Holmes.

THE ADVENTURE OF THE UNIQUE *HAMLET*

VINCENT STARRETT

incent Starrett may not have invented the fictional biography, but he was one of the first to chronicle the life of Holmes as if he were a historical figure. His The Private Life of Sherlock Holmes *is a staple of that ever-expanding subgenre. "The Adventure of the Unique* Hamlet*" combines a thoroughly grounded understanding of its subject, sly humor, and a send-up of that "gentle madness" he shared with so many (this editor included): bibliomania. This particular story is now in the public domain.*

I.

"Holmes," said I, one morning as I stood in our bay window, looking idly into the street, "surely here comes a madman. Someone has incautiously left the door open and the poor fellow has slipped out. What a pity!"

It was a glorious morning in the spring, with a fresh breeze and inviting sunlight, but as it was rather early few persons were astir. Birds twittered under the neighboring eaves, and from the far end of the thoroughfare came faintly the droning cry of an umbrella repair man; a lean cat slunk across the cobbles and disappeared into a courtway; but for the most part, the street was deserted save for the eccentric individual who had called forth my exclamation.

My friend rose lazily from the wicker rocker in which he had been lounging and came to my side, standing with long legs spread and hands in the pockets of his dressing gown. He smiled as he saw the singular personage coming along. A personage indeed he seemed to be, despite his odd actions, for he was tall and portly, with elderly whiskers of the brand known as mutton-chop, and he seemed eminently respectable. He was loping curiously, like a tired hound, lifting his knees high as he ran, and a heavy double watch chain of gold bounced against and rebounded from the plump line of his figured waistcoat. With one hand he clutched despairingly at his silk two-gallon hat, while with the other he essayed weird gestures in the air with an emotion bordering upon distraction. We could almost see the spasmodic workings of his countenance.

"What under heaven can ail him?" I cried. "See how he glances at the houses as he passes."

"He is looking at the numbers," responded Sherlock Holmes, with dancing eyes, "and I fancy it is ours that will bring him the greatest happiness. His profession, of course, is obvious."

"A banker, I imagine, or at least a person of affluence," I hazarded, wondering what curious bit of minutiae had betrayed the man's business to my remarkable companion, in a single glance.

"Affluent, yes," said Holmes, with a mischievous grin, "but not exactly a banker, Watson. Notice the sagging pockets, despite the excellence of his clothing, and the rather exaggerated madness of his eye. He is a collector, or I am very much mistaken."

"My dear fellow!" I exclaimed. "At his age and in his station! And why should he be seeking us? When we settled that last bill—"

"Of books," said my friend, severely. "He is a professional book collector. His line is Caxtons, Elzevirs, Gutenberg Bibles, folios; not the sordid reminders of unpaid grocery accounts and tobacconists' debits. See, he is turning in here, as I expected, and in a moment he will stand upon our hearthrug and tell us the harrowing tale of an unique volume and its extraordinary disappearance."

His eyes gleamed and he rubbed his hands together in profound satisfaction. I could not but hope that Holmes's conjecture was correct, for he had had little to occupy his mind for some weeks, and I lived in constant fear that he would seek that stimulation his active brain required in the long-tabooed cocaine bottle.

As Holmes finished speaking, the man's ring at the doorbell echoed through the apartment; hurried feet sounded upon the stairs, while the wailing voice of Mrs. Hudson, raised in agonized protest, could only have been occasioned by frustration of her coveted privilege of bearing his card to us. Then the door burst violently inward and the object of our analysis staggered to the center of the room, and, without announcing his intention by word or sign, pitched head-foremost onto our center rug. There he lay, a magnificent ruin, with his head on the fringed border and his feet in the coal scuttle; and sealed within his lifeless lips the amazing story he had come to tell—for that it was amazing we could not doubt, in the light of our client's extraordinary behavior.

Holmes quickly ran for the brandy bottle, while I knelt beside the stricken mountain of flesh and loosened the wilted neckband. He was not dead, and when we had forced the nozzle of the flask between his teeth he sat up in groggy fashion, passing a dazed hand across his eyes. Then he scrambled to his feet with an embarrassed apology for his weakness, and fell into the chair that Holmes held invitingly toward him.

"That is right, Mr. Harrington Edwards," said my companion, soothingly. "Be quite calm, my dear sir, and when you have recovered your composure you will find us ready to listen to your story."

"You know me, then?" cried our sudden visitor, with pride in his voice and surprised eyebrows lifted.

"I had never heard of you until this moment, but if you wish to conceal your identity it would be well for you to leave your bookplates at home." As Holmes spoke, he handed the other a little package of folded paper slips, which he had picked from the floor. "They fell from your hat when you had the misfortune to tumble," he added, with a whimsical smile.

"Yes, yes," cried the collector, a deep blush spreading over his features. "I remember now; my hat was a little large and I folded a number of them and placed them beneath the sweatband. I had forgotten."

"Rather shabby usage for a handsome etched plate," smiled my companion, "but that is your affair. And now, sir, if you are quite at ease, let us hear what it is that has brought you, a collector of books, from Poke Stogis Manor—the name is on the plate—to the office of Mr. Sherlock Holmes, consulting expert in crime. Surely nothing but the theft of Mahomet's own copy of the Koran can have affected you so amazingly."

Mr. Harrington Edwards smiled feebly at the jest, then sighed. "Alas," he murmured, "if that were all it were! But I shall begin at the beginning.

"You must know, then, that I am the greatest Shakespearean commentator in the world. My collection of *ana* is unrivaled, and much of the world's collection (and consequently its knowledge of the true Shakespeare) has emanated from my pen. One book I did not possess; it was unique, in the correct sense of that abused word; it was the greatest Shakespeare rarity in the world. Few knew that it existed, for its existence was kept a profound secret between a chosen few. Had it become known that this book was in England—any place, indeed—its owner would have been hounded to his grave by American millionaire collectors.

"It was in the possession of my friend—I tell you this in the strictest confidence, as between adviser and client—of my friend, Sir Nathaniel Brooke-Bannerman, whose place at Walton-on-Walton is next to my own. A scant two hundred yards separate our dwellings, and so intimate has been our friendship that a few years ago the fence between our estates was removed, and each roamed or loitered at will about the other's preserves.

"For some years, now, I have been at work on my greatest book— my *magnum opus*. It was to be also my last book, embodying the results of a lifetime of study and research. Sir, I know Elizabethan London better than any man alive, better than any man who ever lived, I sometimes think—" He burst suddenly into tears.

"There, there," said Sherlock Holmes, gently. "Do not be distressed. It is my business to help people who are unhappy by reason of great losses. Be assured, I shall help you. Pray continue with your interesting narrative. What was this book—which, I take it, in some manner has disappeared? You borrowed it from your friend?"

"That is what I am coming to," said Mr. Harrington Edwards, drying his tears, "but as for help, Mr. Holmes, I fear that is beyond even you. Yet, as a court of last resort, I came to you, ignoring all intermediate agencies.

"Let me resume then: As you surmise, I needed this book. Knowing its value, which could not be fixed, for the book is priceless, and knowing Sir Nathaniel's idolatry of it, I hesitated long before asking the loan of it. But I had to have it, for without it my work could not be completed, and at length I made the request. I suggested that I go to his home, and go through the volume under his own eyes, he sitting at my side throughout my entire examination, and servants stationed at every door and window, with fowling pieces in their hands.

"You can imagine my astonishment when Sir Nathaniel laughed at my suggested precautions. 'My dear Edwards,' he said, 'that would be all very well were you Arthur Bambidge or Sir Homer Nantes (mentioning the two great men of the British Museum), or were you Mr. Henry Hutterson, the American railroad magnate; but you are my friend Edwards, and you shall take the book home with you for as long as you like.' I protested vigorously, I assure you, but he would have it so, and as I was touched by this mark of his esteem, at length I permitted him to have it his own way. My God! If I had remained adamant! If I had only—"

He broke off and for a moment stared fixedly into space. His eyes were directed at the Persian slipper on the wall, in the toe of which Holmes kept his tobacco, but we could see that his thoughts were far away.

"Come, Mr. Edwards," said Holmes, firmly. "You are agitating yourself unduly. And you are unreasonably prolonging our curiosity. You have not yet told us what this book is."

Mr. Harrington Edwards gripped the arm of the chair in which he sat, with tense fingers. Then he spoke, and his voice was low and thrilling:

"The book was a *Hamlet* quarto, dated 1602, presented by Shakespeare to his friend Drayton, with an inscription four lines in length, written and signed by the Master, himself!"

"My dear sir!" I exclaimed. Holmes blew a long, slow whistle of astonishment.

"It is true," cried the collector. "That is the book I borrowed, and that is the book I lost! The long-sought quarto of 1602, actually inscribed in Shakespeare's own hand! His greatest drama, in an edition dated a year earlier than any that is known; a perfect copy, and with four lines in his handwriting! Unique! Extraordinary! Amazing! Astounding! Colossal! Incredible! Un—"

He seemed wound up to continue indefinitely, but Holmes, who had sat quite still at first, shocked by the importance of the loss, interrupted the flow of adjectives.

"I appreciate your emotion, Mr. Edwards," he said, "and the book is indeed all that you say it is. Indeed, it is so important that we must at once attack the problem of rediscovering it. Compose yourself, my dear sir, and tell us of the loss. The book, I take it, is readily identifiable?"

"Mr. Holmes," said our client, earnestly, "it would be impossible to hide it. It is so important a volume that, upon coming into possession of it, Sir Nathaniel Brooke-Bannerman called a consultation of the great binders of the Empire, at which were present Mr. Riviere, Messrs. Sangorski and Sutcliffe, Mr. Zaehnsdorf and others. They and myself, and two others, alone know of the book's existence. When I tell you that it is bound in brown levant morocco, super extra, with leather joints, brown levant doublures and flyleaves, the whole elaborately gold-tooled, inlaid with seven hundred and fifty separate pieces of various colored leathers, and enriched by the insertion of eighty-two precious stones, I need not add that it is a design that never will be duplicated, and I tell you only a few of its glories. The binding was personally done by Messrs. Riviere, Sangorski, Sutcliffe, and Zaehnsdorf, working alternately, and is a work of such enchantment that any man might gladly die a thousand deaths for the privilege of owning it for five minutes."

"Dear me," quoth Sherlock Holmes, "it must indeed be a handsome volume, and from your description, together with a realization of its importance by reason of its association, I gather that it is something beyond what might be termed a valuable book."

"Priceless!" cried Mr. Harrington Edwards. "The combined wealth of India, Mexico, and Wall Street would be all too little for its purchase!"

"You are anxious to recover this book?" Holmes asked, looking at him keenly.

"My God!" shrieked the collector, rolling up his eyes and clawing the air with his hands. "Do you suppose—"

"Tut, tut!" Holmes interrupted. "I was only testing you. It is a book that might move even you, Mr. Harrington Edwards, to theft—but we may put aside that notion at once. Your emotion is too sincere, and besides you know too well the difficulties of hiding such a volume as you describe. Indeed, only a very daring man would purloin it and keep it long in his possession. Pray tell us how you came to suffer it to be lost."

Mr. Harrington Edwards seized the brandy flask, which stood at his elbow, and drained it at a gulp. With the renewed strength thus obtained, he continued his story:

"As I have said, Sir Nathaniel forced me to accept the loan of the book, much against my own wishes. On the evening that I called for it, he told me that two of his trusted servants, heavily armed, would accompany me across the grounds to my home. 'There is no danger,' he said, 'but you will feel better,' and I heartily agreed with him. How shall I tell you what happened? Mr. Holmes, it was those very servants who assailed me and robbed me of my priceless borrowing!"

Sherlock Holmes rubbed his lean hands with satisfaction. "Splendid!" he murmured. "It is a case after my own heart. Watson, these are deep waters in which we are sailing. But you are rather lengthy about this, Mr. Edwards. Perhaps it will help matters if I ask you a few questions. By what road did you go to your home?"

"By the main road, a good highway which lies in front of our estates. I preferred it to the shadows of the wood."

"And there were some two hundred yards between your doors. At what point did the assault occur?"

"Almost midway between the two entrance drives, I should say."

"There was no light?"

"That of the moon only."

"Did you know these servants who accompanied you?"

"One I knew slightly; the other I had not seen before."

"Describe them to me, please."

"The man who is known to me is called Miles. He is clean-shaven, short, and powerful, although somewhat elderly. He was known, I believe, as Sir Nathaniel's most trusted servant; he had been with Sir Nathaniel for years. I cannot describe him minutely for, of course, I never paid much attention to him. The other was tall and thickset, and wore a heavy beard. He was a silent fellow; I do not believe he spoke a word during the journey."

"Miles was more communicative?"

"Oh yes—even garrulous, perhaps. He talked about the weather and the moon, and I forget what all."

"Never about books?"

"There was no mention of books between any of us."

"Just how did the attack occur?"

"It was very sudden. We had reached, as I say, about the halfway point, when the big man seized me by the throat—to prevent outcry, I suppose—and on the instant, Miles snatched the volume from my grasp and was off. In a moment his companion followed him. I had been half throttled and could not immediately cry out; when I could articulate, I made the countryside ring with my cries. I ran after them, but failed even to catch another sight of them. They had disappeared completely. "

"Did you all leave the house together?"

"Miles and I left together; the second man joined us at the porter's lodge. He had been attending to some of his duties."

"And Sir Nathaniel—where was he?"

"He said good night on the threshold."

"What has he had to say about all this?"

"I have not told him."

"You have not told him!" echoed Sherlock Holmes, in astonishment.

"I have not dared," miserably confessed our client. "It will kill him. That book was the breath of his life."

"When did this occur?" I put in, with a glance at Holmes.

"Excellent, Watson," said my friend, answering my glance. "I was about to ask the same question."

"Just last night," was Mr. Harrington Edwards's reply. "I was crazy most of the night; I didn't sleep a wink. I came to you the first thing this morning. Indeed, I tried to raise you on the telephone last night, but could not establish a connection."

"Yes," said Holmes, reminiscently, "we were attending Mme. Trontini's first night. You remember, Watson, we dined later at Albani's?"

"Oh, Mr. Holmes, do you think you can help me?" cried the abject collector.

"I trust so," declared my friend, cheerfully. "Indeed, I am certain that I can. At any rate, I shall make a gallant attempt, with Watson's aid. Such a book, as you remark, is not easily hidden. What say you, Watson, to a run down to Walton-on-Walton?"

"There is a train in half an hour," said Mr. Harrington Edwards, looking at his watch. "Will you return with me?"

"No, no," laughed Holmes, "that would never do. We must not be seen together just yet, Mr. Edwards. Go back yourself on the first train, by all means, unless you have further business in London. My friend and I will go together. There is another train this morning?"

"An hour later."

"Excellent. Until we meet, then!"

II.

We took the train from Paddington Station an hour later, as we had promised, and began the journey to Walton-on-Walton, a pleasant, aristocratic village and the scene of the curious accident to our friend of Poke Stogis Manor. Holmes, lying back in his seat, blew earnest smoke rings at the ceiling of our compartment, which fortunately was empty, while I devoted myself to the morning paper. After a bit, I tired of this occupation and turned to Holmes. I was surprised to find him looking out of the window, wreathed in smiles and quoting Hafiz softly under his breath.

"You have a theory?" I asked, in surprise.

"It is a capital mistake to theorize in advance of the evidence," he replied. "Still, I have given some thought to the interesting problem of our friend, Mr. Harrington Edwards, and there are several indications which can point only to one conclusion."

"And whom do you believe to be the thief?"

"My dear fellow," said Sherlock Holmes, "you forget we already know the thief. Edwards has testified quite clearly that it was Miles who snatched the volume."

"True," I admitted, abashed. "I had forgotten. All we must do then, is find Miles."

"And a motive," added my friend, chuckling. "What would you say, Watson, was the motive in this case?"

"Jealousy," I replied promptly.

"You surprise me!"

"Miles had been bribed by a rival collector, who in some manner had learned about this remarkable volume. You remember Edwards told us this second man joined them at the lodge. That would give an excellent opportunity for the substitution of a man other than the servant intended by Sir Nathaniel. Is not that good reasoning?"

"You surpass yourself, my dear Watson," murmured Holmes. "It is excellently reasoned, and, as you justly observe, the opportunity for a substitution was perfect."

"Do you not agree with me?"

"Hardly, Watson. A rival collector, in order to accomplish this remarkable coup, first would have to have known of the volume, as you suggest, but also he must have known what night Mr. Harrington Edwards would go to Sir Nathaniel's to get it, which would point to collaboration on the part of our client. As a matter of fact, however, Mr. Edwards's decision as to his acceptance of the loan, was, I believe, sudden and without previous determination."

"I do not recall his saying so."

"He did not say so, but it is a simple deduction. A book collector is mad enough to begin with, Watson; but tempt him with some such bait as this Shakespeare quarto and he is bereft of all sanity. Mr. Edwards would not have been able to wait. It was just the night before that Sir Nathaniel promised him the book, and it was just last night that he flew to accept the offer—flying, incidentally, to disaster, also. The miracle is that he was able to wait for an entire day."

"Wonderful!"

"Elementary," said Holmes. "I have employed one of the earliest and best known principles of my craft, only. If you are interested in the process, you will do well to read Harley Graham on 'Transcendental Emotion,' while I have, myself, been guilty of a small brochure in which I catalogue some twelve hundred professions, and the emotional effect upon their members of unusual tidings, good and bad."

We were the only passengers to alight at Walton-on-Walton, but rapid inquiry developed that Mr. Harrington Edwards had returned on the previous train. Holmes, who had disguised himself before leaving the train, did all the talking. He wore his cap peak backwards, carried a pencil behind his ear, and had turned up the bottoms of his trousers; from one pocket dangled the end of a linen tape measure. He was a municipal surveyor to the life, and I could not but think that, meeting him suddenly in the road, I should not myself have known him. At his suggestion, I dented the crown of my derby hat and turned my coat inside out. Then he gave me an end of the tape measure, while he, carrying the other end, went on ahead. In this fashion, stopping from time to time to kneel in the dust, and ostensibly to measure sections of the roadway, we proceeded toward Poke Stogis Manor. The occasional villagers whom we encountered on their way to the station barroom paid us no more attention than if we had been rabbits.

Shortly we came into sight of our friend's dwelling, a picturesque and rambling abode, sitting far back in its own grounds and bordered by a square of sentinel oaks. A gravel pathway led from the roadway to the house entrance, and, as we passed, the sunlight struck glancing rays from an antique brass knocker on the door. The whole picture, with its background of gleaming countryside, was one of rural calm and comfort; we could with difficulty believe it the scene of the sinister tragedy we were come to investigate.

"We shall not enter yet," said Sherlock Holmes, resolutely passing the gate leading into our client's acreage, "but we shall endeavor to be back in time for luncheon."

From this point the road progressed downward in a gentle incline and the trees were thicker on either side of the road. Holmes kept his eyes stolidly on the path before us, and when we had covered about one hundred yards he stopped. "Here," he said, pointing, "the assault occurred."

I looked closely at the earth, but could see no sign of struggle.

"You recall it was midway between the two houses that it happened," he continued. "No, there are few signs; there was no violent tussle. Fortunately, however, we had our proverbial fall of rain last evening and the earth has retained impressions nicely." He indicated the faint imprint of a foot, then another, and another. Kneeling down, I was able to see that, indeed, many feet had passed along the road.

Holmes flung himself at full length in the dirt and wriggled swiftly about, his nose to the earth, muttering rapidly in French. Then he whipped out a glass, the better to examine a mark that had caught his eye; but in a moment he shook his head in disappointment and continued with his examination. I was irresistibly reminded of a noble hound at fault, sniffing in circles in an effort to reestablish the lost scent. In a moment, however, he had it, for with a little cry of pleasure he rose to his feet, zigzagged curiously across the road and paused before a hedge, a lean finger pointing accusingly at a break in the thicket.

"No wonder they disappeared," he smiled as I came up. "Edwards thought they continued up the road, but here is where they broke through." Then stepping back a little distance, he ran forward lightly and cleared the hedge at a bound, alighting on his hands on the other side.

"Follow me carefully," he warned, "for we must not allow our own footprints to confuse us." I fell more heavily than my companion, but in a moment he had me by the heels and had helped me to steady myself. "See," he cried, lowering his face to the earth; and deep in the mud and grass I saw the prints of two pairs of feet.

"The small man broke through," said Holmes, exultantly, "but the larger rascal leaped over the hedge. See how deeply his prints are marked; he landed heavily here in the soft ooze. It is very significant, Watson, that they came this way. Does it suggest nothing to you?"

"That they were men who knew Edwards's grounds as well as the Brooke-Bannerman estate," I answered, and thrilled with pleasure at my friend's nod of approbation.

He lowered himself to his stomach without further conversation, and for some moments we crawled painfully across the grass. Then a shocking thought came to me.

"Holmes," I whispered in horror, "do you see where these footprints tend? They are directed toward the home of our client, Mr. Harrington Edwards!"

He nodded his head slowly, and his lips were set tight and thin. The double line of impressions ended abruptly at the back door of Poke Stogis Manor!

Sherlock Holmes rose to his feet and looked at his watch.

"We are just in time for luncheon," he announced, and hastily brushed his garments. Then, deliberately, he knocked on the door. In a few moments we were in the presence of our client.

"We have been roaming about the neighborhood," apologized Holmes, "and took the liberty of coming to your rear entrance."

"You have a clew?" asked Mr. Harrington Edwards, eagerly.

A queer smile of triumph sat upon Sherlock Holmes's lips.

"Indeed," he said, quietly, "I believe I have solved your little problem, Mr. Harrington Edwards!"

"My dear Holmes!" I cried, and "My dear sir!" cried our client.

"I have yet to establish a motive," confessed my friend, "but as to the main facts there can be no question."

Mr. Harrington Edwards fell into a chair, white and shaking.

"The book," he croaked. "Tell me!"

"Patience, my good sir," counseled Holmes, kindly. "We have had nothing to eat since sunup, and are famished. All in good time. Let us first dine and then all shall be made clear. Meanwhile, I should like to telephone to Sir Nathaniel Brooke-Bannerman, for I wish him to hear what I have to say."

Our client's pleas were in vain. Holmes would have his little joke and his luncheon. In the end, Mr. Harrington Edwards staggered away to the kitchen to order a repast, and Sherlock Holmes talked rapidly and unintelligibly into the telephone for a moment and came back with a smile on his face, which, to me, boded ill for someone. But I asked no questions; in good time this amazing man would tell his story in his own way. I had heard all he had heard, and had seen all he had seen; yet I was completely at sea. Still, our host's ghastly smile hung in my mind, and come what would I felt sorry for him. In a little time we were seated at table. Our client, haggard and nervous, ate slowly and with apparent discomfort; his eyes were never long absent from Holmes's inscrutable face. I was little better off, but Holmes ate with gusto, relating meanwhile a number of his earlier adventures, which I may some day give to the world, if I am able to read my illegible notes made on the occasion.

When the sorry meal had been concluded, we went into the library, where Sherlock Holmes took possession of the big easy chair, with an air of proprietorship that would have been amusing in other circumstances. He screwed together his long pipe and lighted it with a malicious lack of haste, while Mr. Harrington Edwards perspired against the mantel in an agony of apprehension.

"Why must you keep us waiting, Mr. Holmes?" he whispered. "Tell us, at once, please, who—who—" His voice trailed off into a moan.

"The criminal," said Sherlock Holmes, smoothly, "is—"

"Sir Nathaniel Brooke-Bannerman!" said a maid, suddenly putting her head in at the door, and on the heels of her announcement stalked the handsome baronet, whose priceless volume had caused all this stir and unhappiness.

Sir Nathaniel was white, and appeared ill. He burst at once into talk.

"I have been much upset by your call," he said, looking meanwhile at our client. "You say you have something to tell me about the quarto. Don't say—that—anything has happened—to it!" He clutched nervously at the wall to steady himself, and I felt deep pity for him.

Mr. Harrington Edwards looked at Sherlock Holmes. "Oh, Mr. Holmes," he cried, pathetically, "why did you send for him?"

"Because," said my friend, firmly, "I wish him to hear the truth about the Shakespeare quarto. Sir Nathaniel, I believe you have not been told as yet that Mr. Edwards was robbed, last night, of your precious volume—robbed by the trusted servants whom you sent with him to protect it."

"What!" shrieked the titled collector. He staggered and fumbled madly at his heart; then collapsed into a chair. "Good God!" he muttered, and then again: "Good God!"

"I should have thought you would have been suspicious of evil when your servants did not return," pursued Holmes.

"I have not seen them," whispered Sir Nathaniel. "I do not mingle with my servants. I did not know they had failed to return. Tell me—tell me all!"

"Mr. Edwards," said Sherlock Holmes, turning to our client, "will you repeat your story, please?"

Mr. Harrington Edwards, thus adjured, told the unhappy tale again, ending with a heartbroken cry of "Oh, Sir Nathaniel, can you ever forgive me?"

"I do not know that it was entirely your fault," observed Holmes, cheerfully. "Sir Nathaniel's own servants are the guilty ones, and surely he sent them with you."

"But you said you had solved the case, Mr. Holmes," cried our client, in a frenzy of despair.

"Yes," agreed Holmes, "it is solved. You have had the clue in your own hands ever since the occurrence, but you did not know how to use it. It all turns upon the curious actions of the taller servant, prior to the assault."

"The actions of—" stammered Mr. Harrington Edwards. "Why, he did nothing—said nothing!"

"That is the curious circumstance," said Sherlock Holmes, meaningly.

Sir Nathaniel got to his feet with difficulty.

"Mr. Holmes," he said, "this has upset me more than I can tell you. Spare no pains to recover the book, and to bring to justice the scoundrels who stole it. But I must go away and think—think—"

"Stay," said my friend. "I have already caught one of them."

"What! Where?" cried the two collectors, together.

"Here," said Sherlock Holmes, and stepping forward he laid a hand on the baronet's shoulder. "You, Sir Nathaniel, were the taller servant; you were one of the thieves who throttled Mr. Harrington Edwards and took from him your own book. And now, sir, will you tell us why you did it?"

Sir Nathaniel Brooke-Bannerman toppled and would have fallen had not I rushed forward and supported him. I placed him in a chair. As we looked at him, we saw confession in his eyes; guilt was written in his haggard face.

"Come, come," said Holmes, impatiently. "Or will it make it easier for you if I tell the story as it occurred? Let it be so, then. You parted with Mr. Harrington Edwards on your doorsill, Sir Nathaniel, bidding your best friend good night with a smile on your lips and evil in your heart. And as soon as you had closed the door, you slipped into an enveloping raincoat, turned up your collar, and hastened by a shorter road to the porter's lodge, where you joined Mr. Edwards and Miles as one of your own servants. You spoke no word at any time, because you feared to speak. You were afraid Mr. Edwards would recognize your voice, while your beard, hastily assumed, protected your face, and in the darkness your figure passed unnoticed.

"Having choked and robbed your best friend, then, of your own book, you and your scoundrelly assistant fled across Mr. Edwards's fields to his own back door, thinking that, if investigation followed, I would be called in, and would trace those footprints and fix the crime upon Mr. Harrington Edwards, as part of a criminal plan, prearranged with your rascally servants, who would be supposed to be in the pay of Mr. Edwards and the ringleaders in a counterfeit assault upon his

104

person. Your mistake, sir, was in ending your trail abruptly at Mr. Edwards's back door. Had you left another trail, then, leading back to your own domicile, I should unhesitatingly have arrested Mr. Harrington Edwards for the theft.

"Surely, you must know that in criminal cases handled by me, it is never the obvious solution that is the correct one. The mere fact that the finger of suspicion is made to point at a certain individual is sufficient to absolve that individual from guilt. Had you read the little works of my friend and colleague, here, Dr. Watson, you would not have made such a mistake. Yet you claim to be a bookman!"

A low moan from the unhappy baronet was his only answer.

"To continue, however: there at Mr. Edwards's own back door you ended your trail, entering his house—his own house—and spending the night under his roof, while his cries and ravings over his loss filled the night, and brought joy to your unspeakable soul. And in the morning, when he had gone forth to consult me, you quietly left—you and Miles—and returned to your own place by the beaten highway."

"Mercy!" cried the defeated wretch, cowering in his chair. "If it is made public, I am ruined. I was driven to it. I could not let Mr. Edwards examine the book, for exposure would follow, that way; yet I could not refuse him—my best friend—when he asked its loan."

"Your words tell me all that I did not know," said Sherlock Holmes, sternly. "The motive now is only too plain. The work, sir, was a forgery, and knowing that your erudite friend would discover it, you chose to blacken his name to save your own. Was the book insured?"

"Insured for £350,000, he told me," interrupted Mr. Harrington Edwards, excitedly.

"So that he planned at once to dispose of this dangerous and dubious item, and to reap a golden reward," commented Holmes. "Come, sir, tell us about it. How much of it was forgery? Merely the inscription?"

"I will tell you," said the baronet, suddenly, "and throw myself upon the mercy of my friend, Mr. Edwards. The whole book, in effect, was a forgery. It was originally made up of two imperfect copies of the 1604 quarto. Out of the pair, I made one perfect volume, and a skillful workman, now dead, changed the date for me so cleverly that only an expert of the first water could have detected it. Such an expert, however, is Mr. Harrington Edwards—the one man in the world who could have unmasked me."

"Thank you, Nathaniel," said Mr. Harrington Edwards, gratefully.

"The inscription, of course, also was forged," continued the baronet. "You may as well know all."

"And the book?" asked Holmes. "Where did you destroy it?"

A grim smile settled on Sir Nathaniel's features. "It is even now burning in Mr. Edwards's own furnace," he said.

"Then it cannot yet be consumed," cried Holmes, and dashed into the basement. He was absent for some little time, and we heard the clinking of bottles, and, finally, the clang of a great metal door. He emerged, some moments later, in high spirits, carrying a charred leaf in his hand.

"It is a pity," he cried, "a pity! In spite of its questionable authenticity, it was a noble specimen. It is only half consumed, but let it burn away. I have preserved one leaf as a souvenir of the occasion." He folded it carefully and placed it in his wallet. "Mr. Harrington Edwards, I fancy the decision in this matter is for you to announce. Sir Nathaniel, of course, must make no effort to collect the insurance."

"I promise that," said the baronet, quickly.

"Let us forget it, then," said Mr. Edwards, with a sigh. "Let it be a sealed chapter in the history of bibliomania." He looked at Sir Nathaniel Brooke-Bannerman for a long moment, then held out his hand. "I forgive you, Nathaniel," he said, simply.

Their hands met; tears stood in the baronet's eyes. Holmes and I turned from the affecting scene, powerfully moved. We crept to the door unnoticed. In a moment the free air was blowing on our temples, and we were coughing the dust of the library from our lungs.

III.

"They are strange people, these book collectors," mused Sherlock Holmes, as we rattled back to town.

"My only regret is that I shall be unable to publish my notes on this interesting case," I responded.

"Wait a bit, my dear doctor," advised Holmes, "and it will be possible. In time both of them will come to look upon it as a hugely diverting episode, and will tell it upon themselves. Then your notes will be brought forth and the history of another of Mr. Sherlock Holmes's little problems shall be given to the world."

"It will always be a reflection upon Sir Nathaniel," I demurred.

"He will glory in it," prophesied Sherlock Holmes. "He will go down in bookish chronicle with Chatterton, and Ireland, and Payne Collier. Mark my words, he is not blind even now to the chance this gives him for sinister immortality. He will be the first to tell it." (And so, indeed, it proved, as this narrative suggests.)

"But why did you preserve the leaf from *Hamlet*?" I curiously inquired. "Why not a jewel from the binding?"

Sherlock Holmes chuckled heartily. Then he slowly unfolded the page in question, and directed a humorous finger at a spot upon the page.

"A fancy," he responded, "to preserve so accurate a characterization of either of our friends. The line is a real jewel. See, the good Polonius says: *'That he is mad, 'tis true: 'tis true 'tis pittie; and pittie it is true.'* There is as much sense in Master Will as in Hafiz or Confucius, and a greater felicity of expression. . . . Here is London, and now, my dear Watson, if we hasten we shall be just in time for Zabriski's matinee!"

THE ADVENTURE OF THE RED WIDOW

ADRIAN CONAN DOYLE

*A*drian Conan Doyle, it's said, wrote The Exploits of Sherlock Holmes *(in collaboration with John Dickson Carr) on his father's desk; given the quality of his pastiches, a case may be made that the desk was haunted by Sir Arthur's genial ghost. But since Holmes himself said, "No ghosts need apply," perhaps he simply inherited his talent, then built upon it with skill of his own making. It is reprinted by permission of the Sir Arthur Conan Doyle Estate.*

"Your conclusions are perfectly correct, my dear Watson," remarked my friend Sherlock Holmes. "Squalor and poverty are the natural matrix to crimes of violence."

"Precisely so," I agreed. "Indeed, I was just thinking—" I broke off to stare at him in amazement. "Good heavens, Holmes," I cried, "this is too much. How could you possibly know my innermost thoughts!"

My friend leaned back in his chair and, placing his fingertips together, surveyed me from under his heavy, drooping eyelids.

"I would do better justice, perhaps, to my limited powers by refusing to answer your question," he said, with a dry chuckle. "You have a certain flair, Watson, for concealing your failure to perceive the obvious by the cavalier manner in which you invariably accept the explanation of a sequence of simple but logical reasoning."

"I do not see how logical reasoning can enable you to follow the course of my mental processes," I retorted, a trifle nettled by his superior manner.

"There was no great difficulty. I have been watching you for the last few minutes. The expression on your face was quite vacant until, as your eyes roved about the room, they fell on the bookcase and came to rest on Hugo's *Les Misérables*, which made so deep an impression upon you when you read it last year. You became thoughtful, your eyes narrowed, it was obvious that your mind was drifting again into that tremendous dreadful saga of human suffering; at length your gaze lifted to the window with its aspect of snowflakes and grey sky and bleak, frozen roofs, and then, moving slowly on to the mantelpiece, settled on the jackknife with which I skewer my unanswered correspondence. The frown darkened on your face and unconsciously you shook your head despondently. It was an association of ideas. Hugo's terrible sub-third stage, the winter cold of poverty in the slums, and, above the warm glow of our own modest fire, the bare knifeblade. Your expression deepened into one of sadness, the melancholy that comes with an understanding of cause and effect in the unchanging human tragedy. It was then that I ventured to agree with you."

"Well, I must confess that you followed my thoughts with extraordinary accuracy," I admitted. "A remarkable piece of reasoning, Holmes."

"Elementary, my dear Watson."

The year of 1887 was moving to its end. The iron grip of the great blizzards that commenced in the last week of December had closed on the land, and beyond the windows of Holmes's lodgings in Baker Street lay a gloomy vista of grey, lowering sky and white-capped tiles dimly discernible through a curtain of snowflakes.

Though it had been a memorable year for my friend, it had been of yet greater importance to me, for it was but two months since that Miss Mary Morstan had paid me the signal honour of joining her destiny to mine. The change from my bachelor existence as a half-pay, ex-Army surgeon into the state of wedded bliss had not been accomplished without some uncalled-for and ironic comments from Sherlock Holmes but, as my wife and I could thank him for the fact that we had found each other, we could afford to accept his cynical attitude with tolerance and even understanding.

I had dropped in to our old lodgings on this afternoon, to be precise December 30th, to pass a few hours with my friend and enquire whether any new case of interest had come his way since my previous visit. I had found him pale and listless, his dressing gown drawn round his shoulders and the room reeking with the smoke of his favorite black shag, through which the fire in the grate gleamed like a brazier in a fog.

"Nothing, save a few routine enquiries, Watson," he had replied in a voice shrill with complaint. "Creative art in crime seems to have become atrophied since I disposed of the late-lamented Bert Stevens." Then lapsing into silence, he curled himself up morosely in his armchair, and not another word passed between us until my thoughts were suddenly interrupted by the observation that commenced this narrative.

As I rose to go, he looked at me critically.

"I perceive, Watson," said he, "that you are already paying the price. The slovenly state of your left jawbone bears regrettable testimony that somebody has changed the position of your shaving mirror. Furthermore, you are indulging in extravagances."

"You do me a gross injustice."

"What, at the winter price of five pence a blossom! Your buttonhole tells me that you were sporting a flower not later than yesterday."

"This is the first time I have known you penurious, Holmes," I retorted with some bitterness.

He broke into a hearty laugh. "My dear fellow, you must forgive me!" he cried. "It is most unfair that I should penalize you because a surfeit of unexpended mental energy tends to play upon my nerves. But hullo, what's this!"

A heavy step was mounting the stairs. My friend waved me back into my chair.

"Stay a moment, Watson," said he. "It is Gregson, and the old game may be afoot once more."

"Gregson?"

"There is no mistaking that regulation tread. Too heavy for Lestrade, and yet known to Mrs. Hudson or she would accompany him. It is Gregson."

As he finished speaking there came a knock on the door, and a figure muffled to the ears in a heavy cape entered the room. Our visitor tossed his bowler on the nearest chair and, unwinding the scarf wrapped around the lower part of his face, disclosed the flaxen hair and long, pale features of the Scotland Yard detective.

"Ah, Gregson," greeted Holmes, with a sly glance in my direction. "It must be urgent business that brings you out in this inclement weather. But throw off your cape, man, and come over to the fire."

The police agent shook his head. "There is not a moment to lose," he replied, consulting a large silver turnip watch. "The train to Derbyshire leaves in half an hour and I have a hansom waiting below. Though the case should present no difficulties for an officer of my experience, nevertheless I shall be glad of your company."

"Something of interest?"

"Murder, Mr. Holmes," snapped Gregson curtly, "and a singular one at that, to judge from the telegram from the local police. It appears that Lord Jocelyn Cope, the Deputy Lieutenant of the County, has been found butchered at Arnsworth Castle. The Yard is quite capable of solving crimes of this nature, but in view of the curious terms contained in the police telegram, it occurred to me that you might wish to accompany me. Will you come?"

Holmes leaned forward, emptied the Persian slipper into his tobacco pouch, and sprang to his feet.

"Give me a moment to pack a clean collar and toothbrush," he cried. "I have a spare one for you, Watson. No, my dear fellow, not a word. Where would I be without your assistance? Scribble a note to your wife, and Mrs. Hudson will have it delivered. We should be back tomorrow. Now, Gregson, I'm your man and you can fill in the details during our journey."

The guard's flag was already waving as we rushed up the platform at St. Pancras and tore open the door of the first empty smoker. Holmes had brought three travelling-rugs with him, and as the train roared its way through the fading winter daylight we made ourselves comfortable enough in our respective corners.

"Well, Gregson, I shall be interested to hear the details," remarked Holmes, his thin, eager face framed in the earflaps of his deerstalker and a spiral of blue smoke rising from his pipe.

"I know nothing beyond what I have already told you."

"And yet you used the word 'singular' and referred to the telegram from the county police as 'curious.' Kindly explain."

"I used both terms for the same reason. The wire from the local inspector advised that the officer from Scotland Yard should read *The Derbyshire County* Guide and *The Gazetteer*. A most extraordinary suggestion!"

"I should say a wise one. What have you done about it?"

"*The Gazetteer* states merely that Lord Jocelyn Cope is a Deputy Lieutenant and county magnate, married, childless, and noted for his bequests to local archaeological societies. As for *The Guide*, I have it here." He drew a pamphlet from his pocket and thumbed over the pages. "Here we are," he continued. "Arnsworth Castle. Built reign of Edward III. Fifteenth-century stained-glass window to celebrate Battle of Agincourt. Cope family penalized for suspected Catholic leaning by Royal Visitation, 1574. Museum open to public once a year. Contains large collection of martial and other relics, including small guillotine built originally in Nimes during French Revolution for execution of a maternal ancestor of the present owner. Never used owing to escape of intended victim, and later purchased as relic by family after Napoleonic Wars and brought to Arnsworth. Pshaw! That local inspector must be out of his senses, Mr. Holmes. There is nothing to help us here."

"Let us reserve judgment. The man would not have made such a suggestion without reason. In the meantime, I would recommend to your attention the dusk now falling over the landscape. Every material object has become vague and indistinct, and yet their solid existence remains, though almost hidden from our visual senses. There is much to be learned from the twilight."

"Quite so, Mr. Holmes," grinned Gregson, with a wink at me. "Very poetical, I am sure. Well, I'm for a short nap."

It was some three hours later that we alighted at a small wayside station. The snow had ceased, and beyond the roofs of the hamlet the long desolate slopes of the Derbyshire moors, white and glistening under the light of a full moon, rolled away to the skyline. A stocky, bowlegged man swathed in a shepherd's plaid hurried towards us along the platform.

"You're from Scotland Yard, I take it?" he greeted us brusquely. "I got your wire in reply to mine and I have a carriage waiting outside. Yes, I'm Inspector Dawlish," he added in response to Gregson's question. "But who are these gentlemen?"

"I considered that Mr. Sherlock Holmes's reputation—" began our companion.

"I've never heard of him," interposed the local man, looking at us with a gleam of hostility in his dark eyes. "This is a serious affair and there is no room for amateurs. But it is too cold to stand arguing here and, if London approves his presence, who am I to gainsay him? This way, if you please."

A closed carriage was standing before the station, and a moment later we had swung out of the yard and were bowling swiftly but silently up the village high street.

"There'll be accommodation for you at the Queen's Head," grunted Inspector Dawlish. "But first to the castle."

"I shall be glad to hear the facts of this case," stated Gregson, "and the reason for the most irregular suggestion contained in your telegram."

"The facts are simple enough," replied the other, with a grim smile. "His lordship has been murdered and we know who did it."

"Ah!"

"Captain Jasper Lothian, the murdered man's cousin, has disappeared in a hurry. It's common knowledge hereabouts that the man's got a touch of the devil in him, a hard hand with a bottle, a horse, or the nearest woman. It's come as a surprise to none of us that Captain Jasper should end by slaughtering his benefactor and the head of his house. Aye, head's a well-chosen word," he ended softly.

"If you've a clear case, then what's this nonsense about a guidebook?"

Inspector Dawlish leaned forward while his voice sank almost to a whisper. "You've read it?" he said. "Then it may interest you to know that Lord Jocelyn Cope was put to death with his own ancestral guillotine."

His words left us in a chilled silence.

"What motive can you suggest for that murder and for the barbarous method employed?" asked Sherlock Holmes at last.

"Probably a ferocious quarrel. Have I not told you already that Captain Jasper had a touch of the devil in him? But there's the castle, and a proper place it looks for deeds of violence and darkness."

We had turned off the country road to enter a gloomy avenue that climbed between banked snowdrifts up a barren moorland slope. On the crest loomed a great building, its walls and turrets stark and grey against the night sky. A few minutes later, our carriage rumbled under the arch of the outer bailey and halted in a courtyard.

At Inspector Dawlish's knock, a tall, stooping man in butler's livery opened the massive oaken door and, holding a candle above his head, peered out at us, the light shining on his weary red-rimmed eyes and ill-nourished beard.

"What, four of you!" he cried querulously. "It b'aint right her ladyship should be bothered thisways at such a time of grief to us all."

"That will do, Stephen. Where is her ladyship?"

The candle flame trembled. "Still with him," came the reply, and there was something like a sob in the old voice. "She hasn't moved. Still sitting there in the big chair and staring at him, as though she had fallen fast asleep with them wonderful eyes wide open."

"You've touched nothing, of course?"

"Nothing. It's all as it was."

"Then let us go first to the museum where the crime was committed," said Dawlish. "It is on the other side of the courtyard."

He was moving away towards a cleared path that ran across the cobblestones when Holmes's hand closed upon his arm. "How is this!" he cried imperiously. "The museum is on the other side, and yet you have allowed a carriage to drive across the courtyard and people to stampede over the ground like a herd of buffalo."

"What then?"

Holmes flung up his arms appealingly to the moon. "The snow, man, the snow! You have destroyed your best helpmate."

"But I tell you the murder was committed in the museum. What has the snow to do with it?"

Holmes gave vent to a most dismal groan, and then we all followed the local detective across the yard to an arched doorway.

I have seen many a grim spectacle during my association with Sherlock Holmes, but I can recall none to surpass in horror the sight that met our eyes within that grey Gothic chamber. It was a small room with a groined roof, lit by clusters of tapers in iron sconces. The walls were hung with trophies of armour and mediaeval weapons, and edged by glass-topped cases crammed with ancient parchments, thumb rings, pieces of carved stonework, and yawning man-traps. These details I noticed at a glance, and then my whole attention was riveted to the object that occupied a low dais in the centre of the room.

It was a guillotine, painted a faded red, and, save for its smaller size, exactly similar to those that I had seen depicted in woodcuts of the French Revolution. Sprawling between the two uprights lay the body of a tall, thin man clad in a velvet smoking jacket. His hands were tied behind him and a white cloth, hideously besmirched, concealed his head, or rather the place where his head had been.

The light of the tapers, gleaming on a blood-spattered steel blade buried in the lunette, reached beyond to touch, as with a halo, the red-gold hair of the woman who sat beside that dreadful, headless form. Regardless of our approach, she remained motionless in her high, carved chair, her features an ivory mask from which two dark and brilliant eyes stared into the shadows with the unwinking fixity of a basilisk. In an experience of women covering three continents, I have never beheld a colder nor a more perfect face than that of the chatelaine of Castle Arnsworth, keeping vigil in that chamber of death.

Dawlish coughed.

"You had best retire, my lady," he said bluntly. "Rest assured that Inspector Gregson here and I will see that justice is done."

For the first time, she looked at us, and so uncertain was the light of the tapers that for an instant it seemed to me that some swift emotion more akin to mockery than grief gleamed and died in those wonderful eyes.

"Stephen is not with you?" she asked incongruously. "But, of course, he would be in the library. Faithful Stephen."

"I fear that his lordship's death—"

She rose abruptly, her bosom heaving and one hand gripping the skirt of her black lace gown.

"His damnation!" she hissed, and then, with a gesture of despair, she turned and glided slowly from the room.

As the door closed, Sherlock Holmes dropped on one knee beside the guillotine and, raising the blood-soaked cloth, peered down at the terrible object beneath. "Dear me," he said quietly. "A blow of this force must have sent the head rolling across the room."

"Probably."

"I fail to understand. Surely you know where you found it?"

"I didn't find it. There is no head."

For a long moment, Holmes remained on his knee, staring up silently at the speaker. "It seems to me that you are taking a great deal for granted," he said at length, scrambling to his feet. "Let me hear your ideas on this singular crime."

"It's plain enough. Sometime last night, the two men quarrelled and eventually came to blows. The younger overpowered the elder and then killed him by means of this instrument. The evidence that Lord

Cope was still alive when placed in the guillotine is shown by the fact that Captain Lothian had to lash his hands. The crime was discovered this morning by the butler, Stephen, and a groom fetched me from the village, whereupon I took the usual steps to identify the body of his lordship and listed the personal belongings found upon him. If you'd like to know how the murderer escaped, I can tell you that too. On the mare that's missing from the stable."

"Most instructive," observed Holmes. "As I understand your theory, the two men engaged in a ferocious combat, being careful not to disarrange any furniture or smash the glass cases that clutter up the room. Then, having disposed of his opponent, the murderer rides into the night, a suitcase under one arm and his victim's head under the other. A truly remarkable performance."

An angry flush suffused Dawlish's face. "It's easy enough to pick holes in other people's ideas, Mr. Sherlock Holmes," he sneered. "Perhaps you will give us your theory."

"I have none. I am awaiting my facts. By the way, when was your last snowfall?"

"Yesterday afternoon."

"Then there is hope yet. But let us see if this room will yield us any information."

For some ten minutes we stood and watched him, Gregson and I with interest and Dawlish with an ill-concealed look of contempt on his weather-beaten face, as Holmes crawled slowly about the room on his hands and knees, muttering and mumbling to himself and looking like some gigantic dun-coloured insect. He had drawn his magnifying glass from his cape pocket, and I noticed that not only the floor but the contents of the occasional tables were subjected to the closest scrutiny. Then, rising to his feet, he stood wrapped in thought, his back to the candlelight and his gaunt shadow falling across the faded red guillotine.

"It won't do," he said suddenly. "The murder was premeditated."

"How do you know?"

"The cranking-handle is freshly oiled, and the victim was senseless. A single jerk would have loosed his hands."

"Then why were they tied?"

"Ah! There is no doubt, however, that the man was brought here unconscious with his hands already bound."

"You're wrong there!" interposed Dawlish loudly. "The design on the lashing proves that it is a sash from one of these window-curtains."

Holmes shook his head. "They are faded through exposure to daylight," said he, "and this is not. There can be little doubt that it comes from a door-curtain, of which there are none in this room. Well, there is little more to be learned here."

The two police agents conferred together, and Gregson turned to Holmes. "As it is after midnight," said he, "we had better retire to the village hostelry and tomorrow pursue our enquiries separately. I cannot but agree with Inspector Dawlish that while we are theorizing here, the murderer may reach the coast."

"I wish to be clear on one point, Gregson. Am I officially employed on this case by the police?"

"Impossible, Mr. Holmes!"

"Quite so. Then I am free to use my own judgment. But give me five minutes in the courtyard, and Dr. Watson and I will be with you."

The bitter cold smote us as I slowly followed the gleam of Holmes's dark lantern along the path that, banked with thick snow, led across the courtyard to the front door. "Fools!" he cried, stooping over the powdered surface. "Look at it, Watson! A regiment would have done less damage. Carriage wheels in three places. And here's Dawlish's boots and a pair of hobnails, probably a groom. A woman now, and running. Of course, Lady Cope and the first alarm. Yes, certainly it is she. What was Stephen doing out here? There is no mistaking his square-toed shoes. Doubtless you observed them, Watson, when he opened the door to us. But what have we here?" The lantern paused and then moved slowly onwards. "Pumps, pumps," he cried eagerly, "and coming from the front door. See, here he is again. Probably a tall man, from the size of his feet, and carrying some heavy object. The stride is shortened and the toes more clearly marked than the heels. A burdened man always tends to throw his weight forward. He returns! Ah, just so, just so! Well, I think that we have earned our beds."

My friend remained silent during our journey back to the village. But, as we separated from Inspector Dawlish at the door of the inn, he laid a hand on his shoulder.

"The man who has done this deed is tall and spare," said he. "He is about fifty years of age with a turned-in left foot and strongly addicted to Turkish cigarettes, which he smokes from a holder."

"Captain Lothian!" grunted Dawlish. "I know nothing about feet or cigarette holders, but the rest of your description is accurate enough. But who told you his appearance?"

"I will set you a question in reply. Were the Copes ever a Catholic family?"

The local inspector glanced significantly at Gregson and tapped his forehead. "Catholic? Well, now that you mention it, I believe they were in the old times. But what on earth—!"

"Merely that I would recommend you to your own guidebook. Good night."

On the following morning, after dropping my friend and myself at the castle gate, the two police officers drove off to pursue their enquiries further afield. Holmes watched their departure with a twinkle in his eye.

"I fear that I have done you injustice over the years, Watson," he commented somewhat enigmatically, as we turned away.

The elderly manservant opened the door to us, and as we followed him into the great hall it was painfully obvious that the honest fellow was still deeply afflicted by his master's death.

"There is naught for you here," he cried shrilly. "My God, will you never leave us in peace?"

I have remarked previously on Holmes's gift for putting others at their ease, and by degrees the old man recovered his composure. "I take it that this is the Agincourt window," observed Holmes, staring up at a small but exquisitely coloured stained-glass casement through which the winter sunlight threw a pattern of brilliant colours on the ancient stone floor.

"It is, sir. Only two in all England."

"Doubtless you have served the family for many years," continued my friend gently.

"Served 'em? Aye, me and mine for nigh two centuries. Ours is the dust that lies upon their funeral palls."

"I fancy they have an interesting history."

"They have that, sir."

"I seem to have heard that this ill-omened guillotine was specially built for some ancestor of your late master?"

"Aye, the Marquis de Rennes. Built by his own tenants, the varmints, hated him, they did, simply because he kept up old customs."

"Indeed. What custom?"

"Something about women, sir. The book in the library don't explain exactly."

"*Le droit du seigneur*, perhaps."

"Well, I don't speak heathern, but I believe them was the very words."

"H'm. I should like to see this library."

The old man's eyes slid to the door at the end of the hall. "See the library?" he grumbled. "What do you want there? Nothing but old books, and her ladyship don't like—oh, very well."

He led the way ungraciously into a long, low room lined to the ceiling with volumes and ending in a magnificent Gothic fireplace. Holmes, after strolling about listlessly, paused to light a cheroot.

"Well, Watson, I think that we'll be getting back," said he. "Thank you, Stephen. It is a fine room, though I am surprised to see Indian rugs."

"Indian!" protested the old man indignantly. "They're antique Persian."

"Surely Indian."

"Persian, I tell you! Them marks are inscriptions, as a gentleman like you should know. Can't see without your spyglass? Well, use it then. Now, drat it, if he hasn't spilled his matches!"

As we rose to our feet after gathering up the scattered vestas, I was puzzled to account for the sudden flush of excitement in Holmes's sallow cheeks.

"I was mistaken," said he. "They are Persian. Come, Watson, it is high time that we set out for the village and our train back to town."

A few minutes later, we had left the castle. But to my surprise, on emerging from the outer bailey, Holmes led the way swiftly along a lane leading to the stables.

"You intend to enquire about the missing horse," I suggested.

"The horse? My dear fellow, I have no doubt that it is safely concealed in one of the home farms, while Gregson rushes all over the county. This is what I am looking for."

He entered the first loose box and returned with his arms full of straw. "Another bundle for you, Watson, and it should be enough for our purpose."

"But what is our purpose?"

"Principally to reach the front door without being observed," he chuckled, as he shouldered his burden.

Having retraced our footsteps, Holmes laid his finger on his lips and, cautiously opening the great door, slipped into a nearby closet full of capes and sticks, where he proceeded to throw both our bundles on the floor.

"It should be safe enough," he whispered, "for it is stone-built. Ah! These two mackintoshes will assist admirably. I have no doubt," he added, as he struck a match and dropped it into the pile, "that I shall have other occasions to use this modest stratagem."

As the flames spread through the straw and reached the mackintoshes, thick black wreaths of smoke poured from the cloakroom door into the hall of Arnsworth Castle, accompanied by a hissing and crackling from the burning rubber.

"Good heavens, Holmes," I gasped, the tears rolling down my face. "We shall be suffocated!"

His fingers closed on my arm.

"Wait," he muttered, and even as he spoke, there came a sudden rush of feet and a yell of horror.

"Fire!"

In that despairing wail, I recognized Stephen's voice.

"Fire!" he shrieked again, and we caught the clatter of his footsteps as he fled across the hall.

"Now!" whispered Holmes and, in an instant he was out of the cloakroom and running headlong for the library. The door was half open but, as we burst in, the man drumming with hysterical hands on the great fireplace did not even turn his head.

"Fire! The house is on fire!" he shrieked. "Oh, my poor master! My lord! My lord!"

Holmes's hand fell upon his shoulder. "A bucket of water in the cloakroom will meet the case," he said quietly. "It would be as well, however, if you would ask his lordship to join us."

The old man sprang at him, his eyes blazing and his fingers crooked like the talons of a vulture.

"A trick!" he screamed. "I've betrayed him through your cursed tricks!"

"Take him, Watson," said Holmes, holding him at arms' length. "There, there. You're a faithful fellow."

"Faithful unto death," whispered a feeble voice.

I started back involuntarily. The edge of the ancient fireplace had swung open, and in the dark aperture thus disclosed there stood a tall, thin man, so powdered with dust that for the moment I seemed to be staring not at a human being but at a spectre. He was about fifty years of age, gaunt and high-nosed, with a pair of sombre eyes that waxed and waned feverishly in a face that was the colour of grey paper.

"I fear that the dust is bothering you, Lord Cope," said Holmes very gently. "Would you not be better seated?"

The man tottered forward to drop heavily into an armchair. "You are the police, of course," he gasped.

"No. I am a private investigator, but acting in the interests of justice."

A bitter smile parted Lord Cope's lips.

"Too late," said he.

"You are ill?"

"I am dying." Opening his fingers, he disclosed a small empty phial. "There is only a short time left to me."

"Is there nothing to be done, Watson?"

I laid my fingers upon the sick man's wrist. His face was already livid, and the pulse low and feeble.

"Nothing, Holmes."

Lord Cope straightened himself painfully. "Perhaps you will indulge a last curiosity by telling me how you discovered the truth," said he. "You must be a man of some perception."

"I confess that at first there were difficulties," admitted Holmes, "though these discovered themselves later in the light of events. Obviously the whole key to the problem lay in a conjunction of two remarkable circumstances—the use of a guillotine and the disappearance of the murdered man's head.

"Who, I asked myself, would use so clumsy and rare an instrument, except one to whom it possessed some strong symbolic significance, and, if this were the case, then it was logical to suppose that the clue to that significance must lie in its past history."

The nobleman nodded.

125

"His own people built it for Rennes," he muttered, "in return for the infamy that their womenfolk had suffered at his hands. But pray proceed, and quickly."

"So much for the first circumstance," continued Holmes, ticking off the points on his fingers. "The second threw a flood of light over the whole problem. This is not New Guinea. Why, then, should a murderer take his victim's head? The obvious answer was that he wished to conceal the dead man's true identity. By the way," he demanded sternly, "what have you done with Captain Lothian's head?"

"Stephen and I buried it at midnight in the family vault," came the feeble reply. "And that with all reverence."

"The rest was simple," went on Holmes. "As the body was easily identifiable as yours by the clothes and other personal belongings which were listed by the local inspector, it followed naturally that there could have been no point in concealing the head unless the murderer had also changed clothes with the dead man. That the change had been effected before death was shown by the bloodstains. The victim had been incapacitated in advance, probably drugged, for it was plain from certain facts already explained to my friend Watson that there had been no struggle and that he had been carried to the museum from another part of the castle. Assuming my reasoning to be correct, then the murdered man could not be Lord Jocelyn. But was there not another missing, his lordship's cousin and alleged murderer, Captain Jasper Lothian?"

"How could you give Dawlish a description of the wanted man?" I interposed.

"By looking at the body of the victim, Watson. The two men must have borne a general resemblance to each other or the deception would not have been feasible from the start. An ashtray in the museum contained a cigarette stub, Turkish, comparatively fresh and smoked from a holder. None but an addict would have smoked under the terrible circumstances that must have accompanied that insignificant stump. The footmarks in the snow showed that someone had come from the main building carrying a burden, and had returned without that burden. I think I have covered the principal points."

For a while, we sat in silence broken only by the moan of a rising wind at the windows and the short, sharp panting of the dying man's breath.

"I owe you no explanation," he said at last, "for it is to my Maker, who alone knows the innermost recesses of the human heart, that I must answer for my deed. Nevertheless, though my story is one of shame and guilt, I shall tell you enough to enlist perhaps your forbearance in granting me my final request.

"You must know, then, that following the scandal which brought his Army career to its close, my cousin Jasper Lothian has lived at Arnsworth. Though penniless and already notorious for his evil living, I welcomed him as a kinsman, affording him not only financial support but, what was perhaps more valuable, the social aegis of my position in the county.

"As I look back now on the years that passed, I blame myself for my own lack of principle in my failure to put an end to his extravagance, his drinking and gaming and certain less honourable pursuits with which rumour already linked his name. I had thought him wild and injudicious. I was yet to learn that he was a creature so vile and utterly bereft of honour that he would tarnish the name of his own house.

"I had married a woman considerably younger than myself, a woman as remarkable for her beauty as for her romantic yet singular temperament, which she had inherited from her Spanish forebears. It was the old story, and when at long last I awoke to the dreadful truth it was also to the knowledge that only one thing remained for me in life—vengeance. Vengeance against this man, who had disgraced my name and abused the honour of my house.

"On the night in question, Lothian and I sat late over our wine in this very room. I had contrived to drug his port, and before the effects of the narcotic could deaden his senses I told him of my discovery, and that death alone could wipe out the score. He sneered back at me that in killing him I would merely put myself on the scaffold and expose my wife's shame to the world. When I explained my plan, the sneer was gone from his face and the terror of death was freezing in his black heart. The rest you know. As the drug deprived him of his senses, I changed clothes with him, bound his hands with a sash torn from the door-curtain, and carried him across the courtyard to the museum, to the virgin guillotine which had been built for another's infamy.

"When it was over, I summoned Stephen and told him the truth. The old man never hesitated in his loyalty to his wretched master. Together we buried the head in the family vault and then, seizing a mare from the stable, he rode it across the moor to convey an impression of flight and finally left it concealed in a lonely farm owned by his sister. All that remained was for me to disappear.

"Arnsworth, like many mansions belonging to families that had been Catholic in the olden times, possessed a priest's hole. There I have lain concealed, emerging only at night into the library to lay my final instructions upon my faithful servant."

"Thereby confirming my suspicion as to your proximity," interposed Holmes, "by leaving no fewer than five smears of Turkish tobacco ash upon the rugs. But what was your ultimate intention?"

"In taking vengeance for the greatest wrong which one man can do to another, I had successfully protected our name from the shame of the scaffold. I could rely on Stephen's loyalty. As for my wife, though she knew the truth she could not betray me without announcing to the world her own infidelity. Life held nothing more for me. I determined therefore to allow myself a day or two in which to get my affairs in order, and then to die by my own hand. I assure you that your discovery of my hiding place has advanced the event by only an hour or so. I had left a letter for Stephen, begging him as his final devoir that he would bury my body secretly in the vaults of my ancestors.

"There, gentlemen, is my story. I am the last of the old line, and it lies with you whether or not it shall go out in dishonour."

Sherlock Holmes laid a hand upon his.

"It is perhaps as well that it has been pointed out to us already that my friend Watson and I are here in an entirely private capacity," said he quietly. "I am about to summon Stephen, for I cannot help feeling that you would be more comfortable if he carried this chair into the priest's hole and closed the sliding panel after you."

We had to bend our heads to catch Lord Jocelyn's response.

"Then a higher tribunal will judge my crime," he whispered faintly, "and the tomb shall devour my secret. Farewell, and may a dying man's blessing rest upon you."

Our journey back to London was both chilly and depressing. With nightfall, the snow had recommenced and Holmes was in his least communicative mood, staring out of the window at the scattered lights of villages and farmhouses that periodically flitted past in the darkness.

"The old year is nodding to its fall," he remarked suddenly, "and in the hearts of all these kindly, simple folk awaiting the midnight chimes dwells the perennial anticipation that what is to come will be better than what has been. Hope, however ingenuous and disproven by past experience, remains the one supreme panacea for all the knocks and bruises which life metes out to us." He leaned back and began to stuff his pipe with shag.

"Should you eventually write an account of this curious affair in Derbyshire," he went on, "I would suggest that a suitable title would be 'the Red Widow.'"

"Knowing your unreasonable aversion to women, Holmes, I am surprised that you noticed the colour of her hair."

"I refer, Watson, to the popular sobriquet for a guillotine in the days of the French Revolution," he said severely.

The hour was late when, at last, we reached our old lodgings in Baker Street where Holmes, after poking up the fire, lost not a moment in donning his mouse-coloured dressing gown.

"It is approaching midnight," I observed, "and as I would wish to be with my wife when this year of 1887 draws to its close, I must be on my way. Let me wish you a happy New Year, my dear fellow."

"I heartily reciprocate your good wishes, Watson," he replied. "Pray bear my greetings to your wife, and my apologies for your temporary absence."

I had reached the deserted street and, pausing for a moment to raise my collar against the swirl of the snowflakes, I was about to set out on my walk when my attention was arrested by the strains of a violin. Involuntarily, I raised my eyes to the window of our old sitting room and there, sharply outlined against the lamplit blind, was the shadow of Sherlock Holmes. I could see that keen, hawk-like profile which I knew so well, the slight stoop of his shoulders as he bent over his fiddle, the rise and fall of the bow tip. But surely this was no dreamy Italian air, no complicated improvisation of his own creation, that drifted down to me through the stillness of that bleak winter's night.

> Should auld acquaintance be forgot
> and never brought to mind?
> Should auld acquaintance be forgot
> and auld lang syne?

A snowflake must have drifted into my eyes for, as I turned away, the gas lamps glimmering down the desolate expanse of Baker Street seemed strangely blurred.

My task is done. My notebooks have been replaced in the black tin deed-box where they have been kept in recent years, and, for the last time, I have dipped my pen in the inkwell.

Through the window that overlooks the modest lawn of our farm-house, I can see Sherlock Holmes strolling among his beehives. His hair is quite white, but his long, thin form is as wiry and energetic as ever, and there is a touch of healthy colour in his cheeks, placed there by Mother Nature and her clover-laden breezes that carry the scent of the sea amid these gentle Sussex Downs.

Our lives are drawing towards eventide, and old faces and old scenes are gone forever. And yet, as I lean back in my chair and close my eyes, for a while the past rises up to obscure the present, and I see before me the yellow fogs of Baker Street, and I hear once more the voice of the best and wisest man whom I have ever known.

"Come, Watson, the game's afoot!"

THE MYSTERIOUS CASE OF THE URN OF ASH; OR, WHAT WOULD SHERLOCK DO?

DEBORAH MORGAN

eborah Morgan is an award-winning writer of both fiction and nonfiction. Her five antique-lover mystery novels were published by Berkley, and are now available in eBook format. Although she has published short stories in both the western and mystery genres, this is her first featuring the main character of her novels, antiques picker Jeff Talbot. This story is a clever take on how Jeff, a newcomer to the canon, becomes hooked on the indomitable Sherlock Holmes—and how he stumbles upon a Holmes-worthy case when he acquires an old trunk full of Sherlockian memorabilia. Published here for the first time, by permission of the author.

Let go a single sheet of paper, observe it as it slowly slices through air before alighting nowhere near your predicted destination for it, and you will understand how ethereal an object it is. Or, watch the solitary snowflake, near weightless in its lacy form, as it floats and drifts toward a soundless landing.

Put thousands of either together, and you'll need some muscle to move them.

Jeff Talbot fought the urge to supervise as the two stout men lifted the mammoth camelback trunk from the back of the panel wagon. Before their arrival, he had brought a pushcart from the carriage house near his home's back door. He'd pointed it out more than once to the pair.

Jeff rubbed his shoulder. The wound had healed—it had been a year since he'd been shot—but it most certainly limited him when it came to chores that involved much lifting. Now, too, he had his own built-in barometer, which often was on active duty (a curse of living in the Northwest). He was barely into his forties, and the necessity to hire movers went against the grain.

With a Queen Anne home full of Victorian antiques, Jeff didn't often acquire large or heavy items. This, however, couldn't be passed up.

It had belonged to an old woman who, until her death the day prior, had been a resident of a local nursing facility since before the new millennium. She had no relatives to list as next of kin, and since it was required that *someone* be listed in order for her to become a resident, she had used her medical doctor. That doctor, Michael Danville, was a friend of Jeff's, and had called him when the woman passed. "I have no clue what's in it," Mike had said, "and I don't want to know. She was adamant about keeping it, but I'm told it hasn't been opened since 1986, when she moved in. To tell you the truth, she was adamant about everything. I don't need any reminders of her.

"Take it, Jeff. I'm off to Japan tomorrow, so I've already told the director of nursing that you'll be picking it up."

Jeff jotted down the information. An antiques picker by trade, he offered a fair sum to his friend, who turned it down.

"Being listed as next of kin happens more often than you might think. The last thing I need is another trunk full of a musty old woman's musty old belongings. You're doing me a favor."

Musty old women's musty old belongings were Jeff's bread and butter, so he accepted.

The trunk was as near pristine a specimen as Jeff had ever encountered. Its polished wood, richly embossed leather, and brass fittings had been well maintained over the years. He had stopped by the facility, made the necessary arrangements, along with a cursory glance inside when he checked that the key worked, then arranged for a moving company to do the heavy lifting.

Now he hovered, anxious to get the beautiful, beastly thing inside and commence digging through it. The weather was perfect for an indoor treasure hunt. Cold and rainy, with a lingering fog. It felt like London, and Jeff had spied an old London map in the trunk. He took comfort in pairings such as that. They satisfied like the snapping together of puzzle pieces.

The men hoisted the mammoth trunk and, ignoring the pushcart, started up the steep steps, the smaller of the two going backwards. They were used to moving furniture in Seattle, Jeff could tell.

Greer, a pleasant-looking young man and the Talbots' butler since his graduation from butling school a decade before, waited patiently at the top of the steps. He held in his hands a perfectly folded bar towel.

"How many bodies you got in here?" the younger of the two men asked.

"To tell you the truth, I don't know what's in it," Jeff said.

The men stopped dead in their tracks.

"I mean, I glanced inside. Ephemera, mostly, from what I could tell. But the one thing I know is *not* in it is a body."

"Ephemera?" the younger mover said.

"Papers and such," said his partner.

"Oh, I thought that was ethereal," he said as they resumed climbing.

The trunk was placed on a tarp in the library, where Greer wiped it down with the towel. Jeff scratched out a check, then the butler led the workers from the room.

Jeff retrieved the key from his jacket pocket and unlocked the hasp. The hinges creaked and groaned as he lifted the lid. A century earlier, when either train or steamship was the chosen mode of travel, impatient travelers preferred these domed trunks, as they could only be stacked at the top, and thus were the first unloaded at depot or port.

Greer had cleared all items from the large library table, and Jeff commenced filling it, taking care to group according to subcategory. As he did so, he noted that the European maps, journals, newspaper clippings, bound sheaves of papers, and small publications boasted one theme and one theme only: Sherlock Holmes.

The scent of mimeograph ink lingered. Or was it from a Ditto machine? Although he couldn't recall which machine produced the often-blotchy purple ink that stained the memories of mid-twentieth-century schoolchildren, the scent itself was unmistakable.

The copies—dozens, by his estimation—were of short stories written by Sir Arthur Conan Doyle about Sherlock Holmes. Each story, held together by a paper clip that had left its rusty impression, was worn and dog-eared, the margins heavy with annotation.

London maps had once been thumbtacked to walls; that was easy to deduce by pinholes in the center of rust-edged circular imprints at every corner. Jeff unfolded one and spied a dot of light shining through it. Closer examination revealed that a place on Baker Street had once been pinpointed. He wasn't a fan of Sherlock Holmes, but even he had heard of the famous address at 221B.

Copies of *The Serpentine Muse*, slim publications with various dates from the 1970s but with cover designs that looked more like apothecary labels from Victorian times, carried the subtitle *A Quarterly Publication of the Adventuresses of Sherlock Holmes*.

A women's group dedicated to Sherlock Holmes? Jeff made a mental note to investigate further.

Bundles of letters, along with larger envelopes—those would be greeting cards—were tied with soft silk ribbons in dove grays, blues, pinks. He fluttered the upper right corners of several stacks, noting that most of the postmarks were from the 1970s and '80s.

At 4:00 P.M., Greer entered the library with the coffee tray and found Jeff sitting in an armchair near the fireplace, reading from a slender stack of copy paper. The butler announced that the newspaper had not yet been delivered.

Jeff looked up. "Elementary, my dear Watson."

Greer raised a brow, barely discernible. "Sir?"

He thumped the stack with a knuckle. "Looks like most of this loot has to do with Sherlock Holmes."

"Interesting, sir." Greer set down the tray, poured coffee from a silver-plated pot. "If I may take the liberty of saying so, that particular phrase was never written by Sir Arthur Conan Doyle."

It was Jeff's turn to raise a brow. "Greer, don't tell me you're a Sherlockian."

"I am well acquainted with the stories, but have never been so zealous as to attend meetings, dress in costume, or take part in quizzes."

"Quizzes? You're not serious."

"If you mean to ask whether quizzes are taken, then I assure you I am serious."

"So, these meetings . . . ?"

"The Baker Street Irregulars. There are scions, as well, and—" The phone rang. "Excuse me, sir," Greer said as he left the room.

Jeff took a drink of the strong coffee, one of his favorite Tully's blends, then placed the cup on the hearth and returned to the story. While he read "The Adventure of the Dancing Men," the beverage, forgotten, grew cold. He set aside the papers when he had finished the last page, reflecting upon his childhood and a long-forgotten love of cryptographs, like those used in the story.

Other duties called him, but Jeff managed to spend every available moment over the next few days on the task of unpacking the trunk. Carefully, he set aside the bundles of ribbon-bound correspondence, not yet wishing to dismantle them for fear of separating the contents from their respective envelopes. Maps, magazines, and clippings were also stacked for future perusal.

The copied short stories, however, were another thing. They beckoned him, captured him. Invariably, he would glance at one, meaning only to read the opening, and, without conscious thought, would settle himself once again into his armchair by the fire, consumed by yet another tale.

Although it was difficult to ignore the annotations meticulously printed along the margins and in the tiniest of hands, ignore them he must. He'd never read Sir Arthur Conan Doyle's works, and he didn't want someone else's take on the games afoot to sway him, or give away the solution before he'd had his own go at it.

He barely noticed when Greer entered to tend the fire or serve coffee, as he was caught up in noticing many inconsistencies among the stories, as well as downright errors about some elements. Oddly, though, that didn't stop him from reading. He was hooked on the characters, and this fact thoroughly surprised him.

However, as Jeff's new obsession continued, he buttonholed Greer at every turn, engaging him in conversations about Sherlock Holmes, asking him questions, pointing out discovered errors.

Greer, always the dutiful butler, answered questions, shared knowledge, even loaned his employer some books on the subject: *The Encyclopaedia Sherlockiana*, *The Private Life of Sherlock Holmes*, and *The Complete Adventures and Memoirs of Sherlock Holmes: A Facsimile of the Original* Strand Magazine *Stories, 1891–1893*. This last title Jeff found to be a real treat, as it included original illustrations by Sidney Paget.

Sheila, who had been busy helping plan the annual harvest fair, popped her blonde head in from time to time to check on her husband. On day five of The Adventure of the Trunk in the Middle of the Room, she walked in and said, "How can you stand it, not knowing what else is in there?"

Jeff rose and kissed her. "You must be finished with your committee work."

She reached toward the trunk, then paused. "May I?"

"Of course. Just put the ones like these—" he held up his current reading material— "at this end of the table." He returned to his chair.

Sheila clearly wasn't distracted by the stories. She moved quickly, stacking mimeographed sheets where her husband had indicated, and the rest of the papers with their like-minded groups on the large table.

"Would you look at this?" She lifted from the trunk a large department store box, ivory with a floral bouquet image, and tilted it so that Jeff could see the lid. The logo was written in an elegant script that read, "The Bon Marché Fur Salon."

He said, "That department store has been defunct for years."

Sheila withdrew more boxes like the first, stacking each like it on a nearby chair.

"Aren't you going to open them?"

"Not until we see what else is in here."

Momentarily, she caught her breath. "Look at this! I've never seen such exquisite stitching."

She lifted a segment to reveal a Victorian crazy quilt, done up in rich shades of silk and velvet and heavily embellished with fancy embroidery. When she started to pull more of the quilt from the trunk, a clunking sound came from inside. "It's wrapped around something."

Jeff jumped up to help. He searched out the shape of the solid object, and carefully lifted it from the deep trunk. The pair worked together, removing the velvet wrappings. He hoisted the large receptacle onto the library table, then both he and Sheila stepped back to study it.

The large bowl shape with a footed pedestal was of chased silver with porcelain cabochons depicting pastoral scenes. The lid's silver finial was in the shape of an acorn.

"Is that what I think it is?" Sheila asked.

"I believe so. Heavy, too."

"Do you think it contains ashes?"

He shrugged. "There's a good chance it does."

"Well, I don't know what you plan to do with it, but it's not staying here."

"Wonder who it is?"

"Does it really matter? You said yourself the old woman had no relatives. What on earth do people do with ashes when there's no one left to claim them?"

"I can't very well just dump them in the garbage. At the very least, that seems disrespectful. Might even be illegal."

Greer entered the room, and handed a package to Sheila. "Missus, this just arrived for you."

"Thank you, Greer."

Jeff said, "Greer, it appears there was a body of sorts in the trunk, after all."

Greer studied the urn. "It appears so, sir."

"Would you get me the phone number of that nursing home?"

"Rose Trellis Nursing Facility. Yes, sir." Greer started toward the door.

"Jeff, what are you going to do?" Sheila asked.

Jeff called the butler back.

"Sir?"

"What would Sherlock do?"

"The same thing you're about to do, sir: Follow the clues to a logical conclusion."

"But what if there isn't one? A logical conclusion, I mean."

"To quote Mr. Holmes: 'When you have eliminated the impossible, whatever remains, however improbable, must be the truth.'"

Sharon Swan's office was small, well organized, and busy. The director of nursing had warned him on the phone that she wouldn't have much time, because corporate was expected in the building, two residents were due back from the hospital, and an aide had called in sick.

Jeff sat in a chair in front of her desk, and waited as a parade of smocked employees, EMTs, and suits filed through. His promise to be brief had him scrambling to come up with the most pressing questions.

"Like I told you on the phone, there's not much I can divulge. I follow HIPAA to the letter."

"Understood." Jeff shifted in the small chair. "To the point: There's an urn with ashes in the bottom of the trunk."

The woman shrugged. "Happens all the time."

Pragmatic. He liked that. "I'd like to know whose ashes they are, so I can decide the best way to process them. A husband's, perhaps?"

"That would be in public records, so I can tell you there was a husband." She turned, opened a credenza that held a lateral file system. "As I recall, he passed several years ago."

She skimmed contents of a folder labeled ELDER, VERONICA. "Here it is. Richard Elder died April 2, 1984, in Portland, Oregon. Worley Funeral Home." She stood. "I hope they can help you, Mr. Talbot."

Back home Jeff searched online for the funeral home, but couldn't locate one with that name. He bookmarked a page listing funeral

141

homes in Portland, and begrudged the task before him of contacting the dozens on the list. As much as he wanted to know the answer, he wasn't in the mood to be on the phone making cold calls the rest of the day, so he shelved the chore.

He tried to read, but the urn—its contents, rather—distracted him. He tried to call Mike Danville about the discovery, but when the call went straight to voicemail he remembered that Mike was currently on a Japanese clock. He tried to call Sharon Swan to ask if there was any other information she could divulge. Again, voicemail. Finally, he gave up and moved to the trunk.

There was some sort of satchel inside. He retrieved it; a valise, black leather, plain but in good shape. He opened it, found a deerstalker cap, Inverness coat with the cape (just like the ones he'd seen in Paget's illustrations), ebony-handled magnifying glass, and a Calabash pipe.

Holmes smoked one or another of many pipes in the stories he'd been reading. The trunk had belonged to a woman, that much he knew. But what about these items? Had they belonged to her husband? Or had the woman herself dressed in the likeness of Sherlock Holmes, right down to propping the pipe between her lips?

Jeff next wondered whether any female characters in the canon had smoked a pipe. He made a mental note to ask Greer. But when Greer appeared a few minutes later, that wasn't the question he asked.

"Do you know anything about pipes?"

"Yes, sir. What would you like to know?"

"How to sterilize a pipe's stem, for one thing." Jeff showed him the Calabash.

"I'll see to that for you, sir."

"Just don't let Sheila see it. For now, anyway."

"Yes, sir."

Waiting on callbacks caused him as much angst as the hovering task of making all those funeral home calls. No wonder Sherlock Holmes often grew impatient and turned to vices. Jeff certainly didn't condone the cocaine, but the pipe? He pondered the stories he'd read so far, and began to understand. He found himself gaining a new appreciation for the pipe, and by the time Greer returned with the sterilized stem, he had decided to give it a try.

Of course, he had no tobacco, no tamping tools, no pipe cleaners. But he could pretend. This was all about pretending, wasn't it?

He grabbed the next short story from the stack and sank into his chair. The curved pipe stem bobbed precariously between his teeth, making the large bowl ebb and flow in his sights. It crossed his mind that a man might turn green as much from the motion as from the tobacco.

Upon Greer's recommendation, he started watching TV adaptations of the canon every evening before going to bed. The paisley prints on vests, ascots, and smoking jackets reminded him of a vintage jacket that had belonged to his grandfather. Jeff rummaged in the attic until he found the item of clothing, which became his new livery while reading more stories, watching more episodes, and stacking more letters on the table from the trunk's contents.

From time to time, during his career as a picker, he had stumbled upon a mystery connected to an antique. At times, being dragged into those mysteries had become more harrowing and challenging than anything he'd tackled during his years with the FBI. Now, with the influence of Sherlock Holmes under his skullcap, he found himself attaching mysteries to most of his finds throughout the course of his daily work. He watched for bicycle marks on boots, and wax drips on hats, and footprints on practically everything.

The next morning, Jeff left to take a stab at making a living. He'd been gone from home less than an hour when Greer called his cell to relay messages. "Sir, Dr. Danville reports that no DNA can be ascertained from the ashes, and that if it turns out to be necessary for some reason, he'll help you obtain dental records of Mrs. Elder."

"What about Sharon Swan at the nursing home?"

"Actually, sir, it was a receptionist who called. She wanted you to know that Miss Swan is away at a conference."

Jeff thought a moment, then said, "Might be the perfect time to swing by there."

No one seemed to notice him as he entered the nursing home, so he kept moving. At the end of the east corridor was a cleaning cart, and as he strolled toward it, a young lady in pink scrubs walked out of a room, deposited a bundle of sheets into the bin, then pumped a dollop of sanitizer into her palm. Jeff seized the opportunity to strike up a conversation.

"Thank goodness for that stuff, huh?" He threw a nod toward the large dispenser.

"You got that right. I don't know *what* they used to do."

Jeff fought the urge to say, *soap and water*. He gave her his name, and used Dr. Danville and the trunk as his connection to Veronica Elder. "Did you know her?"

"Sure. Everybody knew her, nobody liked her."

The girl wiped excess sanitizer on her pant legs. "She was hard on everyone, for sure, but she was a lot like my grandmother, so I usually didn't let her get to me." She picked up a folded set of bedding from one of the cart's shelves. "It got harder, though, not to get dragged down by her, especially when she'd get confused. She was at her worst then."

"Confused? In what way?" He leaned against the wall in order to appear nonthreatening.

"Oh, she'd forget where she was, even what town she was in, sometimes. Or she wouldn't know her name, so it'd *really* set her off when we called her 'Miss Ronnie.' She'd tell us that was her older sister's name. You know, things like that."

"Sister? I was told she had no one."

"Exactly." The girl raised a brow. "Like I said, confused."

Someone called out from one of the rooms.

"Sorry, I have to get back to work."

Jeff smiled. "Thanks. You've been most helpful."

He hurried home and virtually locked himself in the library. Systematically, he went through the bundles of letters.

They were tied in batches according to year, and the batches were conveniently in chronological order. That not only saved time, but also helped give flow to the conversation. By the time he was well into them, he could practically guess what the letters *to* the woman named Violet Chilson had said.

"*Violet?*" Greer said, when Jeff reported his findings. The butler placed the day's mail on Jeff's desk, then picked up a stack of books from the credenza.

"Unbelievable, isn't it?" Jeff studied the return address on the envelope in his hand, printed under the once-required line reading *After Five Days Return To*. "That must've been Conan Doyle's favorite name for a woman, since he used it so many times in the stories."

"You could be right, sir."

Jeff paced. A notion was forming. When he had it worked out, he said, "What would Sherlock do?"

Greer looked up from the books he was returning to their shelves. "Sir?"

"I'm serious, man! What would he do?"

"Well, sir, he would tell Watson to pack a toothbrush, then a message would be wired, and they would be on the next train to interview the subject."

"Precisely!" Jeff slapped the envelope against his palm. "Let's go, then. Pack our bags, and check the train timetable. The game's afoot, Watson!"

He looked at Greer, whose mouth was gaped open. Jeff, having rarely seen the butler display shock, snapped back to reality almost as quickly as Greer's jaw snapped shut.

"Greer, old fellow," he said, "you'll have to be both Dr. Watson and Mrs. Hudson on this trip."

Greer nodded once, then was off like a shot.

Forty minutes later, they were at King Street Station, boarding the 507 to Portland, Oregon.

The Amtrak car was nothing like the wood-paneled beauties that Jeff had imagined Holmes and Watson journeying on in England during the late 1800s. Still, it had been too long since his last trip by rail.

Greer sat next to him, reading. Jeff closed his eyes and settled back for the short journey, happy for the time to contemplate what he knew about the case so far.

He was asleep almost instantly. When Greer awakened him, he remembered why he rarely accomplished anything while rocking on rails.

McMinnville, Oregon, was located southwest of Portland. Greer had arranged for a rental car that, to Jeff's surprise, was equipped with GPS. The butler deftly entered the woman's address, then followed the spoken directions.

Jeff thought about the online search he'd done while Greer packed their bags, and he wasn't sure which fact surprised him more—finding the woman's phone number online, learning that she still lived at the same address printed on thirty-year-old envelopes, or garnering an invitation from her for that very afternoon.

Forty-five minutes later, they pulled into the driveway beside a stately Italianate on the corner lot of a neighborhood with tree-lined sidewalks and well-maintained historic homes.

The sun was shining, but a crisp breeze swept the valley, carrying with it the perfume of wine country and the bite of autumn chill. They were greeted at the door by an elderly butler who, for all intents and purposes, might well have been an original fixture of the historic home.

Jeff held out his business card, and the man took it, then swept his arm in a gesture of invitation. Out of nowhere, a petite woman seized the card from the butler's hand while grabbing reading glasses from atop her head. "Such a bother getting older," she said while reading the card. She looked up and smiled.

From the letters, Jeff knew her to be in her mid-sixties, but her appearance suggested someone much younger. Her glittery silver pixie cut was spiked on top, and her stylish blue jeans and fitted white shirt outlined a slender figure. The shirt showcased a necklace assembled from vintage findings that caught Jeff's eye, among them faceted chandelier rondelles that refracted the light and sprinkled the woman's face with tiny rainbows. Sheila would call her trendy.

"Mrs. Chilson?" Jeff held out his hand. "Thank you for seeing us."

"How could I not? Likely you know more about my early life than I'll ever remember." She shook his hand firmly. "Call me Vi. Since you've been reading my letters, you know me by no other name."

She was on the move. "Let's go to the sunroom, shall we? I've asked Whitcomb to set up tea out there so that we might enjoy this wonderful autumn day."

As they followed her through the well-appointed home, Jeff noted that the furniture choices were true to its architectural style. The only thing that didn't seem to fit in was the woman herself.

"Whitcomb, I'll serve Jeff. Why don't you and Greer take tea in the atrium, then you can give him the cook's tour of the place."

"Yes, Mum."

Greer and Jeff exchanged glances before the young butler followed Whitcomb from the room, and Jeff suspected they were thinking the same thing: Both Sherlock Holmes and Dr. Watson had often garnered vital information from the servant class. Jeff hoped Greer might do the same.

"Sit, please." Vi motioned to a chair, then poured two cups. "I see Whitcomb has forgotten the lemon slices."

"I'm fine without them," Jeff said, but the energetic woman was gone and back before he could protest further.

She seated herself across from him. "Whitcomb won't show it, but he was thrilled to learn that you employ a butler. I'm sure he's doubly thrilled now to see that young people are still going into service. Mr. Chilson, God rest his soul, promised Whitcomb a place here till either he or I pass on. I argued the point, but could never bring myself to turn him out. And God knows he won't retire. Chilson's promise actually made Whitcomb more loyal, if that's possible."

"Greer was first hired for the benefit of my wife. She's agoraphobic, so having someone to run errands has been a lifesaver. Of course, I've come to rely on him, too. Being an antiques picker keeps me on the road."

"So that's how you ended up with Ronnie's trunk?"

Jeff nodded. "She left it to her doctor—apparently more common than one might think—who's a friend of mine."

"And you said it's full of Sherlock Holmes memorabilia? I'm surprised she kept all that stuff."

"Are you still one of the Adventuresses of Sherlock Holmes?"

"ASH, we call ourselves." She smiled. "We meet on Ash Wednesday, just like the bona fide ones in New York do. I was one of the originals, you know."

"I didn't know. Sorry, I haven't read the copies I found of *The Serpentine Muse*."

"Not to worry. I was in college in Connecticut when a group of us girls discovered a shared love of the Holmes canon. Back then, the Baker Street Irregulars didn't allow women to attend meetings, so we started our own.

"After graduation, I married Mr. Chilson, who brought me from one side of the world to the other—or so it seemed at the time. I found more like-minded women out here, so I started holding meetings."

Jeff nodded. "About the letters. To tell you the truth, I've barely scratched the surface. As I mentioned on the phone, I'm simply trying to learn whose ashes are in the urn I discovered."

"Did you bring the letters with you?"

Jeff withdrew a small bundle from his jacket pocket, and placed it before her on the table. "Two larger bundles are in the car. Greer will bring them in before we leave. I'll ship any others I find when I've finished going through the trunk."

She spread the ones before her like one would a hand of gin rummy, then chose a large envelope and removed its contents. She clapped her hand over her mouth. After a moment, she removed it and said, "I remember purchasing this very card for her."

Jeff gave her a moment before he spoke. "What about letters and cards she sent to you? Was she as prolific as you were?"

"Yes, she was." Vi paused. "Bear in mind, I was both shocked and deeply hurt by the things she said to me the last time I saw her. We were having one of our meetings, and the rest of the women were here in the sunroom. She was late arriving, but she didn't join us. Whitcomb told me that she was waiting for me in the parlor.

"I went in there, and she wouldn't even show her face. I suspected that her brute of a husband had hit her. But after she lambasted me, I wondered if it was simply because she didn't have the nerve to look me in the eye."

Vi paused again, then continued. "That night, I ripped up all of her letters and threw them away. I regretted it later."

"Do you recall your last conversation with her before that one?"

"We rarely spoke on the phone back then, before long distance plans and unlimited minutes. It was a big deal that she drove an hour each way for the meetings. Nowadays, an hour is nothing—plus, we have cell phones in case we break down. Back then, you were at the mercy of whoever might stop—if anyone came along at all. I always tried to get Ronnie to spend the night, but she wouldn't do it.

"The month before, she stayed after the others left, long enough to tell me that the private eye she had hired several months earlier had located a younger sister. Turned out they were separated as toddlers when their parents were killed, and didn't know each other existed. Ronnie's paternal grandmother raised her, told her that there was no other family. When her grandmother passed, Ronnie found family memorabilia that indicated otherwise.

"Anyhow, she contacted the sister, and begged her to come to Portland for a visit. She was as excited as anyone can be. It was short-lived, though. I received one letter during that month between those two ASH meetings. Ronnie wrote that it wasn't going very well between her and her sister, Vickie. She said that the woman hadn't enjoyed a nice upbringing, like she'd had. Apparently Vickie drank a lot, and dressed a bit trashy. Ronnie also said that her husband had taken quite a shine to the woman, though, and that the more those two got along, the more she was being squeezed out."

"You don't think . . . ?"

"That there was some hanky-panky going on? It crossed my mind. Maybe that's why Ronnie was so upset when I last saw her. She didn't want to lash out at her newfound sister, and she didn't dare lash out at her husband, so I was her scapegoat."

"Or," Jeff said, "she did lash out at him, and got her mouth mashed for her trouble."

After a moment, Vi said, "I can tell you one thing: If those ashes in the urn you told me about are her husband's, they're probably still burning."

Jeff let that thought settle, then told Vi that those who knew Ronnie in her later years said she was hard to get along with.

"I wouldn't have believed it, if I hadn't experienced that side of her firsthand. She always had the sweetest spirit. Whatever transpired during those weeks with her sister seems to have altered the rest of her life.

"Even so, a few weeks later I sent her a funny little card, hoping her actions were caused by hormones or the like. I didn't hear back. I kept trying, though, but she never replied. My last one was returned stamped, 'Moved. Forwarding Address Unknown.'"

She took a deep breath, as if she'd been physically chasing the story she relayed to Jeff, then blew it out in a gust. "It took me years to get over her. She was my best friend. Then, suddenly, she wasn't my friend at all."

Jeff touched the woman's hand, then stood. From their conversation, he knew she had nothing to offer as evidence of whose ashes were in the urn.

Vi rose from her chair. "ASH has a motto: *Gutta cavat lapidem, non vi sed saepe cadendo.* It's from Ovid. It means, 'A drop carves the rock, not by force but by persistence.' It was only after she moved that I realized I should've driven to her house when I had the chance. I should've been more persistent."

During the drive back to Portland, the two men exchanged information. Jeff shared the high points from his conversation with Vi, then said, "Did you learn anything from Whitcomb?"

"He's a wealth of knowledge—or could be, I believe. Unfortunately, he seemed always to be searching mental files for pieces of information. It was a sobering afternoon. A good one, too, but sobering."

"The current ways are better," Jeff said. "You're our employee, not our servant. You're not bound by an unreasonable loyalty, and you have the benefits of a retirement plan. Everyone should be prepared so they don't have to work into their eighties, particularly if they aren't able. I would never make you promise to stay with Sheila to the end if something happened to me."

"Thank you, sir, but I assure you, the sense of loyalty is a part of who we are, a part that is honed, polished during our training. Whitcomb's loyalty is as much to his oath and his station as it is to Mrs. Chilson."

Jeff had never thought of it from that angle. Not knowing what else to say on the subject, he changed it. "I'm having second thoughts about our staying in Portland. By now, the funeral homes are closed, and calling them will take all day tomorrow."

"That's up to you, sir, but I would think you could just as easily find Richard Elder's obituary in newspaper archives online."

"*You* could just as easily, but it's rare for me to have the kind of luck I had today when I found Vi Chilson's number."

"If you wish, sir, we can return home now. I'll use my iPad and search for it while we're on the train."

"Greer, is there ever a time you aren't prepared?"

"I hope not, sir."

The next day, when Sheila entered the library and announced that lunch was ready, she found, instead of her husband, the very image most people have of Sherlock Holmes: a man wearing a deerstalker cap and Inverness coat, with a Calabash pipe clenched between his teeth and a magnifying glass in his grasp.

"Well, if it isn't Jeffrey Holmes, Amateur Sleuth."

Jeff looked up, smiled sheepishly. Something glinted in his right hand. "I thought the costume might help me find a clue. Besides, I need to occupy myself while Greer does some research for me."

"Occupy yourself by joining me for lunch." She started to turn, then said, "Just as soon as you shed the Sherlock."

"Are you interested in this?" He held out a large rhinestone fur clip he'd found in one of the Bon Marché boxes. "It's an Eisenberg."

THE MYSTERIOUS CASE OF THE URN OF ASH;

"If I went anywhere to wear it, I might. You'll turn a good profit on it, since it's a marked piece."

Sheila left, and Jeff sighed. He held out little hope that his wife would ever attend a large event—whether or not it called for a fur or, indeed, a vintage fur clip. The Internet was a two-edged sword, and, although it gave his agoraphobic wife access to the outer world, he feared it also had further ensconced her inside the elaborate walls of his inherited mansion.

His mind wandered, pictured Sherlock Holmes deducing the solution to a mystery here among the labyrinth of rooms and hidden passageways.

"Jeff," Sheila called from the kitchen, "your lunch is getting cold."

"Be right there," he said, then muttered, "I doubt it'll ever get as cold as this case."

He laid the pipe and glass on the library table, then walked around it to hang the hat and coat on the hall tree.

When he turned, he had a vantage point not before seen. Sunlight illuminated the right front corner inside the trunk, revealing what looked like a tear in the print fabric lining. Facing the trunk—one's typical approach—made it all but impossible to see those deep, dark corners at the bottom.

Jeff picked at it with his fingernail and discovered that it wasn't the lining at all, but a minuscule loop of dark green ribbon that blended into the greens of the foliage print. He grabbed a letter opener from his desk, used its tip to hook the loop, and pulled. A panel lifted, sucking the airless space as it did and causing a flutter of papers underneath.

A false bottom.

Jeff cursed under his breath. Why hadn't he thought to check for one when they had emptied the thing? *I just proved that I'm anything but a Sherlock Holmes*, he thought.

He gathered the pieces and took them to his desk. It didn't take long to conclude that they were reports from the private eye's search for Ronnie's sister, along with a few ticket stubs and photos Jeff knew must have been compiled during their brief visit.

He grabbed one of the photos, announcing where he was going as he loped through the kitchen.

Greer handed him a printout, along with the statement that Richard Elder had not been cremated. Jeff seized the paper on his way past.

Sheila's voice, asking about lunch, trailed him as he bolted out the back door.

Jeff swung open the door and stepped inside the Rose Trellis lobby. He had one more question for the housekeeper he had talked to before. He chastised himself for not remembering her name, and could almost feel Holmes's disappointment in him once again. He would start with the corridors.

"I remember you." Jeff turned toward the voice. A white-haired gentleman in a wheelchair sat alone in a room with two couches, several armchairs, and a piano. "This is the third time in a week you've been here, and you have yet to stop and visit."

Not wanting to be rude, Jeff walked over and shook the man's hand. "You're right, sir. I apologize." Jeff took a seat across from the man.

The gent waved him off. "Happens all the time. Most people think that just because our bodies fail us, our brains do, too. You're the one who picked up Ronnie's old steamer, aren't you?"

"Not much gets past you, I'll bet."

"Helps keep me sharp, keeping an eye on the comings and goings."

Jeff thought about that one. "You know, I never met her. Were you friends?"

The gent grunted. "Nobody was friends with her, she didn't want that. But we'd talk on occasion, when she let her shield down. She was a pretty thing." He leaned in a bit, said, "I would've made the moves on her, if she hadn't been so danged bitter all the time."

"A real looker, huh?"

"You got that right."

"I'd like to show you something." Jeff reached inside his breast pocket, retrieved the old photo, and handed it to the man.

"Is this some sort of joke?"

"No, sir, I assure you it's not. I realize it was taken a long time ago. Is Ronnie in that picture?"

With a gnarled finger, the old man pointed to a knockout brunette, a beauty mark just above her lip. "Make no mistake, that's her. Told you she was a looker."

"Thank you. I wish I had met her." Jeff stood.

"You're leaving?"

"Afraid so. Duty calls."

"Don't be a stranger," the old man called after him.

When Jeff returned home, he asked Greer to set up a blackboard and easel in the library. He wished he had done it sooner.

He sketched triangles and jotted findings. He drew circles and connecting arrows. He erased and re-grouped theories and bits of information until, at last, he was satisfied that he had conclusively solved the mystery.

After positioning two chairs before the blackboard, he called Sheila and Greer into the library.

"Before I left earlier to substantiate the final piece of this puzzle, I discovered a secret panel in the trunk."

Both audience members leaned forward.

"Beneath it—" He held up a manila envelope. "—the results of the P.I.'s investigation."

"As you both know, Veronica Elder—Ronnie—hired him after the paternal grandmother who raised her had died, and she learned that she had a sister. The girls' parents were killed in a train derailment when the girls were toddlers.

"The private eye tracked down said sister, who had been raised by an aunt and uncle of the biological mother.

"They were born into this world as Veronica and Victoria Elder, identical except for one small difference: a mole above Victoria's lip."

"*Twins?*"

"Twins." Jeff told them about his conversation with the old gent at the nursing home, then handed over the photograph he'd shown the man. It was of the two women on the day they were reunited.

Greer said, "They have just come from the beauty parlor, followed by a shopping trip for matching outfits. They're exactly the same, except for the perfectly circular mole."

"Greer, you're absolutely right," Sheila said, looking at the photo again before turning back to her husband. "How did your old gent react?"

"He thought I was playing a joke, but he quickly picked out the one with the mole, and said that was the Ronnie who'd been living in the nursing home all these years."

"What about the 'younger sister, older sister' stuff?"

"Veronica was older—by three minutes. From everything I've learned, Victoria was a vain woman. Remember, the only info we had about one being older was what Ronnie told Vi the night before she met Victoria—Vickie."

Sheila's eyes widened. "Are you saying that she killed her own sister?"

"That's what everything adds up to."

Greer said, "Why do you think she kept the trunk with all those things of her sister's—even her ashes—if she basically had no relationship with her?"

"In a way, they did have a relationship, built on remorse after experiencing firsthand the abuse of Richard Elder. It created a warped sense of camaraderie between Vickie and the sister whose life she had taken.

Or the life the husband had taken—there's not enough evidence to determine who killed her, and who was an accessory."

Sheila waved her hands as if shooing away confusion. "So, you're saying that the real Veronica Elder is in the urn?"

Jeff said, "I'm afraid that's right."

"Very sad story, sir."

Sheila looked as if a fog had cleared. "I've got it now: The woman who died last week at the nursing home was Victoria Elder."

"Right. No, wait." Jeff searched the blackboard. "Actually, Victoria Larson. She was never an Elder. Her beauty mark, along with a lusty, bohemian approach to life, captivated her sister's husband from the start. Ronnie alluded to it in a letter to Vi Chilson. Difficult to predict who seduced whom; probably a two-way attraction. They had an affair two short weeks after Victoria entered her married sister's life."

"How could you possibly know that?" Sheila asked.

He waggled the manila envelope and grinned. "The P.I. had met both women and, apparently, he was fascinated by their being nearly identical. He followed Vickie and her brother-in-law to a nearby town, saw them check into a motel."

"As a wife, I must ask: Didn't he report his findings to the wife?"

"He thought he did. There's a note here stating that he went to the home and talked to Mrs. Elder. From what I have deduced, it was Vickie. She even fooled him.

"To continue the ruse after the murder, Vickie attended—as Ronnie—one last meeting of the Adventuresses of Sherlock Holmes. She concealed her face from Vi, remember, Greer? What she didn't know was that Ronnie had always held a soft spot in her heart for Whitcomb. While Greer brought in the blackboard, he told me about a phone call he got from the old butler while I was gone.

"Whitcomb said that he remembers her visit that last night, and he never believed that the woman who came to the house was Veronica

Elder. But he had nothing tangible to offer, nor the compulsion to step out of his station and question it."

Jeff handed photos to them. "Here's a pair of school pictures from when they were eighth graders—same pose, different clothing, different towns, of course. In Vickie's, the beauty mark is already distinctive."

"So is the 'here comes trouble' spark in her eye." Sheila shook her head.

"Victoria Elder was masquerading as her deceased sister—and continued doing so in order to collect a widow's pension when Richard Elder died of a massive heart attack shortly after. She effectively wrote her own life sentence, a most nefarious femme fatale who clearly didn't look beyond her immediate desires.

"I wouldn't doubt that Richard Elder had a bizarre existence during those few months between Ronnie's death and his own."

Sheila shuddered. "Can you imagine killing someone who has an identical twin, then . . . *being* with the twin? Creepy."

Greer glanced at Sheila, then asked Jeff, "How do you suppose they were able to have her cremated?"

"Good question. All I can figure is a pay-off of some sort."

Greer and Sheila stood. She walked up and hugged her husband. "I'm impressed with both of you for your work on this. Somehow, I believe her soul can now rest in peace.

"One more question: What are you going to do with her ashes?"

"The way I see it, there's only one proper thing to do, right, Greer?"

"Agreed, sir."

"I've already called Vi Chilson, told her what we discovered."

Greer said, "She must be quite relieved."

"She is. And she said she'd be honored if we'd give her Ronnie's ashes. She and the rest of her ASH group will conduct a ceremony, with a burial in the flower garden outside her sunroom."

"Whitcomb will be quite pleased as well, sir."

"I'd better get dinner started," Sheila announced.

After she left the room, Jeff draped a shawl over the blackboard. He had a strange sense that Holmes would've wrapped up this case in similar fashion, since he often doled out his own sense of justice. There was no one to bring to justice in this situation, and he took some comfort in the fact that the bitter old woman had unwittingly delivered her own sentence—a life lived out as a lie, long after the principals were gone.

"I have to hand it to Sherlock Holmes and his keen skills of deduction. Can you imagine doing all of this during Victorian times?"

Greer said, "We're fortunate. Sir Arthur Conan Doyle actually spurred the advancement of forensic medicine."

"And to think, each clue in this mystery seemed to be just a trifle."

"But there's nothing so important as trifles."

Jeff thought a moment. "I know that story. 'The Man with the Twisted Lip,' right?"

Greer smiled. "'The Man with the Twisted Lip.'"

THE END

THE ADVENTURE OF THE DEADLY INTERLUDE

JAMES O'KEEFE

*E*ssayist, novelist, short-story writer, and veteran of several scion societies of the national Baker Street Irregulars, James O'Keefe turns to pastiche for the first time in "The Adventure of the Deadly Interlude," and one wonders what took him so long. This poignant story of a legendary friendship is both solid detective writing and textbook "buddy" fiction. Along the way, the author solves a mystery that has puzzled scholars for decades: Just when did Watson learn of the existence of Professor Moriarty? Published here for the first time, by permission of the author.

"... *him whom I shall ever regard as the best and wisest man whom I have ever known.*"

I laid down my pen and stared at my obituary to Sherlock Holmes, consumed by memories of hansom rides through night-time London or some remote village, en route to some mysterious, often dangerous encounter, filled with the excitement I thought I had left behind in Afghanistan when I had alighted from the ship into the teeming multitudes of the Great City, so many years ago. There were adventures as yet unrecorded, which Holmes had felt should be saved for later for so many reasons. Would I be able to write them when the time came? I could not do so now, though I was recalling one.

It began with a warning from someone named Porlock, a spy in the ranks of someone Holmes refused to name beyond calling him "a shifty and evasive personality." Porlock was attempting to prevent the murder of one John Douglas; but he was too late. Inspector Alec Mac-Donald of the Yard informed us Douglas had died of a shotgun blast to the face at his estate in Birlstone. Holmes seemed to have some idea of who was behind it, and dismissed me so that he might speak to the inspector alone. He rarely treated me thus.

My friend never told me who was behind the strange events that had begun in a part of the United States called Vermissa Valley or, as I was to come to think of it, the Valley of Fear; but as I paced my office, I had no doubt of that mastermind's identity.

What recalled the episode to my mind was a village we passed through on the way to Birlstone. It seemed a cosy little place in the Sussex hills, with its shops and pubs on either side of a cobblestone street, the few great secluded houses atop those hills, and a lake where one could sink one's lure, lean back, and forget all cares. Was this the spot to relieve, if only slightly, my grief, or would it remind me of the thrills we had shared among such scenes?

I was still contemplating this over breakfast, which I am almost certain was excellent, as was most of what our cook prepared, though I cannot recall what it was. I tried to hide my mood from Mary, whose health had begun to bother me; but I could tell by her eyes that I could keep nothing from her.

I was reading *The Times* and she was sewing that evening when she looked up. "It's no good, John."

"What?"

"He haunts your every step—you know who I mean. I loved him, too, not the least for bringing us together; but I see every day how you are suffering. I must believe your practice is suffering."

"And you and I?"

She smiled wanly. Too many of her smiles were wan these days. "Nothing this side of the grave could harm that. There are several men who could see to your practice while you took a brief leave to put some of this behind you. It hurts to say the game will never be afoot again; but if you do not remove yourself from all this, the Reichenbach may claim a third victim."

I laid aside *The Times*. "As a matter of fact, I was thinking only this morning of a place that might serve, the village of Dickencroft. We could be there—"

"Not we, John—you. You must be alone with your thoughts."

I found myself at Paddington Station the following morning. Mary was there to see me off. I was glad of that. Holmes and I had begun so many adventures from this place, and I could not bear to be alone.

I shall not weary my readers with the thoughts that occupied me on that journey, so reminiscent of those I had taken with Holmes, or how much Dickencroft reminded me of the scenes of those adventures, save that I dismissed the first curious incident there as my musings working on my imagination. I was wandering the main street, trying to lose myself in the mood such hamlets often produce in me, when I saw a man across the street. He had a small moustache and a goatee on his jutting chin. His eyes projected strength, or so it seemed at that distance.

I was convinced I had seen him somewhere before. This impression was strengthened when he saw me and those eyes widened. He hurried his pace and, as I watched him, occasionally glanced back at me. I had no doubt I had just encountered someone I had met before in Holmes's company. He had recognized me, and was not happy about the encounter.

I had no desire to investigate. Those days were over.

I was dining at The Laughing Friar when something similar happened. I was washing down an excellent shepherd's pie with stout when I noticed a man at a table along the opposite wall of the pub. He was also bearded, though his was black and much fuller, as were his slick head of hair and the heavy brows that made him seem all the more sinister. He was dressed in grey, and his wardrobe was obviously expensive. I tried to convince myself I was again imagining something, that the light was too dim to be sure; but there was no mistaking those narrow eyes staring at me.

Holmes had often recalled cases before our association when something had reminded him of them; but as we had passed through Dickencroft on the way to Birlstone, he had made no mention of anything that might have happened here.

I was awakened the following morning by the proprietor's plump wife, who held out a folded piece of paper. "Gentleman told me to give you this, doctor. He's waiting for a reply." It was a note written, it seemed to me, in a fine, flowing hand from which Holmes might have deduced much:

> *Doctor:*
> *I understand you were the companion of the late Sherlock Holmes.*
> *I am holding a soirée this evening at my home, Maple Meadow. I*

should be delighted if you would attend. Please inform my man if he might call for you at 7:30.
Sir Cecil Dandridge

"Tell him I shall be delighted."

It did not occur to me to wonder why she seemed apprehensive. "Very well, Doctor."

I spent the rest of the morning strolling the streets and even venturing into the countryside, trying to enjoy the simple beauty of the area beneath a cloudless late spring sky. It was no use. There seemed an invisible wall between myself and all this; and it had little to do with Holmes. How had Sir Cecil Dandridge learned of my presence when, as far as I knew, we had never met? Only now did it occur to me how uneasy the proprietor's wife had seemed. She knew of Sir Cecil; and, for some reason, she did not like him.

I was returning to prepare for the evening when I noticed a figure astride a fine-looking chestnut on a nearby hill. I could not mistake that slim build or that black beard; and, once again, he seemed to be watching me.

I stopped at a tailor, as I had brought no formal wear.

A barouche pulled up to the door of The Laughing Friar shortly past the appointed time. The journey, chiefly along a country road, seemed roughly half an hour and ended at the cedar-lined drive leading to a great red-bricked, multi-gabled structure gleaming in the last rays of the sun.

A tall, gaunt butler with a few white hairs led me along the polished chequerboard floor of a wood-panelled hall to a grand ballroom, illuminated by a gigantic chandelier hanging from a frescoed ceiling. The men in their tailcoats and women in elaborate gowns might have overflowed some gatherings; but here, their numbers seemed sparse. A fat little fellow with wild copper hair played passages from Mozart's *The Magic Flute* on a grand piano before one of the numerous picture windows.

The butler announced me; my host approached almost immediately. Sir Cecil was a big man in height and girth with dark brows and chiseled features that, before the wrinkles and slight double chin, must have cut quite a figure with the ladies. He had wavy black hair with streaks of gray.

"Dr. Watson, Dr. Watson," said he, shaking my hand with almost frightening vigour, "what an honour, what a singular honour. I must introduce you immediately."

I was terribly impressed with all the distinguished-looking folk towards whom he practically dragged me. I had been to several such gatherings in my profession and in the company of Holmes, but not since the tragedy at Reichenbach, and never as guest of honour.

I confess I recall only two of these people: Trevor Atkins, who frankly made me feel more comfortable than Sir Cecil, and Atkins's charming companion.

Atkins was a short, trim man without a hair on his head or chin. His voice reminded me of a well-fed cat. "Ah, Dr. Watson." His handshake was nearly as hearty as my host's. "I was devastated, as all good Englishmen must be, to hear of your friend's fate—England's own Dupin."

"Indeed."

"And I should have liked to tell him so personally."

"He would have been thrilled." Why tell him Holmes's actual low opinion of "by no means such a phenomenon as Poe seemed to imagine"?

"And this is Mlle. Marie L'Espanaye."

The young woman had large, brown, child-like eyes. Her white ruffled gown hugged her slim figure and displayed her shoulders, over one of which hung her long, dark brown tresses. "*Enchantée.*"

Her smile and the way she took my hand both lacked enthusiasm. Was she wondering if she would meet anyone here her own age?

Atkins leaned towards me and lowered his voice. "I fear she speaks little English."

"If you will excuse us," said Sir Cecil, taking my arm, "I have something to discuss with Dr. Watson in the garden."

He seemed less congenial as he preceded me along a path to a stone bench by a pond spanned by a wooden bridge, visible in the last vibrant light of day. He motioned me to sit, but remained standing.

"I did not invite you totally as a guest of honour." There was no trace of cordiality in his voice or expression. "The fact is that when someone like Sherlock Holmes dies and there is no trace of a body, and when, furthermore, his dearest friend shows up in this area, I worry; and I think you know why."

"Perhaps you would care to elucidate?"

"I do not think that is necessary."

"Forgive me, Sir Cecil, but I have no idea to what you are referring."

"Forgive me, doctor, but I do not believe you."

I shot to my feet. "See here, sir, I am here precisely because Holmes is dead. There can be no mistake. I came to Dickencroft to contemplate what my future will be without him and those adventures, which so enriched my life. I came to this house to have one night to think of other things, to rest my mind, to be refreshed for—I don't know. If you are some enemy of Holmes, and invited me here out of guilt and anxiety, how cruel. I have a good mind to go to the authorities. And don't get any ideas. Your guests know we came out here together, so if anything happens to me—"

His laugh was so raucous I thought the man had lost his senses. "The authorities know far more than you; and they don't know enough to make a case." He turned and walked away. "I shall give you a chance to say your goodbyes, and then my driver will take you back to The Laughing Friar. If you are telling the truth, if you stay out of my way, you will find your little idyll to be all you expected. Dickencroft really is quite charming."

I was standing there alone, pondering my next move, when I heard a heavily accented voice: "I should listen to him, *monsieur le docteur.*" He stepped out of the small forest I had barely noticed behind me—the bearded man I had twice noticed watching me. "I have read several of your accounts of the great Sherlock Holmes. I particularly recall how dangerous he felt rural areas to be, in many ways more dangerous than any metropolis. I assure you, his words could be no truer than when applied to innocent-looking Dickencroft. I should take the first train to London tomorrow."

"I believe I can deal with Sir Cecil Dandridge. I survived Afghanistan, and you've read how well Holmes and I survived more formidable foes."

"Forgive my insensitivity, *monsieur le docteur*; but your friend lies at the foot of the Reichenbach, and he always struck me as being more resourceful than yourself."

I shrugged. The remark stung; I was not about to reveal it to this fellow.

"Two things you should consider, *mon ami*: first, I have my own way of dealing with Sir Cecil Dandridge—never mind how."

"And the second?"

His eyes narrowed. "If you do not leave tomorrow, you may also have to deal with me."

As he turned to leave, I said: "As I do not know your name, I have no idea of whether that is mere bluff."

He smiled. "Ah, I know you; but you have not had the pleasure. I am Jean-Baptiste Thibadeau. You will forgive me for not shaking hands."

I watched his retreating back until I saw him no more, then returned to the house. I scanned the room for my host, vowing to learn what all this was about, especially the mysterious M. Thibadeau.

"Doctor." It was Atkins; and he was alone. "Dandridge seemed so grim when he invited you into the garden. I hope it was nothing serious."

I was about to assure him there was not when something occurred to me. "Do you have reason, other than his manner, to think something might be serious?"

"I'm—afraid I don't understand."

"I never heard of Sir Cecil until I was invited to this gathering. He admitted it was due to my association with Sherlock Holmes. I have reason to suspect there is more than hero worship involved."

"And what made you think that?"

"My question first."

He considered. "I know he is mysterious. I am not the only one who has often seen him glancing about with obvious apprehension. I know he takes frequent trips, often to the Continent. He will tell us nothing of them; and from his manner, we have come to the conclusion it is not a good idea to ask."

"Wait." Something had occurred to me—an observation, I was proud to think, worthy of Holmes. "If he never told you anything about his trips, how do you know he went so often to the Continent?"

"Ah, there you touch upon one of his most interesting secrets. Several of his acquaintances have seen him in various parts of France, in the company of a certain gentleman. He swears they must have mistaken someone else for him, that he never knew anyone of this fellow's description; and he seemed, as he made these denials, extremely uneasy."

"Do you recall this fellow's description?"

"Tall and slim, dark hair—brown or black, I'm not sure as they never saw him closely—expensively dressed, with a rather remarkable beard."

"Ladies and gentlemen." So shrill was the voice that the attention of all turned to the badly shaken butler, standing halfway up the elaborate staircase. "I have terrible news. Sir Cecil has just been murdered."

I pushed through the crowd at the foot of the stairs, with apologies, to find myself blocked by the butler.

"I am a doctor."

"There is nothing that can be done."

"I should decide that." I ascended to his bedchamber, where the servant told me he lay.

He was sprawled across a four-poster, his eyes staring at the ceiling in frozen horror. An ornate letter opener protruded from his chest. Blood stained the rose counterpane. I saw all this by the light of a single lamp on the table beside the bed. I felt for a pulse, though one look confirmed the butler's statement.

I examined the room, finding nothing significant, uncertain what I hoped to find, possibly behaving out of habit from my years with Holmes. His absence was never more intensely felt than at this moment. How much he might have seen.

I returned to the ballroom to find an Inspector Thompson and a constable. The latter, a slim sandy-haired youth, never spoke, giving the impression of an avid student absorbed by his professor's lesson.

The inspector approached, smiling, hand extended. "Dr. Watson." He was a tall, athletically built man somewhere past fifty, with a bulbous nose and pale blond hair parted in the middle. "I did not have the honor of meeting Mr. Holmes, but meeting you . . . ." The smile broadened. "Naturally, any help you might give us, based on your experiences with him, would be most welcome."

"I might accommodate you there sooner than you think."

He raised a brow.

"There is a gentleman I have encountered three times since my arrival in Dickencroft. He was here tonight, though I am certain he was not invited. I do not think he was on good terms with Sir Cecil, though I have learned he—at least, a man of his description—was observed several times with Sir Cecil on the Continent."

"Perhaps you could give us this description?"

The young constable withdrew notebook and pencil from his uniform.

"I can do better than that. He gave me his name—or rather, a name: Jean-Baptiste Thibadeau."

They stared at each other. They obviously found the name familiar and not at all pleasant.

"I should still," said Thompson, "like a description."

"Tall—about your height—dark hair, dark beard, prosperously dressed every time I saw him. English is most certainly not his first language."

"That's Thibadeau, all right." His gaze seemed fixed on something behind me. "McGregor, give the doctor a copy of our address. I should like to see you at ten o'clock tomorrow—if that is convenient?"

"Who is this Thibadeau?"

"All in good time, doctor." He turned and signaled McGregor to follow him. "All in good time."

The constabulary was on Cherry Lane in the middle of Dickencroft. A stone wall surrounded it. I passed through an iron gate and along a short walk to the two-storey red brick structure.

The inspector looked up as I entered. "Dr. Watson." He had lost some of his joviality. "Please be seated."

I lowered myself into a dark hardwood chair.

"I do not enjoy what I am about to say." He seemed to consider. "Several witnesses claim to have heard words between yourself and Sir Cecil Dandridge shortly before the tragedy. Is this correct?"

"It is. He seemed to feel my visit here was somehow connected to him, that I knew something that might not be to his benefit. Naturally, I denied this."

"Naturally?"

"I don't understand."

"Your friend, the late Mr. Holmes, never mentioned him?"

"I am quite certain he did not; and what if he had?"

171

"Someone, who wished to avoid unpleasantness by remaining anonymous, recalled rumours about Sir Cecil—rumours which, if true, might have given you cause for animosity."

"I swear, I knew nothing of the gentleman before last night and know of no reason to dislike him."

"Including rumours—unsubstantiated, I assure you—of his connection with the man you must hold responsible for your friend's death?"

"Professor Moriarity?"

"The same. I should reject the suggestion that, since the man who killed Holmes died as well, your revenge might have been directed against a surviving member of his organisation, but for the unpleasantness between yourself and Sir Cecil and one other fact. There is no evidence of direct contact between Sir Cecil and Moriarity; but we have witnesses to both having been seen in the company of the same man, a scoundrel guilty of every sin that has a name, suspected of murder, selling secrets to unfriendly powers, and some unfit to be discussed between gentlemen."

"One Jean-Baptiste Thibadeau?"

"Exactly. He avoided being photographed; but the Sûreté had a sufficiently good idea of what he looked like to be certain the body was his."

I sat up. "Body!"

His gaze in my direction hardened. "Correct, doctor. They had a hard time making a case against him; but when they finally did, with the help of an anonymous note that arrived at their headquarters, they tracked him to a village thirty miles from Paris. He killed three gendarmes before they got him. Identification was verified by one Yvette Rousseau, who'd sheltered him for at least a year. She claimed to have known nothing of his activities—which, given her own reputation, the French authorities doubted. That was also why they sought further corroboration of his identity. Oh yes, doctor, he's dead, could not have been in that garden last night, could not have killed Sir Cecil." I was considering all this when he added: "There is, of course, the possibility it was someone else, someone who knew what he looked like and that there were no photographs, who hoped he would be blamed when they killed Sir Cecil."

"That is very generous of you, inspector."

"Indeed it is. It is a straw I am clinging to rather than accuse the best friend of the late Sherlock Holmes of committing a revenge murder and trying to blame it on a dead man. There is no reason for this conversation to go beyond this room for the present. You may return to London, where you have a wife, a home, and a medical practice, all of which should keep you where we may find you, should the need arise. I hope you also have, especially after your years with Holmes, the good sense to realise how unfortunate it might prove if you were not where we might find you. Good day, Doctor."

I took the next train home, more depressed than when I had arrived. Only one person noted my disquiet: Mary, who took it for continued grief over Holmes's death.

I have since wondered whether it might not have been a blessing that, a few months later, she passed away believing it.

"... 'Here's British Birds, and Catallus, and The Holy War—a bargain every one of them. With five volumes you could just fill that gap on the second shelf. It looks untidy, does it not, sir?'

"I moved my head to look at the cabinet behind me. When I turned again, Sherlock Holmes was standing smiling at me across my study table . . ."

We watched the police hansom bearing away the second most dangerous man in London.

"Let us hope," said I, "our next adventure proves less catastrophic."
"This one is not quite over," said Holmes. "There is one more link
in the chain—at least, I hope there is. It will involve a short trip, after
a good night's sleep, to a village called Dickencroft."

This was my second shock of the day, equal to that following the
"strange old book collector" indicating the gap on the second shelf.
"Holmes, since we are going there anyway—"

"It's the same matter, Watson." He raised a hand as I stared at him.
"I should prefer discussing it tomorrow."

The train was well underway the following morning when Holmes
gave me the account. "I was in the beautiful city of Antwerp a year and
a half ago, partly to relax, partly to consider my next move. Given Bel-
gium's proximity to England, I wore one of my favourite disguises—"
He grinned. "—which I shall discuss in greater detail later. I am
tempted to say what happened there was due to some clue that drew
me to a certain sidewalk café; but the fact is, it was—I blush to say I,
of all people, should benefit from such—blind, stupid luck. A man
approached my table at a sidewalk café, greatly chagrined. It seems I
was supposed to have lain low after killing a man, a certain Leonard
Trelawney, in Lyon a few months earlier."

"Trelawney—I recall the case." Leonard Trelawney was an officer
at the Royal Lion Bank, one of the most prestigious in England. He
was married with three children and lived in a country house not far
from the City. He was thought to be the soul of discretion until he left
one spring morning and never returned. Seventy thousand pounds
in securities disappeared with him. Scotland Yard learned of several
alleged business trips, about which the bank knew nothing, and holi-
days with his wife and children, about which they also knew nothing.
His body, with a dagger in the back, was found floating in the Saône
early in June. The case was more than two years old, the assassin and
the securities yet to be located.

"Though this opportunity had been due to blind chance, instinct gave it a little help. I claimed I'd had no choice but to come here; and that it was dangerous to talk openly. I made an appointment to meet him that night at a certain corner where I would tell all. Naturally, I slipped out of the city, changed disguises, and looked into the matter further. The investigation took a little over a year. There wasn't that much to it; but you know my methods—learning all the details, separating rumour from fact, then verifying and re-verifying everything I'd learned. The facts are basically these: Leonard Trelawney had made the acquaintance of a certain peer, who had squandered enough of his fortune to be willing to enter into certain questionable enterprises to restore the life to which he had become accustomed. They had met through another officer of the Royal Lion Bank—like Trelawney, a gentleman with an apparently unimpeachable reputation. His friends knew he liked an occasional game of whist. Others knew how completely cards had possessed him, despite his miserable luck.

"This associate was undoubtedly the one who brought Trelawney into the operation. He would have known of Trelawney's beautiful wife with expensive tastes, who insisted that her children be educated at only the best schools and that she and her husband live in such a fine house.

"The question was how this associate had come in contact with the peer; not a large detail, but helpful in making a connection between all involved. Imagine when blind fortune led me to that which I should have sensed all along. The associate played cards with an acquaintance of the peer—one Sebastian Moran, which meant that, at the end of this chain of embezzlement and murder, was almost certainly the late Professor Moriarty. But Trelawney was still alive and healthy when the Professor and I battled at the edge of the Reichenbach, which meant the operation continued after its founder's death."

"Obviously Moran." I threw up my hands. "Which means the whole affair is at an end."

"Then who killed the peer, Sir Cecil Dandridge, five months ago? Because I was following Moran when that tragedy happened; and he was nowhere near England that night."

"How about this associate?—who, by the by, you haven't named yet."

He smiled. "I try not to name names until I have proof, especially against those with pockets deep enough to launch slander suits. You may now have guessed Professor Moriarity was behind that business of the Valley of Fear; and you may recall Inspector MacDonald and I seemed reluctant to name the man we believed to be behind the presumed murder of John Douglas. Ah, I see by the way you stare at the opposite wall, it has all come back to you."

"I—uh—I don't know what you mean." I did—at least, I thought I did—but it seemed too insane to enunciate.

He leaned back. "Many years ago, in an area of California known as the Vermissa Valley, there existed a group of men known as the Scowrers. They claimed to represent Irish miners, but were actually hoodlums spreading terror and death throughout the area, causing that valley to be called the Valley of Fear. A man named Jack McMurdo insinuated himself into the gang, aided by erroneous reports of his criminal activities in Chicago. He was actually a Pinkerton detective named Birdy Edwards, who effectively brought down these wretches, including their leader—or Bodymaster—McGinty. He then fled the States to avoid reprisal.

"Some time later, a man named Jack Douglas was shot in the face; and as it was connected to a man I was investigating, whom I did not choose to name at the time, I looked into it, only to discover the real victim was a man sent to kill Douglas, whom Douglas accidentally shot during a struggle. Douglas was not tried, since it was obviously self-defense. He and his wife fled England. He was later reported washed overboard. We had no doubt the Scowrers or this unnamed mastermind—more likely both—were involved."

"I am aware of the story. I had some idea of writing it someday as a remembrance of you."

"Feel free to pretend you knew about Moriarity at the time. How many of your readers will quibble about your claim to have only heard of the man before our departure for Reichenbach? But please, for the sake of a noble, gallant man, do not mention having seen McMurdo-Edwards-Douglas alive and healthy on a street in Dickencroft a few months ago."

"Then, he was not lost overboard near St. Helena?"

"And his wife, despite her heart-wrenching letter, knew it. Moriarity undoubtedly took credit for it, because one cannot take credit for too many murders if one wishes his power; and he cannot be paid for a murder he had nothing to do with. Moriarity probably assumed someone else killed him. Birdy Edwards had, and undoubtedly still has, many enemies—another good reason to pretend he fell, or was pushed off, the boat to Palmyra that night."

"How long does he think this is going to work, pretending to be dead again—if Moriarity's people are still out there?"

"It worked for me; and I have reason to believe our troubles with him and his people are coming to an end."

Something else struck me as we neared Dickencroft station. "But hiding out a short distance from where they tracked him down before?"

"From what I know of Birdy Edwards, it is conceivable he saw himself as a human purloined letter." I settled back when something occurred to me, something I had meant to mention before we had gotten on the subject of Edwards. "Holmes."

"Yes?"

"Speaking of men who are supposed to be dead . . . ." I glanced at him. He retained the stony look I had so often seen. "Do you recall a man named Jean-Baptiste Thibadeau?"

"I know of him well, much more than I'd like to."

"I know that the Sûreté was supposed to have tracked him down and killed him; but I encountered him, or someone claiming to be him, the night of the murder. He indicated he had ways of dealing with Sir Cecil and that Dickencroft might be made highly undesirable for me, and that any unpleasantness I might suffer might be at his hands. Inspector Thompson insisted the man was dead, but conceded that whomever I had encountered matched his description."

"Thibadeau had an understandable aversion to being photographed; but many knew what he looked like, and there are a number of police sketches. A disguise that might fool someone like yourself who had never encountered the real man is conceivable."

There was something odd about Holmes. I may not have seen him for several years; but he seemed strangely uninterested in the mysterious Frenchman.

We sat in Inspector Thompson's office late that afternoon.

"This is an honour, Mr. Holmes. I only wish we had met under happier circumstances."

"I take it you do not mean the death of Sir Cecil Dandridge. If you know me at all, you know that is the sort of thing I live for; but from the way you glanced at Dr. Watson, I take it you mean that my friend is a suspect?"

The inspector studied the back of his left hand. "He did give a satisfactory explanation for his quarrel with Sir Cecil; and while I would not ordinarily give great weight to his suggested motive, he did try to steer suspicion from himself with what must almost certainly be a lie."

I rose, snarling: "I did see that man. As God is my witness, I did see Jean-Baptiste Thibadeau."

"Sit down, Watson," said Holmes. "That is hardly prudent behaviour for a murder suspect."

I resumed my seat.

"My reputation was not built on being blind to a man's guilt even if he is my dearest friend. Watson did not sneak into Maple Meadow. Sir Cecil invited him; and as for that disagreement, it is consistent with everything I know about the man, about his fears that I was still alive and on his trail, that my friend might be there at my behest. In other words, if Watson lied, it was based on information he could not possibly have had. And the evidence shows Sir Cecil repaired to his bedchamber with some unnamed person who, since there was no sign of a struggle, he trusted sufficiently for this person to get close enough to plunge that letter opener into his chest. Does that fit your theory of Dr. John H. Watson, avenging angel?"

"And I did speak to this Thibadeau."

"*Imbecile.* If *Monsieur l'inspecteur* says I am dead, I am dead." I could not mistake Thibadeau's voice even months later; but as I looked about, I saw only Inspector Thompson and a grinning Sherlock Holmes. "As I said on the train, one of my favourite disguises. I tried to warn you away from danger; and you thought it was a threat. I assured you I had my own ways of dealing with Sir Cecil Dandridge; and you thought I was hinting at my intention of killing him—which, by the way, the real Thibadeau would have been far too crafty to do." He shrugged with a chuckle. "I rather suspected something of that sort. That said, he was rather a disappointment as members of Moriarity's organization go. He would never appear in public without false eyebrows, attached with the aid of spirit gum, his own being rather thin. He would alter his voice and his nose; and he had an encyclopedic memory of whom he had encountered with which voice and which nose. He grew the beard to draw the eye to it and, of course, those brows. He would dispose of both should the police ever make a case against him. There was some talk of his having a pair of spectacles on hand, just to make recognising his real self the more difficult."

"Sounds ingenious to me," said I.

"And to me," said the inspector.

"It was—unless, of course, someone like myself is on one's trail, in his own disguise, with the notion of impersonating one. Jean-Baptiste Thibadeau did such an excellent job of confusing everyone he came in contact with that it was simple to deceive those who'd encountered him several times. He might have gone on forever had the organization, for their own reasons, not betrayed him to the Sûreté. I have speculated how much trouble I might have saved them by telling him what a fool I'd made of him, handing him a pistol, and reminding him what honourable Frenchmen do when they have been so humiliated." He sighed. "He probably would have done so after shooting me. Anyhow, I am certain I should have recalled plunging a letter opener into Sir Cecil Dandridge's chest."

"Holmes," said I, "what about that other fellow? You know, the one involved in that other business we were discussing on the train—" I glanced uneasily at Inspector Thompson, uncertain how many people Holmes would want to let in on that particular secret. "—the one who is supposedly no longer with us?"

"You mean," inquired the inspector, "Jebediah Watts?"

"Who?"

"His latest *nom de guerre*," said Holmes. "You don't suppose, after all the trouble he went to, convincing Moriarity and his crew that John McMurdo, Birdy Edwards, and John Douglas were dead, that he would be so foolish as to use any of those names again? His wife is now Mary Watts. He makes his living as a blacksmith; they have one child. What about him?"

"How long could he and Sir Cecil reside in the same area before Sir Cecil discovered his secret? And could our friend of the many names have decided to get rid of Sir Cecil—"

Holmes's fit of laughter was nearly apoplectic. "Forgive me, my friend." He took a moment more to gain full control. "I—I suppose he had something of a motive; but in making deductions, it is always best to think them through before speaking." He leaned over and squeezed my arm. "Again, forgive me. But there are so many objections to it. Dandridge was not one of Moriarity's best men; but he would have given Watts no hint he had been exposed until blow fell against Watts. And you have been to *soirées* like that one often enough to know that no one but invited guests, and their guests, could have gotten past that butler."

"I recall," said I, "a gentleman calling himself Jean-Baptiste Thibadeau who seemed to get in without going through the butler."

"Ah, Watson's revenge—I feel so much better, though you must admit someone as cunning as I could manage it, where many couldn't. But even if he could have procured evening clothes—on a blacksmith's salary?—and blended in with the rest, we have the same objection I offered in your defense: getting close enough to Sir Cecil Dandridge in the man's own bedchamber to deliver the fatal blow without a sign of a struggle."

"Actually," said the inspector, "we knew this fellow's secret and kept an eye on him. He and the victim did business several times over the years—no sign of suspicion, no unpleasantness between them."

"Speaking of the actual guests at this gathering," said my friend, "was one of them an employee of the Royal Lion Bank, one Trevor Atkins?"

"I recall his being there," said I, "along with a most charming companion."

"I also remember him, Mr. Holmes. You suspect he may have been involved in the crime?"

"I strongly suspect it."

"Then I have bad news. Mr. Atkins was engaged in a discussion of the status of the pound, beginning before Sir Cecil went upstairs and lasting until the crime was announced. There are a number of reliable witnesses."

Holmes chuckled. "You see, Watson, why one should not blurt out one's deductions?" He rose.

"Good day, inspector. I have no doubt we shall talk again."

Holmes and I had taken a room at The Laughing Friar. We had each ordered shepherd's pie, along with the house red wine, when he leaned across to me. "Now, Watson, I wish every detail of that evening, everything you can recall."

I may not read faces as well as he; but I pride myself I read his rather well that night. He listened to my narrative without expression, inserting what seemed trivial questions here and there, until his face suddenly brightened. "They are all alike, these scoundrels who plot crimes, then arrange flawless alibis. We must return to London."

He seemed deep in thought on the train, but did not discuss the matter again until some time later, as we stood on the platform at Norwood, having completed a case with some features similar to the Birlstone affair. "We are not going home, Watson. We are returning to Dickencroft."

The train was leaving the station when he handed me a photograph. "This came from the Sûreté just before our departure from Baker Street. Does she look familiar?"

I recognised her almost immediately. "This is Atkins's companion—I believe her name is Marie L'Espanaye?"

Holmes suppressed a laugh. "Ah, yes, you did mention him comparing me to Dupin. Why shouldn't he give her the surname of the victims in that fellow's first case, and the given name of the title character in the second?"

"I take it you know her real name?"

"Yvette Rousseau."

"The woman who was sheltering Thibadeau just before the French police tracked him down and killed him?"

"Their relationship went far beyond that. She loved him passionately enough to kill the man who'd betrayed him, which proved convenient for Trevor Atkins, who had his own reasons for disposing of

Sir Cecil Dandridge or, more likely, was following the orders of those who did."

"I don't recall seeing her with him at the time of the crime."

Neither, it turned out, did most of the witnesses.

We laid the case before Inspector Thompson, who immediately alerted Scotland Yard.

Sadly, we were too late. Atkins and the woman had not been seen for months. His body was later found in an alley off an obscure boulevard in Paris. He had been stabbed hours before. Mlle. Rousseau/ L'Espanaye also met a violent end, beaten to death and found in a small pasture not far from Marseilles. She had so many enemies, particularly male, that there seemed little hope of solving it.

"I shouldn't care to look into it," said Holmes when he read the account.

"Because you couldn't solve it, or wouldn't want to?"

He considered. "I don't know."

THE ADVENTURE OF THE ROUNDED OCELOT

LARRY D. SWEAZY

lthough a newcomer to pastiche, Larry D. Sweazy is an award-winning writer of historical western short stories, novels featuring Josiah Wolfe, Texas Ranger, and a forthcoming mystery novel that promises to become a series. "The Adventure of the Rounded Ocelot" presents us with, in addition to a priceless cat sculpture, a story of close friendship, an exotic client, and the blue Caribbean, in contrast to the fog-laden streets of London. Published for the first time, by permission of the author.

1.

I had lost count of how many times Sherlock Holmes had paced by the window, stopping for a brief moment at every pass, like he was checking a clock for the time, then moving on. It was quite unlike him to be so impatient, so anxious for the arrival of a potential client.

"You should have a cigarette," I said, peering over the tabloid that had yet to capture my full attention.

Holmes stopped pacing, looked down his hawklike nose at me, and scowled. "How can you possibly think about a pleasure at a time like this?"

"Perhaps I don't know what time it is."

"Oh, very well." He rolled his eyes, marched directly to the window, and stood frozen in wait.

"You're acting very cagey. Is there something I need to know?" A direct question sometimes did the trick, but again Holmes ignored me, so I was left with no alternative but to return to the sordid rag in my hands.

He was not acting himself, so I thought he may have participated in a moment of weakness recently. I had often encouraged him to give up his cocaine habit, but as of yet my advice had fallen on deaf ears. A man of Holmes's dual nature, prone to rising and falling extremes in mood, did not need any additional agitators in my medical opinion. As it was, he seemed like a lit fuse about halfway to the point of explosion. I had a deep suspicion that something had set him off, had sent him to the needle, out of my sight once again. I could only sigh at his silence.

After several minutes, he finally said, "Do you mind, Watson? Really, it is quite impossible to share every detail of my day with you."

I tossed the tabloid to the table, and stood up. "Then I shall depart."

"Don't be silly. I need you here."

"Whatever for?" I demanded.

At that moment, the bell rang and Holmes stiffened. "Ah, have a seat, Watson. I am absolutely positive that you will find this interesting, and glad to have taken the time for."

Being educated in the ways and manners of Sherlock Holmes, I had no choice but to act as a three-year-old and do as I was told. He wanted me to have a look at something, that was certain. I sat down eagerly, and waited for whatever was to come next.

I had been through the procedure before, more than once, but something was out of order, like the turn of a kaleidoscope had not fallen exactly into place. Holmes confused me and confounded me. That was normal, as was his intensity. But he was acting like a schoolboy waiting for the girl of his dreams. And that was not ordinary, at all.

I heard Mrs. Hudson meet the door, followed by murmured voices, then footsteps echoed up the stairs. I have to say, I was not prepared for what came next, for the sight that entered the door, even with all of Holmes's apparent—and completely founded—excitement.

Mrs. Hudson burst in first, of course, heavy-footed, nearly stomping in with an unnecessary announcement of her Scottish heritage. I almost laughed out loud once when Holmes complimented the landlady, offering that she "fixed a fine breakfast, for a Scottish woman." He was lucky he wasn't served haggis for every meal for weeks thereafter. It would have served him right, if you ask me.

"A lady to see you, Mr. Holmes," Mrs. Hudson offered, dusting flour from her apron. If jealousy had a face, it would have chosen the one Mrs. Hudson was wearing.

I saw the woman's shadow first, tall, slender, sharp-jawed, the perfect outline of Nefertiti. If I had said that out loud, Holmes would have denounced my choices right away with an offer that I was on the completely wrong continent. And, as always, he would have been correct. She was not from Africa at all.

The woman's entrance into the room quite simply took my breath away.

She was black-skinned, not a crease or a wrinkle showing on her perfectly sculpted face, with the most penetrating sunflower-brown eyes I had ever seen. There was no question that she stood six feet tall. Her dress was unusually colorful, patterned with the blooms of big flowers against a white background, with a wrap across her ample breasts of the same red color. Multiple gold hoop earrings dangled from her ears, quite visible because her tightly curled hair was cut short to the scalp, almost like a man's.

It felt as if I were in the presence of royalty, and I stood up immediately. I think my face must have flushed, because I saw Holmes smirk as stealthily as he could.

"Madame Taru, it is a great pleasure finally to meet you in person," Sherlock Holmes said, rushing across the room with an extended hand.

The woman, who looked to be in her early thirties at the most, was carrying a large red flower that looked like a lily of some kind in her left hand. She met Holmes's handshake firmly, then handed him the flower.

"Ah, a *Bougainvillea glabra*," Holmes said, gladly taking the blooming gift.

He turned to me, and offered the big red flower. "Don't mistake the leaves for flowers, Watson. The flower itself is white, if you pay close attention to the tiny blooms in the center. Most people call it the Paper Flower."

I forced a smile, noticed the small blooms, then handed off the Paper Flower to Mrs. Hudson, who seemed far more curious about it than I was. She smiled, then hurried out of the room with it, presumably to put the beauty in a vase somewhere.

"Thank you for meeting with me, Mr. Holmes," Madame Taru said. Her voice had an island lilt to it, like an easy, rolling wave that never crashed ashore, just spread out onto the sand, then eased back into the ocean from which it came. "It is a matter of great importance that we speak in person." She cast an uncertain glance my way.

"This is John Watson, medical doctor, my Boswell, if you will, veteran of Afghanistan, and as discreet a man as you will ever meet." The authority in Holmes's voice was unquestionable, and Madame Taru's shoulders seemed to relax immediately at the pronouncement of his trust in me.

I offered my hand, and she returned in kind, placing her silky palm in mine. Her flesh was warm, like she had soaked in the sun before arriving—even though the London sky was a typical grey, with the promise of freezing rain. Her grip was as powerful as any man's that I had ever encountered. I was completely intrigued, and slightly smitten, though I would have never admitted such a thing out loud.

"It is a pleasure to meet you, as well, Dr. Watson," the woman said.

"Please, please," Holmes offered with a sweep of his hand toward a simple chair reserved for clients, "have a seat."

Madame Taru smiled, and the beauty of her ivory teeth brought some much-needed light into the room. She sat demurely, on the edge of the cushion, looking all about the room in a comfortable manner.

"Would you care for some tea?" I asked.

"Oh, no, thank you. I must be here for only a moment. Perhaps some other time, kind sir."

"That would be lovely," I said. I was tempted to ask her about the weather on her island, or her journey to Baker Street, just so I could hear her speak again, but I felt the hard glare of Holmes's insistence that I retreat on the back of my neck, so I restrained myself.

"The governor sends his regards, Mr. Holmes," Madame Taru said.

"I am pleased to hear that. I'm fond of Governor Parker's attempt at office, though I understand he longs for the craggy shores of Nova Scotia over the sandy beaches of your home country."

"There is nothing worse than a man stricken with homesickness," she said.

"But that is not the purpose of your visit, is it?" asked Holmes.

I stood in my place, waiting for the reason for my presence to show itself. Of course, there was nowhere else I would have rather been at that moment—well, perhaps a little closer to Madame Taru than I was, but that was out of the question. There was obvious business at hand.

"No, I am afraid not, sir. The cure for such a thing as homesickness requires something more than a consulting detective."

"But theft usually does require a service like mine," Holmes said.

"Yes. You are most perspicacious, as I expected that you would be. A fine trait for a man in your line of lift and toil." The last word bounced off the walls like a song, reverberating in my ear. The word *toil* had never sounded so pleasant, so void of labor.

"Oh, trust me, Madame Taru, it is not work that I conduct here. It is an adventure in curiosity. Isn't that right, Watson?"

"What? Oh, yes," I said. I must have been staring at the woman. I was totally enamoured by her very being, and my obsession had obviously annoyed Holmes past the point of a glare. It wasn't the first time that had happened. "My friend here is a specialist in observation. Or in the observation of trifles, as he likes to say."

Holmes looked right through me. "How is it that this theft concerns the governor, Madame Taru?"

She reached inside her dress to a hidden pocket and produced a newly printed photograph, then handed it to Holmes. "This is the piece that has disappeared from the residence. It is only a faux piece of art, as I am sure you can tell."

"Quite," Holmes said. "It is not original, but cast of a mold, meaning there are more like it."

"Yes, the piece has been replaced," the woman said. "So no one will be the wiser of the theft of the rounded ocelot. Even if they were, the contents would be unknown to them."

"Why would the governor use this as a container for his personal papers? Does he not have a better place for safekeeping, out of sight?"

Holmes handed me the photograph. "Notice the shadow underneath, Watson. It sits up slightly on an opening."

Madame Taru stood up then, taking my attention away from the piece of art that was her quarry.

"You are exactly the right man for the job. Will you take it, kind sir?" she asked.

"Of course," Holmes said. "But the art has yet to leave the island, and there is only one way I will able to retrieve it."

"And how is that, Mr. Holmes?" the woman asked.

"I must journey to the Bahamas myself, for at the moment, I have no clue where it might be stowed away."

2 .

The last bag was loaded onto the carriage, and the driver seemed in a hurry to depart. But Sherlock Holmes had lost his impatience from the day before, and had replaced it with a slow qualification that every item packed for the trip be in the exact order that he wanted it in. He fussed over the last trunk, making sure the buckles were especially tight, then stood back and pronounced, "Well, Watson, that should do it. Are you ready to sail?"

Traveling by sea evoked complicated and painful memories for me. Long before I had met Sherlock Holmes, I served as a surgeon in the army, where, ultimately, I ended up attached to the Berkshires, and was injured in the second Afghan war. I was shot in the shoulder, the bone shattered and the artery grazed. It was a very painful experience that removed me from the battlefield and put me on a trip home aboard the HMS *Orontes*, a three-hundred-foot troopship less suited for battle than the larger *Euphrates* class of troopships, armed with only three 4-pounder guns. Thankfully, there was no need for the guns on that voyage. I saw little of the deck of Ol' Ste, as I was confined to my bed with a rollicking case of seasickness. Beyond the pain and delirium of my wound, I jerked and hurled back and forth, thanks to an aggressive set of waves brought on by a petulant storm that followed us all the way to Portsmouth.

I had never informed Holmes of my lack of tolerance for the rocking of a ship. I could only hope that we encountered good weather, and my previous misfortune had been brought on by the severity of my wound. Only time would tell.

"Yes, of course, I'm absolutely ready for a change of scenery," I answered.

Holmes looked at me curiously, but said nothing. I feared he knew of my weakness for waves, but he was too much a gentleman, when he was in his most lucid state, to chide me about it.

We both made our way into the carriage, and before long we were clacking toward the docks.

It was a nice enough day, the sky calm with very few clouds to show for weather. The rain from the previous day had not fallen, and it had not frozen, either; a promise left unfulfilled, for the moment. I hoped the sea was just as calm as the sky, a perfect reflection of what was overhead.

"If I do say so, Watson, you're looking a little green around the gills at the prospect of this journey. Perhaps some sun will do you good."

I looked at Holmes oddly. His concern for my health was a surprise. "Perhaps it will," I said, settling back into the plush red velvet seat for the rest of the ride.

Holmes only smiled, and stared back out the window.

It didn't take long to get to the docks, a constantly vibrating, forever moving scene that had always fascinated me, but did little to assuage the dread of the impending forty-three-hundred-mile journey.

There had been no explanation from Holmes as to the important nature of the trip. All I knew was that it pertained to a theft, a governor, and a beautiful island woman with the most radiant smile I had ever seen. He had taken cases that seemed less interesting, but there was rarely as lengthy a journey involved as there was with this case. Even more perplexing was that Sherlock Holmes appeared to be giddy about the prospect of getting out of London.

Our accommodations were first class aboard the White Star steamship *Gothic*, a four-hundred-and-ninety-three-foot cargo liner that made its way to New Zealand via the Caribbean.

I tried not to show my lack of enthusiasm as the steward, a short little French gent with a thin mustache perched on his lip that looked more like a blackbird's feather than facial hair, fussed about us, getting us settled into our prospective accommodations.

Holmes's cabin was next to mine. Both were functional with a thin bed, chair, and porthole. The steward—Pierre, of course—directed us to the facilities that would serve us for the trip, at the bow of the ship.

"Is there anything I can do for you?" the steward asked, studying me from head to toe. "Other than bring you a deep pail to keep close?"

It was going to be a very long trip.

3.

Holmes rarely came out of his cabin, so for most of the journey I was left to my own devices.

To my great surprise, the rocky waves of the Atlantic did not send me to the pail. Just the opposite. Once we were in open seas, away from the pluvial skies of London, I was quite comfortable walking the deck or finding my way to the dining room for afternoon tea. The continual presence of the sun and blue skies agreed with me, as did the smooth waters as we sailed into the Caribbean. The persistent ache in my shoulder vanished, and by the time the sight of land came into view, I was feeling better than I had in years.

Of course, there was a downside to the pleasures of travel. With time on my hands and Holmes locked in his cabin, I eventually found my way to the engine room, where I promptly lost every coin in my pocket in a friendly game of poker with the more genial, English-speaking members of the crew.

The breeze had turned into a full wind as we headed into port, and it nearly toppled the hat off my head. When I grabbed upwards, I turned and came face to face with Sherlock Holmes. He looked refreshed, as if he had slept the entire way from London to Nassau.

"You look a little lighter, Watson," Holmes said, standing shoulder to shoulder with me.

"It has been a pleasant journey."

There was little activity around us. I supposed that Pierre was readying our cabins for departure, and as the island drew closer I was anxious to stand on land, with the hope of seeing the Caribbean beauty Madame Taru again, very soon.

Like a million other times since I had taken up residence with Sherlock Holmes, he seemed to be able to read my mind.

"I'm afraid I have some bad news for you, Watson," he said.

"Really, and what, pray tell, would that be?"

"It is highly likely that Madame Taru is dead."

I wasn't expecting such an announcement. For some reason it hit me hard, buckled my knees. I couldn't imagine such a thing of beauty being taken from this world—but, of course, in our line of work, I had seen the worst mankind can do to one another. "How?" I whispered.

"Murdered, of course. She was being stalked in London."

"Why didn't you stop it? Tell her?"

"She knew she would be in danger by engaging our services, Watson. Madame Taru was, and possibly still is, a skilled woman in matters of secrecy."

"What more haven't you told me?" I was indignant, and did not care.

"There's always more to the story, Watson. You should know that by now."

4.

Nassau was a collection of the old and new. While London always felt to me like it had always existed, there were parts of this island that looked as if they had just crawled up out of the ocean, fresh, unmarred by weather or time, and other parts that had remained the same since the time of Columbus.

Even though my mood was dimmed by news of Madame Taru—at least, by the prospect of her death—I was immediately fascinated by the palm trees that dotted the shore.

The view from the *Gothic* as we disembarked was of a flat scrubland seemingly risen out of the sea, and a small two-storey city plopped down on its edge. There were no rising towers or spires crowding each other out against the azure sky, like the skyline I was accustomed to. There was a bell tower, however, a cathedral of some type, but the style of it was less elaborate than any I had ever seen.

Most of the wood frame buildings looked freshly built, and some of the trees were shaved off at the top, as if a brilliantly strong wind had snapped them in half, which of course was the case. A recent hurricane had left some damage in its wake, but had not wrought total devastation upon the charming island.

Even though the Union Jack flapped happily from the flagpole at the end of the dock, it felt to me as if I was stepping onto foreign soil, onto a land so unfamiliar that it would take days, if not decades, to truly get my footing. Holmes, on the other hand, looked like he had been on the island since its creation, though he did stand out like a touring man in his traveling tweeds.

"Did you know, Watson, that there are twenty-nine islands that make up the Bahamas?"

He had offered no explanation for his lack of presence during the journey from London to Nassau, and I had not asked. As it was, he looked less nervous, less frantic than before we left. For all I knew, he had used the voyage as an opportunity to escape his cocaine dependency, and had come out the other side a new man. If such a thing were the case, Holmes, of course, would never mention it. Or the trials it had taken to accomplish such a thing.

"No," I answered, "I don't know much about the islands, but I can say that this one has some of the most beautiful beaches I have ever seen."

Holmes followed my gaze to the white sand that stretched out toward the horizon, and heartily agreed. Before he could launch into the full history of the islands, we were hurried down the dock to a waiting carriage by our steward, Pierre, who seemed rather happy to be rid of us. I would have tipped him, but a fellow Frenchmen with a year's grease under his fingernails had taken my last farthing.

It was then that I realized that we were being watched.

A palm tree, taller than the rest, stood off to the right of the dock, just between the wildness of the scrub and the beginning of civilization; a cut road led straight into Nassau, and buildings sprouted up there right away. On the other side of the tree, inches off the road, a man stood and watched us carefully. His skin looked just as bronze as Madame Taru's, and he had the same strong jaw and penetrating eyes. He was younger than the woman who had visited us in London, no more than twenty, if that, and dressed in casual trousers, a white linen shirt that exposed his bare skin underneath, and no shoes. He did his best to try and not be noticed, but the sun cast his tall shadow across the beach, and there was no mistaking it for anything other than that of a man on a covert mission.

"It looks like we have drawn some notice," I said to Holmes, as quietly as I could.

He looked up, scanned the land in front of us, and promptly said, "I don't see a thing, Watson."

And he was right. There was no sign of the boy at all. It was as if my imagination had conjured him, and then just as quickly pushed him into retreat, as if he was nothing more than a black cloud, fallen to the ground then whisked away by the persistent ocean breeze.

5.

The Victoria Hotel stood atop a hill overlooking the harbor and city, as stately and grand an affair as one could imagine. It stood four storeys tall, was rounded on each end with an elaborate foyer in the center, and was freshly whitewashed so that every board and plank looked brand new.

A cricket field had been cut into the grass at the back of the hotel, and at midday it was dotted with men and women, dressed in the proper whites, having a go at the game. It all looked very familiar, with the exception of the palm trees and the perfect blue sky overhead that never seemed to change.

Holmes and I were quickly ushered to our respective rooms, nearly ten times the size of the accommodations aboard the *Gothic*, and much more stable. My knees still swayed with the rhythm of the sea.

I expected that we would jump right into our search for the piece of art that had been stolen, an odd sculpture of a cat—an ocelot—in a deep sleep, curled in a high circle so that its back was exaggeratedly raised in the air. But that was not the case. Time was given to unwind from the trip, and dinner was soon served as night blanketed the island.

Holmes treated himself to broiled squab on toast, and I indulged in the scope that my palette expected, mutton with a nice caper sauce. Afterwards, we both took pleasure in pear fritters drizzled with a delicate cognac glaze.

Holmes was oddly quiet throughout the meal, and only opened up and seemed at home once he stepped out onto the veranda for an evening cigarette.

"We will return to London on the next ship out," he said after exhaling slowly from a long draw on the cigarette.

"And when will that be?" I stared out into the darkness, fascinated by the starry sky that was reflected on the gentle sea. It looked like smooth oil covered in sparkling diamonds.

"Monday next, if all goes well."

I didn't answer. I was hoping for a month, not days, on the island. The salt air was comforting, as were the gentle waves that washed ashore, the sound of which floated upward to the hotel as if an orchestra was playing softly below us. Given the opportunity at that moment, I would have never returned to London. But I knew that was impossible, just a fancy. Before long I would encounter a deep case of homesickness, and beg to be on the next ship, even if it was a lowly trawler.

"I've been worried about you, Watson," Sherlock Holmes said, standing before me with half a cigarette left to smoke.

"I appreciate your concern, but I have felt the same of you. You have been largely absent on this trip, and beforehand, you were as agitated as a bull being dragged to slaughter."

"I am perplexed by the seriousness of this case."

"It seems fairly simple, though the travel is out of hand; a big to-do on your part, I'd say."

Holmes's right cheek twitched quickly, then straightened out, as if it would pain him to smile. "Some cases are more challenging, and require our presence. I have fortified your accounts for the return trip, if you're concerned about the losses that may need covering after your recent engine room excursions."

My instinct was to demand an explanation as to how Holmes knew what I had been up to, but that would have been ridiculous. Sometimes, I felt as if I had a tick attached to the back of my neck that told him of my every move and deed. I hate ticks.

Instead of protesting, I shrugged. "That's kind of you, Holmes."

"Someone has to look out for you."

I was obsessed by the fate of Madame Taru, and could wait no longer to find out what had become of her. "Do you know what has happened to Madame Taru, Holmes? I am quite hoping that you are wrong about her demise."

"Wrong?"

"You said she was dead."

"No, Watson," he said, taking a final draw of the cigarette, "I said she *may be* dead, but that she was skilled in such matters of secrecy." Holmes smiled fully then, and extinguished the orange tip of the butt on the bottom of his shoe.

At that moment, I heard footsteps approaching from behind us. As I turned, I heard the familiar lilt of an island voice I had dreamed of.

"I assure you, Dr. Watson, I am very much alive."

6.

I was pleased to turn and see Madame Taru, though the look on Sherlock Holmes's face did not match my enthusiasm. He was tight, drawn up like all of his breath had escaped him.

"I did not expect to see you so soon, Madame Taru. Or should I say, Susheena," Holmes said with a hard stare.

Madame Taru—or Susheena, I didn't know which, but assumed the latter was the truth—lowered her head briefly, then returned the glare. "I knew I was taking a risk visiting you, putting you on the trail."

"But you had no choice," Holmes said.

"No, the governor instructed me to contact you."

"I will grant that your means were impressive, but your first failure was hiring your brother as a foil. His left foot is shorter than his right, just like yours. I was curious of the similarity as I watched him stalk you from my window. I was only assured of my suspicion on our arrival, when he watched us and, of course, left his tracks in the sand. I knew that you were alive and had tried to outwit me, and, of course, the governor."

Susheena had lost the regal air that she'd carried in London. She had looked like a dignitary, a proud woman on a mission. Now she looked like a tall servant, dressed in a lowly, simple sack dress, her feet bare, dropping her several levels on the social scale.

"It is not what you think," Susheena protested. "I have come here to beg you not to reveal my involvement to the governor. He will be disappointed in me." Her words were steady, still magical in their lilt, but less so as her true character began to show itself.

I watched Holmes carefully, curious at how he was going to deconstruct this woman's apparent crime.

"I take it," Holmes said, "that the rounded ocelot has been returned to its proper place."

Susheena nodded woefully. "Yes."

"With all of the papers intact? The copies destroyed?"

"Yes, sir. Of course, sir."

Silence returned to the air, only the noise from inside the hotel and the distant waves of the ocean making themselves known.

"There is no shame in what you have done," Holmes finally said. "The governor's papers are private, and it is up to him if he wishes to make the pages of his journals public. I have instructed him to be more careful. He is a man, madam, just a man. Not married, with needs and an appetite that are normal in such a paradise as this."

"I was only trying to protect him," Susheena said.

"Perhaps," Holmes said. "But it was your brother who sought to benefit from the affair. Extortion is a serious crime. Especially extortion of a government official."

"So it was never a matter of theft at all," I said.

"No, Watson. The governor contacted me when he was in London on a recent visit to the Houses of Parliament. I was well aware of his delicate situation before Madame Taru graced our presence. The trick was to tell if it was a real theft, if she was part of the scheme."

"You feared she would be killed in the meantime, if she was not involved," I said.

"The governor has some strong enemies in this country and at home. He is a strict man, who rules with a hard fist, but fairly," Holmes answered. "I was not sure what was at stake. Which is why I chose to come here and see for myself." Holmes looked over to Susheena and said, "I'm sorry to tell you that your brother has been arrested, and has been taken to the local authorities for processing."

Susheena nodded. "He has always been trouble, that boy. I had no idea that he betrayed me. He helped in the replacement of the piece, then put it back once the fear of getting caught was at hand. I was resigned to the papers being where they belonged. It was the governor's choice to document our time together, and I couldn't protect him forever." She paused, looked to the sky, then back to Holmes. "It will all come out anyway, won't it? The knowledge of our love will be a scandal."

"I'm afraid so," Holmes said.

"Is there nothing that you can do?" she pleaded.

"No, I'm afraid not," Holmes said. "I'm afraid not."

7.

The trunks were stacked on the dock, awaiting loading onto the ship that would see Holmes and I back to London. The sky was perfect, cloudless, and the air was comfortable in its temperature. It was as pleasant a day as one could ever hope for in a paradise like the Bahamas.

"I feel bad for the governor," I said, standing in wait next to Holmes. "He had no choice but to resign his office and return home, without Susheena."

"He knew the risk."

"Risk? Do you really think it is that simple, Holmes, that matters of the heart are just a calculation of risk?"

"You really don't want my answer, do you, Watson? So why ask?"

I exhaled loudly. "You are destined to spend your life alone, with nothing more than the thoughts that swirl inside that thick head of yours, and the pleasure of being right more than you are wrong."

"Oh, Watson, please. I am not alone. I have you, and that's not a calculation at all. It's a matter of fact. You are my friend, and there's nothing more that I could wish, or hope for, than that."

for Liz and Chris Hatton

THE ADVENTURE OF THE PLATED SPOON

LOREN D. ESTLEMAN

redating Sherlock Holmes by a year (1886), Nick Carter is the American bridge between Holmes and Bulldog Drummond: clean-cut, two-fisted, cerebral, and a master of disguise. The creation of Ormond G. Smith and John R. Coryell, he appeared in hundreds of dime novels and pulp magazines—including Nick Carter Weekly—*but is virtually forgotten today, despite a 1972 pilot for a TV series starring Robert Conrad. (He's not to be mistaken for the "Nick Carter" who appeared in a flurry of paperback spy novels in the 1970s.) In* The Adventure of the Plated Spoon, *he teams up with Holmes, Watson, and Mrs. Watson to smash a conspiracy that still plagues us: human trafficking. It is published here for the first time, by permission of the author.*

I.

I Misplace My Wife

Readers who are unfamiliar with the chronicles involving my friend, Sherlock Holmes, may not assign much weight to an appalling tale cast with unspeakable villains, all centred upon so homely an item as a table utensil; yet I ask them to be patient until I have presented all the evidence.

In April of 1897, my wife, Mary, and I were preparing to join another couple for an evening at the Lyceum, where Henry Irving and Ellen Terry were appearing in *Hamlet* after a triumphant tour of the Continent. I was laying out my tailcoat when the bell rang.

"It can't be the Anstruthers," said Mary. "It's too early, and we're to meet them on the way."

"Perhaps it's a patient. I'll try to be brief."

It was a commissionaire, with a message:

> Watson,
> I REQUIRE YOUR IMMEDIATE ASSISTANCE IF NOT
> TIED UP.
> P.S. IF TIED UP BREAK YOUR BONDS

"How impertinent." Mary looked sternly at the uniformed courier. "Tell him we weren't at home."

"You know him as well as I," I said, reaching for my overcoat. "He's only brusque in matters of urgency."

"The rest of the time he's merely rude. What about our engagement?"

"We have two hours. If I'm late, I'll meet you at the theatre."

"Be sure you have time to dress. Bad enough to miss the curtain without arriving looking like a vagabond."

I shan't try the reader's patience with the details of our evening's excursion, although they present interest sufficient to support a full accounting elsewhere. The conundrum turned out to be child's play (if only for Holmes), but it took time enough to deprive our friends and my wife of the pleasure of my company in our box.

The house was dark when I returned. I crept up the stairs as quietly as possible, cursing inwardly the lateness of the hour and the impossibility of finding an open florist's shop, however inadequate a bouquet of posies would prove towards raising my marital stock. Grateful as Mary was to Holmes for the affair that had first brought us together, his continuing dependence upon my aid, to the detriment of my domestic responsibilities, had sorely tried her stores of good will.

It was a clear night. A three-quarter moon shone brightly through the bedroom window, falling full upon my tails laid out on the counterpane exactly as I had left them. Mary wasn't there. To her pillow was pinned a note in her hand on her personal stationery:

> John,
> We'll have a good laugh over this message if we read it
> together. Otherwise, you will find me at the Anstruthers' in
> the morning and we shall revisit your relationship with Mr.
> Sherlock Holmes.
> M.

I spent a sleepless night in pursuit of some gesture that would repair the rift; but here at last was one problem even my friend, the world's first (and so far the greatest) consulting detective, could not solve. Bright and early I bathed and shaved carefully, put on the morning coat that was Mary's favourite, and hastened to the Harley Street home of Dr. and Mrs. Anstruther, stopping along the way to buy the showiest floral display in Piccadilly and a five-pound box of Vienna chocolates. The bell was answered by Gloriana, their maid from South America, who informed me her master and mistress had left for a holiday in Scotland by the first train.

"Is Mrs. Watson alone, then?" I was somewhat relieved to know my self-abasement would be private.

The girl's brow creased. "She is not here, sir. It's just me and Cook."

"When did she leave?"

"Sir, she was never here. Doctor and the missus came home alone from the theatre."

II.

At Scotland Yard

I proceeded directly to New Scotland Yard, where a sergeant informed me that Inspector Lestrade was away on an investigation but that his colleague, Inspector Gregson, was at his desk.

Tobias Gregson, a large, bluff, red-faced mastiff of a man, more given to immediate action than his counterpart—and almost invariably misdirected—sat behind a mountain of papers and ledgers, muttering over the necessity of an active soldier in the war against the criminal classes being reduced to the duties of a clerk. So involved was he in his plaint, several moments lapsed before he noticed my presence.

"Humph! Chang without Eng. I should think Barnum would have the whole force out looking for you."

"Holmes and I are not joined at the navel, nor are we Siamese," I retorted. "Might it not have occurred to you—even you—that I might be here upon my own behalf as a British subject?"

As is frequently the case with bullies, my sharp tone put him into retreat. He rose, his face assuming a deeper shade of scarlet, and turned his great bear's-paw of a palm towards the chair facing the desk. "There's no reason to take on so, doctor. It's just that with Lestrade gallivanting off on another of his fool's errands, I'm left with his paperwork as well as my own. Have a seat."

I ignored the invitation and gave him a full account of the reason for my visit. Moment by moment his colour faded to its normal shade of ruddiness. He lowered himself back into his seat, interlaced his fingers across his broad middle, and heard me out.

"I shouldn't be alarmed if I were you," he said when I'd finished. "Where you see a tragedy, I see a tiff between a man and his wife. Odds are she's gone to stay with her mother."

"Her mother died long ago. She has no blood relatives. Will you issue a bulletin?"

"My hands are tied. When an adult goes missing, regulations require twenty-four hours must pass before action is taken."

"Anything could happen in twenty-four hours! Inspector, I entreat you."

"I can't go about flaunting the rules as a favour to a personal acquaintance."

"Shall I go to the superintendent?"

"You'll hear the same from him."

I straightened, seething. "Holmes once said you and Lestrade were the best of a bad lot. He was being diplomatic."

His face darkened again. "At least neither of us has gone and lost track of his wife like an old umbrella."

III.

I Become Holmes's Client

"One moment, Watson."

When I entered the sitting room we once shared at 221B Baker Street, Holmes was perched on the stool before his acid-scarred deal table, looking for all the world like a gigantic bird of prey. He wore his old mouse-coloured dressing gown and was pouring a bilious-looking liquid from one test tube into another, staring intently at the reaction. A greenish cloud of thick vapour rose from the freshly filled vessel, further staining the plaster ceiling directly above the table, a palimpsest created by dozens of chemical experiments and at least one explosion. For a moment after he returned the empty tube to its stand he continued to watch the phenomenon until the last wisp vanished, then to my horror lifted the phial to his lips and drank down the contents at a gulp.

"Holmes! Whatever—?"

"Rest easy, old fellow," said he, touching a handkerchief to his mouth. "The criminal situation isn't so stagnant that I've chosen the Socratic method to escape it. It's a mixture of pulped avocado and quinine, with soda for effervescence." He belched delicately into his handkerchief. "I beg your pardon. I suspect a bad oyster at Simpson's to be the culprit."

"Promise me you'll never do such a thing again without warning me first."

"You have my word. I trust you've made amends with Mrs. Watson for last night's desertion."

"I never told you we'd quarrelled."

"Supposition, aided by evidence. I've prevailed upon your leisure frequently of late. A domestic contretemps seemed as inevitable as the lingering odour of violets and bird-of-paradise on your person. You buy her flowers only when you've transgressed. Old friend, what's happened?"

I'd collapsed into my old armchair, alarming him out of his musings. He was on his feet and halfway towards me in a lunge.

"For once," said I, "I wish you'd deduced it all at a glance. Might I trouble you for a whisky at this improper hour?"

He reached for the siphon at once and poured a stiff tot. I seized the glass and drank off half. "I scarcely know where to begin."

"At the beginning is not only customary but the most conducive to understanding." He sat in his basket chair, tented his long narrow hands, and closed his eyes, as I had seen him do so many times when a problem was being placed before him.

I told all, starting with Mary's disapproval when Holmes's summons came and finishing with my expulsion—polite, but final—from the office of the superintendent of Scotland Yard. Holmes listened without interruption, then:

"Have you the note she left?"

I took it from a pocket and leaned forwards to hand it to him.

"You're certain this is her writing?"

"Yes. I know it as well as my own."

"Not hurried, and I should say not particularly upset. I know from firsthand experience that she is not easily rattled. The affair of the Four might have unsettled the Queen herself." He returned the note. "What say the Anstruthers?"

"Nothing, of course. They're in Scotland, as the maid reported."

"You're distraught. You rarely leave that level head of yours at home with your nightcap. You must wire your friends and ask if Mrs. Watson attended the theatre with them. Then we shall know whether our trail begins when they parted company, or hours earlier when she left the house."

"Of course. I'm a fool not to have considered it."

"You are not Newton, but neither are you Punch. You have had no practise in separating your head from your heart."

I rose. "What will you do in the meantime?"

He smiled thinly. "I shall give you a full accounting in an hour or so."

"Shall we meet here?"

"Wait for me at your house. For all we know your wife is there now, awaiting your apology."

IV.

Mr. Lysander P. Gristle

The Anstruthers kept a country home near Aberdeen. I sent them a brief explanation along with my question, and directed them to address their response to my house. With a quickening heart I returned home, but Mary was still absent. I unstopped my brandy decanter, but deciding that I was no good to anyone in a state of inebriation, I put it back. As the hands crawled round the clock on the mantel, I attempted to interest myself in *The Times*, *The Telegraph*, and finally the Bible, but could not concentrate upon the news of the day and found no solace in scripture. I smoked a cigar without tasting it and paced through all the rooms—all the empty, echoing chambers of my lonely house—until at last someone pulled on the bell.

I tore open the door, but instead of Holmes discovered a lumpy-faced stranger on my doorstep, wearing a loud chequered suit and a flat-crowned straw hat at an insolent angle. His eyes were hidden behind blue-tinted spectacles, and a gold tooth winked in his greasy smile. He smelled offensively of lavender and lime, in which, judging by the strength of the odour, he appeared to have bathed.

He tipped his hat, exposing momentarily a head glistening with pomade. "Beg pardon, guv'nor," said he in a voice that was both high-pitched and unctuous. "Lysander P. Gristle at your service. It is my h'intense pleasure to acquaint you with the h'inwention of the century."

As he spoke, he produced from a voluminous side pocket a slender silver-coloured cylinder.

"I'm afraid someone beat you to it long ago," I said. "It's a pen." I began to push the door shut.

He stopped it with a foot shod in square-toed leather and a bright yellow gaiter. "I 'aven't finished, guv'nor. *This* pen contains its own supply of h'ink in a sealed reservoir, rendering it as portable as a pencil and making the h'inkwell a fing of the past."

"I'm not interested. Please remove your foot."

"'Old on, 'old on, there's more." He placed the ball of his thumb against the nib. "H'inside 'ere is a steel sphere one-tenth the size of a pea, h'allowing the h'ink to glide onto the page like a duck in a pond. No more blobs or scratches, and the pen does all the work. You can write h'all day wifout a cramp. See for yourself." Thrusting the device into my hand, he retrieved a fold of foolscap from another pocket, snatched off his hat, cradled it in the crook of his arm, and spread the sheet on the crown.

Seeing that there was no other way to get rid of the fellow, I placed the nib against the page and began to write my name. It split on contact, spurting ink and staining my cuff.

I cursed—and stopped in mid-syllable upon recognising the sardonic laugh of the stranger at my door. Lysander P. Gristle unhooked his coloured spectacles, exposing the sharp grey eyes of Sherlock Holmes.

"Good Lord! Whatever—?"

"Rest easy, old fellow. It's vanishing ink, made according to my own formula. In five minutes your laundress will be none the wiser."

I opened the door wide and turned to follow him as he entered, peeling away the putty that had altered the shape of his face. "I am at my wit's end, and you stoop to a practical joke?"

Without awaiting an invitation, he threw himself into a parlour chair, pried the gold cap from a perfectly sound tooth, and poked it into his waistcoat pocket. "You must pardon an amateur actor's conceit. Once immersed in a role, I find that time alone can bring me back to the surface. I'm fresh from a successful tour of Harley Street and the stately home of Dr. and Mrs. Anstruther."

"Why? Have they returned?"

"No; and I was glad of that event. It gave me the opportunity to audition my act in private with the maid."

"Are you telling me she knows something she didn't tell me?"

"Not at all. She knows everything and said nothing. When you told me her name is Gloriana and that she is South American, I remembered a certain domestic from Argentina whose *modus operandi* was to join the staff of a wealthy household—armed, naturally, with glowing references, expertly forged—take inventory of the house's contents, and conveniently neglect to latch the back door when her masters weren't at home. She managed this feat no fewer than three times at three different houses before a constable happened upon her companion, one Archie Munch, grappling a Chippendale cabinet down the back stairs with the maid helping to steer it from above.

"Even so," he continued, "I might have misplaced the memory had she not in those days travelled under the *nom de crime* Celeste. It's no great leap from heaven to glory. If we British weren't so insular we would all benefit from a healthy exposure to languages other than our own."

"Pray come to the point, Holmes."

"Forgive me; but at the risk of offending my bent towards the dramatic, please trust me when I say you need have no fear for the safety of Mrs. Watson. No." He stopped me in mid-pounce with an upraised hand. "Without suspense, you will hear nothing of what I have to say. It's critical that you understand."

"Dash it all." I opened the cabinet and poured us both a brandy. When he had his, I perched on the edge of the settee and took a medicinal sip to flatten my nerves.

"Capital. The sun is already under the yardarm in Lhasa."

But he set his glass down untasted and reached inside yet another pocket. By what great powers of organisation he knew which of those many patches and pouches contained the item he sought, I cannot say. He produced a wicked-looking object that appeared to be a cross between a nutcracker and a corkscrew, with a polished wooden handle.

"'Ere, madam," he said, resuming his Cockney cant, "is the h'answer to an 'ousemaid's dream: an instrument that will render everyfing else in the kitchen h'obsolete. It's a h'inwention of my own, which I'm proud to 'ave christened the Gristlizer."

"What does it do?"

"I haven't the foggiest." The device had vanished along with Mr. Gristle's nasal drawl. "On a sudden inspiration I pinched it from the evidence room at the Yard, where it was no longer required after the defense had exhausted every appeal. It was sufficient to get my persistent flogger's foot in the Anstruthers' door, and to steal a moment alone with *Señorita* Celeste-Gloriana-Paraiso; the last being the name she used in Buenos Aires. I helped Lestrade make his original case with a bit of research.

"Abandoning my pose, I put the thing to her quite simply: the truth in return for a head start, and the chance to avoid arrest and deportation to Argentina, which has unfinished business with her, our system having given her her freedom for peaching on Archie Munch. It did not take much persuading, as she feared the wrath of her current companion more than the law in either country. It developed that he had his eye upon your friends' silver candlesticks and a teak chest that had sailed round the world with Drake, and he wouldn't be any too pleased to learn she'd blown them both just when her master and mistress were away and unable to prevent their removal."

"But what have two petty thieves to do with my wife?"

"I shall come to that in due course."

"Holmes, I really must insist."

He sighed. "Very well. If I'm to be forced to leave my tale unfinished, I shall yield the floor to another."

He stood up abruptly, and in three strides was at the door, which he flung open to give my dear Mary entrance to the house we shared.

V.

The Ordeal of Mrs. John H. Watson

She was dressed for the theatre, in her emerald-coloured ball gown, white fur cape, and pearls. As out of place as she looked in broad daylight, at that moment she was the most beautiful creature I'd ever seen. I fell in love all over again, if anything more intensely than I had at the time of the affair of the Agra treasure, which had brought us together the first time.

She nearly fell into my arms. I held her so tight I wonder now how I didn't break some delicate bone. I kissed her feverishly. Only when we separated ourselves by a few inches, some full two minutes later, did I realise that we were alone in the room. Holmes had absented himself, discreetly and as in a puff of smoke.

I apologised for my careless behaviour; she stopped me by placing a gloved hand against my lips.

"John, I don't care. Since I thought I should never see you again, I can hardly hold you to account for an evening's desertion. You were impetuous, I was churlish; please, dear, let us leave it at that. Do you suppose you could pour me some brandy?"

Although I had rarely known her to drink anything stronger than tea—and never even that, at that early hour—I wasted no time in escorting her to a chair and filling another glass. As she touched her lips to it, I saw that although she seemed physically unharmed, she had been through a harrowing ordeal. The tiny fissures at the corners of her eyes, which she loathed and I adored, were etched deeply as if with an engraving tool, and she was as pale as candle-wax.

This was the story she told, when the spirits had helped her to place her thoughts in order:

As arranged, she'd taken a cab to the Anstruthers, still in high dudgeon over my failure to return from my assignation with Holmes in time to accompany her; from there, our party was to proceed to the Lyceum aboard the couple's own coach-and-four. No sooner had the cab pulled away when Gloriana told her at the door that her employers had already left. She could (or would) offer no explanation as to the change in plan. Thereupon, Mary returned to the street to hail another cab. One pulled up immediately, as well it should; for the maid's own accomplice in crime sat in the driver's seat. Somewhere in their association, the partners had agreed to broaden their activities to include abduction.

When the passenger realised the vehicle was heading in the wrong direction, she called out to get the driver's attention. Instantly a whip cracked, the horse broke into a gallop, and she found herself hanging onto the seat with both hands to keep from spilling out onto the cobblestones. She could no more follow the swaying coach's course, or identify the buildings streaming past, than could a seed in a gourd.

When at last the vehicle came to a jarring stop, nearly pitching her forwards over the dashboard, the driver leapt down and, before she could recover herself enough to alight, threw his arms round her in a death-grip.

"No, you don't, little missy," said he. "Old Snipe 'as a sweet treat for you h'inside."

She struggled desperately, but could not break the hold of his sinewy arms, nor escape his fetid breath; his face, all pocked and stubbled under a filthy tile, was inches from hers. So constricted was she that she could not summon the breath to cry for help.

Suddenly the man's expression shifted from triumph to astonishment, then disgust.

"Cor! You h'ain't nofing but a dried-up old 'ag of thirty! What was Glory finking? Nobody'd pay a farthing for the like of you!" Whereupon he freed one hand with the intention of smacking her across the face.

"Great Scott!" I said, horrified, at this point in her narrative. I wanted to hunt down the swine and throttle him barehanded.

But the blow never fell. With only one arm holding her, she managed to shove him away far enough to draw back a foot and kick him on the shin.

No rugby player ever kicked the ball harder or with greater desperation. The man Snipe howled and let go of her to cradle his barked tibia in both hands. In a thrice, Mary spun round and raced off down the street, lifting the hem of her gown and clattering the heels of her pumps on the pavement.

Snipe gave chase, but a glance back over her shoulder revealed a pursuer much hindered by his injury, limping along like a man with a peg leg.

She dared not alter her pace, however, or risk another look back. She wove her way through the press of pedestrians, turned this corner and that, dashed down alleyways with no sense of where she was in London or whither she was headed, determined as she was to put as much distance as possible between herself and the fiend who sought to recapture her.

Finally, thoroughly winded, her heart pounding and her throat raw from her panting breath, she slowed to a stop. No sooner had she done so than a hand touched her shoulder.

She whirled and lashed out with all her might, striking a hard cheek with her small fist; seeing only in the next instant that it belonged to a constable in uniform.

London's Finest are not so easily vanquished, however, and although astonished, the officer kept his footing and caught her in both arms as she swooned. When, assured that she would not be arrested for assaulting a member of the Metropolitan division, she'd recovered herself sufficiently to relate her tale, he looked down and said, "Here, madam, what's this in your hand?"

She looked down, startled to find that in her struggle to break free from her captor she'd snatched something inexplicable from the villain's waistcoat. As it was clenched in the same fist she'd swung at the officer, the fact that he had not been sent reeling spoke leagues about his constitution.

"What was it?" I asked.

"Mr. Holmes will show you," she said. "He gave me a fair turn when the policeman accompanied me by van to the Anstruthers' to identify the housemaid and we found a disreputable-looking stranger hastening down the front steps."

"Thank you for the review," said Holmes, rejoining us from the next room. "I rather think Gristle was one of my least penetrable impostitures."

Although he still wore the loud suit of clothes, he'd removed all traces of the door-to-door barker from his face and was rummaging in another of his multiplicity of pockets. "Perhaps not as unusual a thing to find in a thief's waistcoat as one might think." He held up the object Mary had snatched from Snipe: a thing so common and homely as to elicit laughter under any other circumstances.

"A spoon?" said I.

"No, Watson," said he. "A key. The one that unlocks the secret to this whole affair."

VI.

A Plot Unfolds

"Is it silver?" I asked.

"Plated pewter, almost certainly. The time required to confirm the point with nitric acid and a jeweller's scale would be far out of ratio to its value."

"Then this Snipe is an ass as well as a jackal, to steal something so worthless. Where *is* the bounder? I ask just five minutes with him alone before he's turned over to the police."

"We must possess our souls in patience. Mrs. Watson was in no state to identify the terminus of her unwanted journey, and his accomplice fled out the back door as I was coming out the front. Her liberty was the price of the information she had to give. There was nothing else for it, and of the two fish she was the one small enough to throw back. I believed her when she said she didn't know where Snipe and his captive were headed."

"Twaddle! She lied."

"She can manage a tall story, I'll give you that, but not with me in the audience. She convinced her employers that Dr. and Mrs. Watson had left hasty word by way of an oral messenger that they were to meet them at the theatre rather than at their house. That way there would be two fewer witnesses to the abduction. Snipe must have been pleasantly surprised to learn that the lady was alone, and that the cudgel in his pocket would not be necessary to remove her escort as an obstacle."

"I shall never forgive myself," I said.

Holmes scowled. He alone was standing. I sat on the arm of Mary's chair, holding both her hands in mine.

"Your wife already has, and with good reason. Snipe isn't your ordinary footpad, scampering away at the sound of an advancing tread. Given the nature of his extracurricular activities—I do not speak of mere burglary—he would not scruple to make her a widow in order to achieve his end. You are a courageous man, Watson, formidable in battle; but I daresay a scoundrel with neither mind nor conscience is as deadly as a wounded brute."

Any protest I might have made died when Mary squeezed my hand. "But what *is* his end?" I cried.

He looked at Mary. "Pray do not be distressed by the fellow's vile remarks upon your maturity. Gloriana misjudged your age when she described you as a likely candidate for his enterprise. You may consider that alone, coming from another of your sex, to be a compliment."

"I do not upset so easily," said she coolly, "nor flatter so quickly."

"In any event, it isn't so much fading youth as strength of will and wisdom of experience that he abhors in a victim. Post-adolescent girls are more susceptible to guile, and easier to intimidate once the veil is torn away."

I disengaged myself from Mary and shot to my feet, fists balled at my sides. "Confound it, Holmes! Patience is one thing and torture quite something apart. We are all adults, and as you can see, my wife isn't so fragile she cannot face harsh reality. You're saying that in addition to a cutpurse, this blackguard Snipe is a procurer."

He smiled without mirth.

"A euphemism if ever there was one. He is a white slaver, and this, like the Freemason's apron, is the symbol of his order." He held up the silver-plated spoon.

VII.

The Tale of the Spoon

"Crime, like science, is never static," said Holmes. "If it were, any unlettered charwoman could recognise its patterns and I should be in early retirement. Today's traffic in young girls is not your grandfather's racket."

"Racket?" I raised my brows.

"A term of relatively recent American coinage, but with a six-thousand-year-old pedigree. In Arabic, *rack* is the palm of one's hand, the oldest of weapons. The derivation in Sanskrit means 'to stretch,' a definition which the Spanish Inquisitors took quite literally. Americans regard a *racket* as a raucous noise, and applied it to the rough-and-tumble of housebreaking overheard by neighbours. From there it spread to encompass any organised criminal endeavour. I'm compiling a dictionary of underworld vernacular as a companion volume to my magnum opus, *The Whole Art of Deduction*. It will be the Rosetta Stone the authorities require to de-riddle the secret language of crime."

I gave vent to an oath. Mary had left us temporarily, to freshen up and change; thus my freedom of language. Inwardly I was relieved that she would not be present for what promised to be shocking revelations about that most vicious of smuggling operations, flesh-peddling. "Holmes, this is not the time to discuss scholarship."

"Just so. However, I am not static either. As we speak, Scotland Yard is scouring the city in search of Snipe's lair, armed with a sturdy constable's dead-reckoning based upon where he encountered your wife and the information I gave, based upon her prize." Once again he held up the spoon, as if he expected it to reveal as much as the trusty convex lens he employed to ferret out vital clues.

"That is some comfort," I concluded, "but I confess I'm as much in the dark about the significance of the utensil as ever. What has it to do with enforced prostitution?" My voice fell to a whisper when I used the word.

"A great deal. In the days of the old Bow Street Runners, the traffickers were almost invariably swarthy foreigners, easy objects of suspicion, who worked out of dank cellars, filthy brothels, rat-infested warehouses, and opium dens—*dives*, to use the colourful term suggested by the divans where the addicted fed their habit chasing the dragon. Again, easy targets for the authorities to aim their investigation. When the newspapers turned their crusading efforts in that direction, awakening public indignation and popular pressure, the police stepped up their efforts, raiding those establishments, arresting the inhabitants, often for transgressions decades old, and padlocking their doors.

"Needless to say, whilst the mice were captured, the rats got away; but just as a rat is intelligent enough to abandon a ship in peril and a house where no food is available, the men behind the men who worked the racket turned their attention in less hazardous directions, albeit no less criminal. Not quite as unsavoury, let us say. Outrage was satisfied; after all, a shipment of stolen rum is not the same as a woman snatched off the street in Westminster and sold in Cairo.

"Skip ahead to the Industrial Age," he continued, putting a match to his favourite pipe from a pouch of his odiferous shag (those pockets!). "Cotton is no longer refined by hand, and whilst the police still maintain a weather eye upon bleak dungeons where men of low character congregate, the market in naive young women has moved to rooms reserved for private parties in good hotels, the sculpted gardens of country estates, and the corner ice-cream parlour."

"Ice-cream parlour!" I stared at the spoon.

"Good old Watson. Though the train runs late, it can be depended upon to arrive at the station eventually."

I had grown accustomed to these sly barbs—he was as much a slave to them as to his former drug of choice—and so failed to rise to the bait. To all appearances unvexed, he toyed with the utensil, spinning it between his fingers so that the bowl flashed in the light.

"The libretto may vary, but the music is always the same: A starry-eyed girl from the country is accosted on a railway platform—not by a dark-complected outsider, but perhaps a dashing young Englishman resembling one of the well-dressed blades who are always seen accompanying the Prince of Wales in rotogravures. He tips his hat, remarks upon the young lady's charms, and invites her to a clean, brightly lit public place for a strawberry sundae. The flavour is immaterial; I merely use it to establish the tableau. You have seen how these parlours proliferate, and how they sparkle, with all their white porcelain and gleaming chromium, the starched white aprons worn by the clean-cut men who scoop the sweet confection into cups and bowls. Where is the mother who would not prefer to see her marriageable daughter courted by a gentleman in such a place than by a sinister-looking stranger in a low public-house?"

"But that isn't—"

"As I said, while the storyline sometimes changes, the score remains the same. What does it matter whether the victim is charmed with praise from a man of evident education and good breeding, or seized by a coachman on a respectable street? Who is more invisible than a man who drives a hansom, and what vehicle less notable? The one fixed thing is the destination itself, which is not so easily changed. Your wife could not have chosen a more revealing souvenir of her adventure had she succeeded in obtaining Snipe's fingermarks. The spoon says it all."

"But why was *she* chosen? Naturally, I regard her as the most beautiful woman in London, if not the world; but a lucky man has his prejudices."

"She is fair of hair and complexion, and slender. The type is rare in certain countries, therefore sought after. Every Arab sheikh must have at least one in his harem, or lose face."

"Certainly not every Arab sheikh would stoop to abduction and slavery."

"I daresay most are above suspicion, even if their views on monogamy do not coincide with ours. However, the lower classes haven't cornered the market on evil. I don't judge a man by the colour of his skin, but by the darkness of his soul."

"What takes place in these parlours?"

"Nothing wicked, to the unpractised eye, and assuredly not in most. The odd *poseur* depends upon the trade's reputation for innocent diversion, just as a cracksman may don a clerical collar to gain admission to a stately home. Honeyed words over sweet concoctions, delivered in a low voice. In your wife's case, a clandestine departure by way of a labourer's door into the kitchen—made easier, I should think, with a handkerchief soaked in chloroform—and from there, who can say? A voyage in the hold of a tramp steamer, a turn in an auction lot in the Orient, or delivery directly into the hands of a customer who has placed his order. The scenario is sometimes unique to the testimony of those few who have been rescued. The one detail that remains inviolate is the fact that these shining establishments are the last place any of them are seen in society."

I sat back with my brandy, utterly drained. "We may thank the Lord—and you, of course—that my Mary is out of it."

"*Your* Mary may be," interposed a fresh speaker, "but *my* Mary is not. I shan't be, until all these horrid places are shut down and the creatures that operate them are behind bars."

We rose at Mary's sudden appearance, in a grey frock more in keeping in bright sunshine than her evening dress. Her expression, however, was as troubled as before.

I said, "The matter is in the hands of the police. They will find the place where you made your escape, and handle the rest. Your statement in court will convict Snipe. I would spare you it, but it's necessary. After that you'll be out of it and in a position to forget the whole sordid affair."

"I shan't ever. What of the poor girls who weren't so lucky? Do you think I can ever put them from my mind, knowing what I know? Mr. Holmes told me everything in the cab on the way home."

"I'm not sure I approve of that," I said stiffly. "Some things—"

"They were, yes," broke in Holmes. "Now that she's a veteran, she has every right not to be kept in the dark. To begin with, the police will, in all likelihood, once they find Snipe's parlour, find it deserted. He may be dense enough to pinch a pewter spoon from his employers, thinking it sterling, but self-preservation is instinctive with vermin. A few gallons of cherry-vanilla swirl for the next Orphans' Fund gala will be the sum total of Scotland Yard's best efforts."

"Then we are all powerless," I said.

His smile was as cold as ice cream.

"I never accept absolutes when they are applied to me. What Gregson and Lestrade will surely overlook once they identify the place, Sherlock Holmes certainly will not."

"And to think I disapproved of your association," breathed Mary.

VIII.

A Woman's Will

Scarcely had Holmes made his declaration of war when someone rang at the door. Upon the step stood a stolid oak of a man in the helmet and caped uniform of the Metropolitan Police, sporting regimental whiskers magnificent enough for a general of the Raj—and, I noted, a purple bruise upon one stony cheek. Mary's reaction, when she joined me, confirmed what I suspected, that here was the fellow who had rescued her from her headlong dash down the street, and had gotten a smiting for his trouble.

"Good afternoon, Officer," said she. "You should put a steak on that eye."

"Too late, missus. I've got a fair riding from my fellows for coming off second best in a bout with a lady." He chortled. "I trust you've recovered?"

Holmes, impatient as usual, interrupted this cordial exchange. "What have you for me, Holcomb?"

The constable, who had removed his helmet for Mary, clapped it back on. "Three possibilities, Mr. Holmes, within the lady's running distance in the time she estimated she was at it." Producing a notebook from under his cape, he rattled off three addresses. "These places multiply like rats, I'm grieved to report."

"We shan't paint them all the same shade of black. The worst you can expect from most is an unsettled stomach. Let us concentrate on the one that's closed its doors."

"That's just the thing, sir. They was all shut up tight as a lady's"—he paused, blushing in Mary's presence—"that is to say, as the Bank of England on Sunday."

"Hum. They must all have learnt their methods of communication by way of the Newgate telegraph. Well, there's no law against closing

224

early, and two of the parlours may even be legitimate, hoping to avoid notoriety. We must visit them all." He thanked the man and shut the door in the middle of his farewell. "We'll stop in Baker Street on the way and put Lysander P. Gristle back in mothballs."

"Wherever did you get that alias?" I asked then.

"I spent a season in a music hall in Chelsea, carrying a spear under the name."

"Good Lord, Holmes. How many lives have you had?"

He smiled. "I daresay I'm the envy of most cats."

I excused myself, to return from the bedroom moments later with my service revolver in one pocket and a handful of extra cartridges in another. To my astonishment, Mary stood in the entrance hall, dressed for the street in a becoming hat and woolen wrap over her grey dress, parasol in hand.

"Wherever do you think you're going?" I demanded.

Her eyes were steely. "When has that tone ever worked with me, John?"

"If I may interpose," said Holmes, interposing. "It was my suggestion. In her haste, Mrs. Watson may have forgotten something she saw that would help us pinpoint the scene of the crime. What the seers are conceited to call the sixth sense is often just a matter of jostling the memory."

"Certainly not. It's too dangerous."

"Your argument is with me," said Mary. "Mr. Holmes has taken responsibility for a decision I made upon my own. If I don't accompany you, I shall spend the rest of my life asking myself, 'Is this the place?' whenever I pass an ice-cream parlour. I shan't be able to look at a sorbet without shuddering. And I may be in a position to help."

"It's difficult enough to defend ourselves in times of danger. Will you have one of us take a bullet for fear of what may happen to you?"

"Have I lived in this wicked city all these years and learnt nothing? I'm anything but unarmed."

In demonstration, she drew the pin from her hat, a wicked-looking six inches of razor-pointed steel with a pearl button, replaced it, and raised her parasol. I'd never noticed before how much the end of it resembled a fencer's foil. She executed a neat flourish, slicing the air with a swish and finishing with it demurely resting upon her shoulder, her small hand gripping it near the carved ivory crook. A watch appended to a gold chain swung from the point.

I groped at my waistcoat. My watch was missing.

In all my years of association with Sherlock Holmes, this was the only time I can recall when he absolutely roared with laughter.

"Face it, Watson!" said he, upon recovering himself. "You're undone!"

"Wherever did you learn to do that?" I said sternly.

"Embroidery," said Mary. "The basics are the same."

I marshalled all my arguments, only to relinquish them with a heavy sigh. "Very well. It's a poor soldier who knows not when to retreat from the field."

She smiled at Holmes. "My apologies. Until this moment I never realised John's value to you."

He bowed. "I sometimes overlook it myself."

IX.

A Triple Scoop of Detection

We stopped at 221B just long enough for Holmes to change. He emerged carrying a heavy-knobbed stick and, no doubt, his own revolver under his frock coat. The driver (once Mary had scrutinised him and declared him "not Snipe"), took us at a canter to the first address on our list.

I had never before visited one of those establishments that had recently sprung up throughout London like wildflowers, and knew nothing of what to expect; based upon Holmes's sinister account I envisioned a cross between a low tavern and a pub of questionable reputation.

What I found resembled H.G. Wells's vision of a foreign future: white, dazzling, and spotless, lit brightly through large, polished windows, with shining chromed steel trim. From the pressed-tin ceiling to the ornate taps behind the counter, fashioned into shapes like elephants' heads and the curving necks of swans, there wasn't a splinter of wood in sight. The tables were glass circles the size of bicycle wheels, supported by spindles of wrought iron matching the frames of the chairs, bent into curlicues. It all belonged to the next century, or yet the next.

After speaking with the constable on the scene, Holmes approached the proprietor, a nervous looking man of forty or so named Osbert, with ruddy cheeks, pale hair, and wrists thickened by hour upon hour of scooping hardened ice cream from zinc-lined sinks into receptacles of china and glass. He'd been roused from a back room to reopen his doors for the purpose of official enquiry.

"The police will confirm that nothing suspicious goes on here," he said. "I know of the vipers who befoul this honest business, and I wish you every success in rooting them out. When I learned they'd struck again, I gave all my customers their money back and closed up to spare them an unpleasant encounter with the authorities."

"Who told you what happened?"

"A stranger who poked his head in the door and said, 'You'd best fold your tent before the peelers get here. The white slavers was at it just now.'"

"He said that exactly, 'fold your tent'?"

"Yes, sir. I'd never heard the phrase before, and so remembered it."

"Describe the man."

He pursed his lips. "A ruffian, built thick and smelling so strongly of gin and onions the stench reached me behind the counter. His face was scarred from pox and he wore the clothes of a cab driver, high hat and all, but shabby in the extreme."

Holmes looked at Mary, who nodded with certainty. He excused himself and drew near enough to us to whisper. "Did anything strike you outside as familiar?"

"No," she replied. "I'm afraid that means nothing. I was—"

"Quite so. It's possible this fellow wishes to throw Snipe on the sword to spare himself, but he must know the man would squeak on him when captured. We shall rule him out for now."

We bade the man good day, thanked the constable for his cooperation, and walked to the next address, round the corner and only a few squares away.

I said, "I fail to see how competing enterprises can survive in such close proximity."

"And yet show me a neighbourhood that doesn't boast at least three tobacco shops. Sugar and milk are habits nearly as compelling as Cavendish."

Mary tightened her grip on my arm. "If I ever grow stout, you'll know it was on marrow and potatoes, and not on sweets. Today has cured me."

The second parlour was much the same as the first, except that in place of a man in uniform we found Inspectors Gregson and Lestrade in charge. The latter, more bull terrier than mastiff, was every bit as aggressive as his colleague. "We've got the blighter," he rapped.

"You're out of order," grumbled Gregson. "This is my investigation."

I bridled. "You seemed little enough interested in pursuing it when I brought it to you."

"It wasn't the same thing then, was it? If the Yard was to start barging in on lovers' quarrels, there'd never be an end to it."

Mary turned my way. "Please forgive me. I thought you exaggerated when you told me of these men."

"Thank you kindly, madam." Gregson lifted his hat. "If I was to arrest a man entirely on appearances, I should not hesitate to clap the owner in irons. However, his piteous attempts at evasion quite settle the matter. Lestrade's in agreement."

"If I'm not out of order." The other was plainly seething. There was no love lost between these two comrades in arms.

"What sort of attempts?" Holmes asked.

"To begin with, he pretended not to have any English at all, but there's the bill of fare on the chalkboard, plain as the Queen's."

"Has he no partners or employees?"

"Lestrade asked him point blank. One thing he can manage is to make himself understood. We tripped the bounder up in his own words. He's cook, bottle-washer, and the gent that sweeps the floors."

"You translated that from which language?"

"Italian, which made him suspicious right off. They're all of them the same, these Mediterraneans, thick as chowder. He shook his head and said, 'No, no, no' when asked if he had anyone with him in the business."

"I see. Lestrade spoke slowly and loudly, which as we all know transcends all tongues, and interpreted the response as an answer to his question. As to his ethnicity as evidence for conviction, we must consult with Plutarch and Garibaldi before we lay it before the bench. May I speak with him?"

Gregson looked at Lestrade, who shrugged. "He's in back with a constable, though what good it will do you I can't say."

Holmes asked to be alone with the man, to which Mary and I agreed, although we were able to watch the interrogation through a circular window in the swinging door leading to a storage room. There among the sacks, jars, and cartons, he drew a chair so close to where the proprietor sat that their knees almost touched, with yet another stalwart in blue standing by wearing an expression of determined comprehension. Dumb show that it was for us, the discussion was clearly no more within the officer's grasp.

The man under guard was youthful in appearance, with black hair cut close to the crown, a long, sallow face, and modest moustaches by the standards of his people. He wore an immaculate white smock and a military stripe on his trousers. That the pair were conversing in Italian seemed obvious by the way both men waved their arms energetically while speaking; the Romans are a demonstrative race. The fellow being interrogated shook his head violently to some questions, nodded animatedly to others, listened with a thoughtful mien when he was silent, and, when Holmes leaned closer and appeared to whisper in his ear, responded with a show of gravity. Presently Holmes shook his hand and returned to the main room.

"His name is Antonio Valardi," he reported. "He came here from Genoa when he was fourteen years old, after his parents perished in a diphtheria epidemic, and saved his labourer's wages for ten years until he had enough money to lease this space and purchase equipment and supplies. He hopes to make enough to bring all his cousins here from Italy, and knows nothing of the white slave trade."

"Why wouldn't he?" said Lestrade with a snort.

"He said also that he employs a boy part-time to sweep up and write the bill of fare on the chalkboard. When you asked him if he had anyone with him in the business, he shook his head and said 'no' because he didn't understand the question."

Gregson said, "He's changed his story."

"It's easy enough to confirm or deny. He expects his boy to report to work any moment."

"How can anyone live in London ten years and not pick up a word of English?" barked Lestrade.

"The Italian Quarter is an insular society. Many have lived their entire lives there communicating entirely in their native dialect."

"We'll break him yet," said Gregson.

"I have no doubt you will, if you employ your usual methods. However, you will be helping the true criminal to escape justice. He has a good memory for phonetics. When I whispered the phrase 'fold your tent' in his ear, he told me that's exactly what the stranger said."

"What stranger?" Both inspectors spoke in unison.

"The one the constables who visited the two other parlours will tell you about, who warned the proprietor to close up shop for his own good. You'll find he answers to the name of Snipe."

"He does, does he?" Gregson said. "What's this 'fold your tent' business, I should like to know?"

"'Let us fold our tents and steal away.' It's an Arab saying, not well known in Britain. Of course it made no sense to *Signor* Valardi, but it was said with such urgency he thought closing up the better part of valour. But here, if I'm not mistaken, is the lad who will confirm at least part of his story."

Outside the plated-glass entrance stood a boy of sixteen or seventeen, whose surprise at finding the door locked at that hour was evident on his face. On his way out, Holmes held it open for him, and we left the inspectors blaming each other in strident tones.

Our visit to the third and last parlour is swiftly summarised. The manager was a lady of genteel manners who operated the establishment for her absentee employer, a Welsh entrepreneur well known to the press, and a confidant of the Prince of Wales. She told the same story as the others, and nothing about the neighbourhood awakened anything in Mary's memory.

"Perhaps the first constable underestimated the length of her flight," I suggested. "The search must be widened."

Holmes's face was dark. "I am the one who is guilty of underestimation. I misjudged the cunning of our enemy. We have already met Snipe this day."

X.

Snipe's Flight

We fairly leapt aboard the first four-wheeler that stopped, Holmes first, I gripping Mary's wrist, effectively pulling her over the stirrup-step.

"A sovereign to you if you can get us there in five minutes," he called out to the driver.

As we lurched forwards, flung back into our seats, Holmes fetched the floor a sharp blow with the ferrule of his stick. "I am a dunderpate, Watsons, worse than Lestrade and Gregson rolled into one arrogant fool! I count myself clever for taking in the doctor with a simple disguise and then fail to detect one far more obvious."

"What do you mean?" I was far at sea, for the address he'd given the driver belonged to the first parlour we'd been to.

"Of course, I did not meet Snipe in his fancy dress, but I should have marked the signs in his alter ego. I attributed the redness in his cheeks to high emotion, or possibly accelerated circulation, a medical condition, when I should have taken note of his overall fairness and the likelihood of an allergic reaction to greasepaint."

"Osbert, the ice cream man?" said Mary. "Snipe in disguise? Impossible!"

"That was no disguise; not in the physical sense of the term. There is no Snipe."

"No Snipe!" we exclaimed together.

"He is a wig, putty, and paint, with a dash of gin and onion to taste: an old country recipe for impersonation. I ought to have known from Mrs. Watson's description, echoed by Osbert, that the man is a caricature out of Dickens, too broad for truth."

"Surely Gloriana described her accomplice to you," I said.

"Letter perfect. Salt in the wound, and well earned. Of course she would not provide me with the picture of the real man, lest he return for retribution. Pray, Watson, write this one up. No man can live up to the paragon you've made me out to be."

He lit a cigarette, took two nervous puffs, and threw it outside. "Beekeeping in the South Downs looks better and better. To err this way or that would cost but the lives of two or three hundred Apidae, which regenerate by the month."

I squeezed Mary's hand, communicating to her the futility of any attempt to draw Holmes out of his characteristic bouts of melancholy.

Finally—within the requisite five minutes, but hours in the imagination—we arrived at our destination. Holmes tossed the driver his disk of gold whilst the coach was still rocking on its springs, and was at the door of the parlour before I could help my wife down to the pavement.

The constable who had greeted us before let us in. When Holmes demanded the whereabouts of Osbert, he said, "Why, he's in back, sir. When I told him the inspectors will want to ask him some questions, he went in to settle his nerves with a pot of tea. There it goes now."

The kettle could be heard whistling from the other side of the door behind the counter. Holmes raced that way with Mary and me close upon his heels.

It was a plain storage room much like the one at Valardi's, but with a coal stove in one corner, atop which the kettle was pouring steam towards the ceiling. No one was inside. As I removed the noisy thing from the stove, Holmes snatched up a shaggy wig from a pile of soiled clothing, padded ticking, and a disheveled tall hat on the floor. Mary took one look and nodded.

"Here is the rest of him," said Holmes, indicating a stained rag on a table with a shaving mirror propped upon it surrounded by sundry jars and bottles. "Cold cream to strip off the makeup, and peppermints to cover the spirits and onions that finished the disguise. I'll wager a quid our man Osbert trod the boards at one time or another."

He held a palm above the stovetop. "Ten minutes at least to bring the pot to a boil at this temperature. Ten hours would not be less convenient to us." He opened a door that looked into an alley behind the building.

"He seemed quite harmless," suggested the constable, who had followed us into the room. "I overheard you say it yourself."

"So I did. You are not the blunderer." He turned towards Mary. "I failed you. Believe me when I say that whatever disappointment you feel about my performance I share tenfold."

She shook her head. "You have been instrumental in foiling a foul business. Osbert, or Snipe, can hardly continue his activities while he is in hiding."

"At all events," said I, "it would take much time and money to create another establishment such as this. You must consider this a victory, measured in the number of women you have saved potentially from his clutches."

"Osbert was a flea on the back of the hyena, Watson, and a trained one at that. There are others. I shall not rest until I make an example of him that will shatter their complacency."

"Surely the fellow will never again show his face in England."

"He may never have shown it anywhere else."

"But, 'fold your tent'—"

"Snipe, of course, alarmed his legitimate competitors in order to stir up dust to cover his tracks. Don't you think he'd choose his language towards the same purpose? Anyone casually acquainted with *The Thousand and One Nights* knows the phrase. Our lecherous sheikh is a comforting image, lulling us into the belief that no fellow countryman would ever stoop to manipulate a machine so vile, yet the brothels are always recruiting, and the poorhouses are never in short supply of broken women. We look at Snipe and think, 'There's a fellow worthy of his work,' and look right past an Osbert because of his tidy appearance. Our culprit may have shared a box with the Anstruthers, and gone backstage to shake Irving's hand and bow over Terry's."

"Perish the thought," I said with a shudder.

Mary lifted her chin. "Mr. Holmes, you may count upon us."

He smiled for the first time since we'd left the third ice-cream parlour. "Then Mr. X must be on his guard, for we are a formidable force."

XI.

The Society of the Spoon

I must now ask the reader to consider that four months passed after my wife's adventure, with little but the usual to occupy our time. When our friends returned from Scotland, curious about the reason for our abandonment of them on theatre night and my mysterious wire, we explained that I had been called away to attend to a patient, and Mary had stayed home with a sudden headache. Upon returning home and finding no sign of her, I'd acted without stopping to consider that she had gone to a chemist's for powders. They were an amiable couple, who accepted our apologies for neglecting to cancel, and there seemed no point in troubling them with the truth.

"I was certain it was something of that nature," said Anstruther. "Henrietta fretted, but we had an early train, and little enough time as it was to rest before our journey."

Throughout this period I saw almost nothing of Holmes. He was some ten weeks on the Continent, probing an affair of such delicacy on behalf of the state that he could not share the details even with me, and then, with nothing taking place in the criminal world to excite his attention, spent many days and nights in the reading room of the British Museum and the libraries of the city's newspapers researching *The Whole Art of Deduction*, his own equivalent of Darwin's *On the Origin of Species*. It was grueling work, and on those few occasions when I dropped in upon him I did not stay long, marking his plain exhaustion.

Osbert the ice-cream man vanished like a drop of water on a hot stove. A likeness based upon his description appeared in all the papers, and a reward posted by *The Times* for information leading to his apprehension, but no one came forward with anything useful. There was no record of a man bearing that name and resembling him to be found, and it was quickly decided that Osbert was an alias as surely as Snipe. With nothing new to report (and with Gregson and Lestrade's stern admonition not to mention the parts played by Holmes, Mary, and myself), the entire episode was soon supplanted by other items of interest.

Soon the columns were filled with the mysterious disappearance of Jane Chilton, the grown daughter of Sir James Chilton, whose textile mills in Middlesex produced uniforms for the British military. She was an heiress, and it was at first conjectured that she had been kidnapped for ransom, but when the anticipated demand failed to materialise, a darker suggestion emerged, that she had been slain for her purse and jewels and the body discarded. Grisly sensation was the specialty of the house in those days, and the illustrators found no limit of inspiration in Eugene Aram and Sweeney Todd. Given my own recent association with a vanishing-woman case, I had suspicions of my own; however, as there was no mention of her ever having been seen anywhere near an ice-cream parlour, I assigned them to personal sensitivity.

Holmes was abroad when the story reached its crescendo. It presented some arcane features I felt sure would attract his curiosity when he returned; but then Sir James received a letter in his daughter's hand, postmarked San Francisco, informing him that she had eloped with that fixture of romantic fiction, a penniless young man Not Suitable for marriage with a woman of good breeding, and after the inevitable flurry of sentimental claptrap, the curtain descended upon this act as well.

In the middle of August, with the streets hot and fetid and a white sun nailed to a burnt-out sky, I found my friend bright-eyed and cheerful, his feet propped upon an ottoman beside an open window and holding something close to his face. With a start I recognised it as the silver-plated teaspoon Mary had torn from the waistcoat pocket of the man she'd known as Snipe.

"Not my favourite trophy by any means, in view of the unsatisfactory conclusion," he said. "Why it should fascinate me enough to interrupt my work in my magnum opus has posed a vexation until this very hour. Exercise your faculties, Watson. What do you surmise is the reason?"

"Dissatisfaction, as you indicated. To you an unsolved case is worse than a failed chemical experiment."

"The reasoning is sound, but the explanation is inapplicable. I never dwell on past mistakes, only seek not to repeat them. Does nothing else occur to you?"

I sat down opposite him, defeated. "You've remarked before upon my matchless talent for grasping the obvious. I've fired my one round."

"I was a prize ass to accuse you of a crime I've committed myself. When the spoon first came to light, we both assumed that Snipe had stolen it out of old habit. At that time we thought him to be a thief who had expanded his operation—"changed his lay," as the Americans say—to embrace abduction. Now that we know he owned the establishment to which the spoon undoubtedly belonged, the theory is groundless. Why, then, did he have it on his person?"

"Perhaps it was his answer to a lucky rabbit's foot."

"Possibly. Criminals are often superstitious. It's a hazardous vocation, after all. But let us widen our loop and consider other solutions. Gogol tells us the Zaporozhye Cossacks carried their dining utensils on their belts wherever they went, but there was nothing remotely Eurasian about Osbert's features. Judging by the lice in Snipe's wig, he wasn't overly fastidious, so we can eliminate any phobias about filth."

He pointed the spoon at me, like a conductor his baton. "Do you remember something I said about fraternal organisations? I thought it profound at the time."

I produced the notebook I am seldom without. In time it will join its hundreds of ancestors in the box I keep at my bank for the edification of future generations. I paged back four months, scanning my personal shorthand. "Of Snipe, you said, 'He is a white slaver, and this, like the Freemason's apron, is the symbol of his order.'"

"Hum. I remembered it as more lyrical. I should have listened more closely to myself in any case, because I believe I had hit upon the truth. In the absence of a more compelling argument, I consider this to be Snipe's bona fides, providing access to others in his racket. These types haggle and trade amongst themselves, bartering in human chattel, and they are constantly on the lookout for infiltrators. A tangible badge of office saves paragraphs of challenge and response."

"Surely anyone can obtain a spoon."

"All the more reason to keep it secret. And should a suspicious constable waylay and search you, a cheap utensil would hardly be cause for arrest. For want of a better name, let us call this baleful brotherhood the Society of the Spoon, and put the hypothesis to the test."

"What sort of test?"

He remarked that it was hot, and asked if I had a yearning for ice cream.

XII.

The Leopards Change Their Spots

"I shall go with you," said Mary.

I shook my head. "Not this time. If you won't heed my advice about the danger, consider that having a woman along would tip our hand."

"Will you dress up as gypsies, with rings in your ears and bandannas wrapped round your heads?"

"Holmes says no, as regards me. My face is not as well known as his, thanks to the illustrators at *The Strand*, so no disguise is necessary in my case. I think also he sought to spare my feelings, as there is more to carrying off a role than fancy dress and a false nose."

"I have never known him to give any thought to your feelings at all." Her expression softened. "I withdraw that remark. I saw quite a different side of him last spring. But surely you're dressed too well to masquerade as a brigand."

She excused herself, to return from the pantry a minute later, dragging a bulky burlap sack. "Here are some of your old clothes I've been saving for charity. See what suits your pretense."

I retired to the bedroom, where I found the favourite pullover I'd missed for weeks. There was plenty of wear left in it in spite of the tiny balls of wool that had erupted upon its surface, but it was too heavy for the season. After clucking my tongue over some other unpleasant revelations (women are born for subterfuge), I selected a seersucker suit, a pair of brogans worn round at the heels, and a bowler beyond blacking. The crowning touch was a cravat a patient had given me one Christmas, with a Balinese dancer hand-painted on it in bright colours. Standing before the glass, I saw a shady character staring back, ready to pick my pocket or offer to sell me the Tower. I stepped back into the parlour and asked how I looked.

"Like something I'd expect to see at the races. Whatever possessed you to buy that suit in the first place?"

"You were away visiting a sick friend, and it seemed a bargain at the time."

At the door she kissed me with particular affection and admonished me to be careful. I lowered one eyelid and patted the revolver in my pocket.

"I keep forgetting you were in the army," she said.

"Would that *I* could."

On this particular clandestine occasion, I had no trouble recognising Holmes when we met in his sitting room. Although a light dusting of freckles and a red wig altered his appearance enough to throw off the casual observer, I was surprised to see that he looked less shabby than I, in broad chalk stripes and a crushable hat with a feather in the band. He took one look at me, shook his head, and relieved me of my cravat.

"Fasten your collar and go without," he said. "These men are low, not stupid."

"I'm sorry, Holmes. This is all new to me."

"Save your apologies, old fellow. Why should the salt of the earth develop a talent for dissembling?"

"But surely you can be recognised."

"Our quarry is doubly suspicious than the ordinary culprit, and double more so since Snipe's close call. They'll be looking for tricks of theatrical magic, whilst the gay attire will throw them off the scent after the fashion of Poe's purloined letter. In any wise, I am counting upon that. This affair is heavy enough with false whiskers and cobbler's wax as it is."

Osbert's parlour, we knew, had been padlocked by order of the superintendent of Scotland Yard. We ruled out the other places we'd visited, first because we'd have been recognised, second because we'd eliminated their personnel as suspects. Holmes, I was not surprised to learn, had acquired an encyclopedic knowledge of all the similar establishments in the city, but when we introduced ourselves to the people in charge—as the Messrs. Sherrinford and Sacker—they regarded with open bewilderment the spoon he produced from his pocket.

One, a burly Irishman, accused us of pinching it from his parlour and demanded its return. When Holmes refused, he tried to snatch it from his hand, much to his immediate regret, as presently we left him lying on the floor upon his back, no doubt wondering how he came to be in that position. In truth, it had all happened so fast I all but missed it, and on our way out I said, "Baritsu?"

"A refined version, which I picked up in Tibet. *Kung fu* is the name. It reaches back to the Zhou Dynasty, a thousand years before Christ."

We had no success in the other half-dozen places we went to, and returned to Baker Street, where I removed my broken-down brogans and massaged my aching feet.

Holmes poured whisky. "I feared this. The Osbert business attracted too much attention for comfort, driving the other slavers to some other cover. There's an argument to be made in favour of allowing one or two known dens of iniquity to remain open, so that justice always has a place to fish."

"Holmes, these creatures trade in human beings, not stolen watches."

"You're right, of course. Meanwhile, we've foundered."

"Perhaps the flesh pedlars were sufficiently frightened to abandon the practice entirely."

"Good old Watson. If I could distill and bottle your optimism like these spirits, I'd be as rich as Gladstone."

I finished my drink and left him in a brown study. I was concerned for him. He was like a horse with the bit in its teeth and no place to gallop, and I knew all too well where that might lead. It was ironic, then, that the most foul of all the foes we'd ever opposed should be the one to rescue him from the lure of the needle.

XIII.

The Chilton Affair

We were experiencing one of the hottest summers in memory, and the English being what they were, I was soon busy treating patients for sunburn and heat exhaustion, prescribing cocoa butter, salt tablets, and cold compresses to wretches more accustomed to overcast skies and declining mercury than sunshine and eighty-degree temperatures. Reverse the situation and imagine South Sea Islanders building snowmen in a freak blizzard, and you may have a fair picture of the epidemic of temporary insanity. As a result, it was a fortnight before I saw or heard anything of Holmes. When I did, it was he who initiated contact.

The telegram arrived as I was explaining to a sufferer that an umbrella was quite as necessary in an August such as we were having as in rainy November. He left, muttering something about a "dashed parasol," and I slit open the envelope.

WATSON
WHAT SAY YOU TO A SPOONFUL OF ADVENTURE
HOLMES

"Really, John," said Dr. Anstruther, when I stopped at his office on my way to Baker Street. "I'm up to my knees as it is in patients scarlet as red Indians. I suppose you're off on another frolic with your friend the bloodhound. You're the only good physician I know who finds time for a hobby."

"All the more reason to bless my good fortune to have such a generous colleague."

I hastened away before he could protest further. As opaque as I find things Holmes regards as elementary, "a spoonful of adventure" to me meant only one thing.

My friend met me at the street door. He was dressed for the country, in his ear-flapped cap and tweeds, but waved off my reservations about my city dress with impatience. "Our client won't issue you any demerits. He's misplaced his daughter, and has engaged us to secure her return."

I accompanied him to Baker Street station, where we caught the four o'clock train north. No sooner had the conductor announced the stops than I said, "Middlesex! It's Jane Chilton then."

I shall treasure forever the look of astonished admiration that appeared upon his face. However, lacking his flair for theatre, I told him all, summarising the newspaper accounts of the search for the textile heiress. Disapproval displaced surprise.

"A chance strike. Five counties were announced, each with a bevy of country homes with grown daughters in residence."

But I was too intrigued to be put off by his chiding. "The investigation was closed when Sir James Chilton received a letter telling him of her runaway marriage. He swore it was written in her hand."

"He is no graphologist; and my own William Thackeray has taken in experts. One dabbles, Watson," he said with a smile. "I had a sabbatical with a book forgery ring in Manchester. I may boast, but given the proper materials I could dash off a Shakespeare First Folio that would put me up comfortably in Sussex for the rest of my days, quietly tending to my bees."

It was the second time in the process of this case he'd mentioned beekeeping and the Downs. In all the years of our association, I never knew when he was having me on.

He returned to the subject. "Sir James is no one's fool, or he should not have beaten out dozens of competitors for his contract with Whitehall. He engaged an American private enquiry agent to investigate the source of the letter posted in San Francisco. The man, whose reputation even I am aware of, could find no trace of the sender. Until convinced otherwise, I suspect some colleague of Osbert's, if not the man himself, had an accomplice in California forge the letter. How he obtained a sample of her script may prove the solution to the affair."

"Still, the gulf between the girl's vanishing and the white slave trade is a long leap."

"I concur. But when a knot reveals the end of the rope, one pulls upon it, on the off chance it's the authentic Gordian."

After this pronouncement he changed the course of the conversation, drawing upon his pipe and directing my attention to some anomalies in the compositions of Sarasate.

We were met at the station by a grey-faced man with impressive white side whiskers, who wrung Holmes's hand, took mine in a grip less fervent, and introduced himself as James Harvey Chilton, Bart., founder of Chilton Mills and father of Jane. Beside him stood a young man, muscular but not bulky, in a sporty suit of a decidedly American cut with a pearl stickpin in his cravat and a tan bowler—*derby*, as it was called on that side of the pond—and displaying a broad handsome face with a determined chin. His slim hand mangled my knuckles in a steely grip.

"This gentleman is the enquiry agent I wrote you about," said Sir James. "He was kind enough to cross the ocean at my request to consult with you."

"How do you do?" said the stranger, in a pleasant, middle-register voice devoid of the broad, nasal tones I associated with American speech. "Nicholas Carter, at your service. Please call me Nick."

XIV.

Mr. Nick Carter

Sir James's carriage conveyed us all to Chilton Hall, a sprawling manor of red and yellow brick laid in chessboard fashion in the midst of rolling green country, dotted with thatched tenant farmhouses and the inevitable sheep. Once ensconced in the library, surrounded by volumes shelved from the floor to the ceiling sixteen feet above, we sat in deep leather chairs and made free with the cigars offered by our host.

"I'm restless, I admit," said Nick Carter, drawing with pleasure upon a dark Havana. "One may be absent from Paris for two or three years, and from London almost a lifetime, and find little changed on his return. But in a few months, New York City will have reinvented itself beyond recognition."

"I can't decide whether you're casting aspersions or singing the praises of any of those places." I was somewhat nettled by his ease of manner in what must have been intimidating surroundings for most of his countrymen.

"Neither, John; I hope I can call you John? We're informal in the States. It comes from twice sending you Brits packing bag and baggage back to Old Blighty."

I felt the blood rise to my face; but Holmes assumed the role of diplomat.

"Gentlemen, we've drawn our lines in the sand. For myself, I envision a future in which the ghosts of our two Georges, Hanover and Washington, address each other as equals, and unite in the commonality of our shared language."

"I'm swell with that." Having delivered this puzzling declaration, Carter unstopped a grin of dazzling American workmanship and sincere good fellowship. "You must make allowances, John." He hesitated. "John, eh?"

I nodded hesitantly.

"Where I come from, we test a man, probing for weakness. A thin skin often means a weak nature; which is nothing you want to take with you into a game of stickball where winner takes all."

Holmes cleared his throat. "I can attest that while Watson may swing at a bad pitch, he can hit a fast ball over the fence."

Carter blew a series of smoke rings. "But can he handle a curve?"

Silence ensued; broken by my own hearty laugh. "I've no earthly idea what a curve is, but show me one and I assure you I'll hit it."

"How much of what this fellow says he can do can he do?" Carter asked Holmes.

"Watson never boasts, idly or otherwise. I trust him with my life, which he has returned to me upon several occasions."

Our host, who had been listening without interrupting, coughed rumblingly. "Gentlemen. Fascinating as this game is, must I remind you that my daughter may be in great peril?"

"None of us has forgotten that for a moment," said Holmes. "As Mr. Carter said, it's as important to familiarise oneself with a new partner as with a tool of recent purchase. Suppose you recount to us in your own words the circumstances of her vanishing."

"And who else's words might I use?" the baronet put in testily. But he proceeded without further delay with a succinct report. The last time he saw Lady Jane was on her way out the door for a shopping excursion in Piccadilly. Her father had arranged to have her presented at Court, and she was determined to find the perfect ensemble to wear for the occasion. She had brought along Emma, her lady's maid, to avoid the impropriety of venturing out into the streets unescorted. In a dress shop with a seal announcing its service to the British royalty, the girl selected a frock and left Emma to wait whilst she tried it on in a dressing room.

She never emerged. When Emma investigated, the room was empty. There was no other door than the one leading into it from the shop, and that entrance was in plain view from where the maid had stood waiting.

"May we speak to her?" asked Carter.

"Of course. She has time on her hands, as I'm sure you can imagine." Sir James rang for the butler, who appeared presently, bowed, and went off to fetch the maid.

Moments later we were joined by a plain-looking woman in livery, who curtseyed and faced her interrogators with hands folded at her waist.

Holmes deferred to the visitor from abroad, who asked her if she'd kept her eyes on the dressing-room door the whole time Lady Jane was gone.

"Yes, sir. I never looked away from it."

"How long did you wait before you decided to see what kept her?"

"I should say half an hour, sir."

"That long?" Carter sounded incredulous.

A grim smile came to the servant's lips. "Your pardon, sir, but from your speech I take it you're new to some of our customs, including ladies' clothing. Twenty minutes or more is not unusual."

"Oh, yes. Stays, bustles, and all that truck. Then what?"

"I called out to my lady to ask if she needed assistance. When there was no reply I knocked at the door. She still said nothing, and that was when I asked the shop girl to let me in."

"The door was locked?"

"Yes, sir. From inside."

Holmes assumed the role of questioner. "You remained standing for thirty minutes and never once looked away from the door."

"Yes, sir. I take my duties seriously. The city can be dangerous. Another pair of eyes is useful."

"And yet a dress shop would seem to be a sanctuary of sorts; unless you saw something suspicious? A sinister-looking clerk or customer, or an unorthodox way of conducting business?"

"No, sir, just a dress shop."

"Stuff and nonsense!" said I, for I could take no more. "Women don't disappear from locked rooms."

Her eyes flashed fire. "I swear it, sir."

Holmes said, "You must pardon Dr. Watson for his customary military directness. However, I concur. You were distracted by something: an attractive pair of gloves, perhaps, or a lace bodice on a form. No one can fault you for that. Such establishments offer the same temptations as a display of new sporting arms to a gentleman."

But she remained defiant even in silence.

Carter crushed out his cigar in a silver tray. "You're sure the shop girl let you into the dressing room? You didn't take the key from her and do it yourself?"

"I did not, sir."

"Then how can you be sure the door was locked from inside?"

"I—" Emma showed confusion for the first time.

Holmes took up the chase. "The girl told you it was locked from inside, did she not?"

After an even longer silence she nodded.

It was then that the two detectives went after her hammer and tongs. I felt almost sorry for the girl as, bit by bit, she crumbled, finally admitting that the shop employee had offered to show her a bolt of calico freshly imported from America stored in the back room. The maid had never seen the material and was curious to see and feel it. She was thus engaged for at least three minutes with no one to watch the dressing-room door. At last she blurted out an apology, broken by sobs.

"I didn't mean to lie, really I didn't. I was afraid I'd be blamed for what happened."

"We'll discuss this later, Emma," said Sir James.

"Oh, sir, please don't sack me!"

"That's your mistress's responsibility, not mine. I shall instruct Hubbard to reassign you to the cleaning staff until further notice."

"Yes, sir. Thank you, sir."

"One more question, Emma," said Holmes. "Can you describe the shop girl who showed you the bolt of fabric and opened the door of the dressing room for you?"

"I can, sir. She was young, black-haired, and pretty. She said her name was Estrella. I remembered it because it's unusual. Or perhaps not, where she comes from."

Carter jumped on that. "Comes from?"

"Yes, sir. She spoke with a Spanish accent."

XV.

The Foreign Quarter

"Holmes!" I exclaimed, once the maid had been dismissed from the room. "Do you suppose it's coincidence?"

"The phenomenon exists; until its own evidence piles up against it. *Estrella* is the Spanish for 'star.' Can there be three young women of Spanish descent named for 'heaven,' 'glory,' and 'star' in the same case? We may proceed as if the answer is no, until we have gathered all the facts."

Nick Carter exhibited a bemused smile. "Please take pity on a traveller three thousand miles from home. I'm out of my element and three steps behind."

Holmes told him of our experience with the white slave trade, from Mary's crisis through Osbert/Snipe's flight. Sir James interrupted but twice, saying, "Good Lord!" both times. Carter said nothing until after the conclusion of the narrative.

"Yes, I'd say that when we find Estrella, we'll find Gloriana, Celeste, and Paraiso all in one package."

"The police questioned the shop girl, but they were inclined to believe her story," said Sir James. "When they went back for another interview in light of recent events, they were informed she'd resigned. No one there seems to have known where she went or even where she resides."

"She won't be there in any event," Holmes said. "We've learned two things, thanks to Emma: Our Hispanic siren is still in the business, and Jane Chilton has become ensnared in it."

"Three things," I corrected. "If Gloriana is involved, Osbert cannot be far behind."

Carter shook his head. "Guesswork. It's just as possible she's latched on to a new partner, or—"

"—the apprentice has become the master," finished Holmes. "I approve of the way you reason. It's always a mistake to theorise—"

"—ahead of the facts."

I declared myself *hors de combat* from this exchange. I had neither the ammunition nor the high ground.

"What now?" demanded Sir James.

"I could go underground," Carter suggested. "I've read of your talent for disguise, Sherlock, but I'm a fair hand with makeup myself, and I have the advantage of being unknown here. All I need is to appear as one who's come down in the world, and pound the bricks, picking up this and that."

"I don't doubt your abilities, even if all your own published exploits are autobiographical." Holmes smiled. "I have a standing order with an American bookseller for anything written on a criminal subject. However, what you suggest can take weeks, and time is critical. Also, as I said to Watson, the mere thought of crowding another bit of Grand Guignol into this case weighs heavily upon my patience. Have you that letter from San Francisco, Sir James?"

The paper was produced forthwith. "It's her hand. I'll swear to that."

"Did you keep the envelope?"

"The police have that. They were more interested in the postmark than the contents, once read."

"They run true to form. Any accomplice, or just someone who will perform a simple act for money, can take delivery of a parcel in America, remove the contents, and mail them to England. It's far more difficult to reproduce a government seal that would fool even a child."

He produced his pocket lens and, standing by the window to study the letter in the sunlight, spent five minutes examining it. "No penman of my acquaintance did this. You'll pardon me for not taking your word at face value."

"I've an eye for detail, Mr. Holmes. I started my business with a needle and thread."

"I believe you. There's nothing new about forcing a captive to write a letter and address an envelope." He offered the sheet to Carter, who declined with a smile. I disliked him a little less for that demonstration of faith.

Holmes returned the letter. "I suggest we make use of the journals."

"An advertisement?" I brightened. His subterfuges by way of the agony columns had never failed to turn up something useful.

"It's far less expensive than a costume, and reaches more people than walking about London with a sandwich board. What do you think, Carter?"

"I'm all for smoking a raccoon out of the attic."

"What the devil is a raccoon?" I asked.

"A rodent that conducts its raids wearing a mask."

I sat back, vexed by the American penchant for spinning yarns.

Holmes began the creative session by asking how the notice should read.

"In Spanish, for starters," said Carter.

There was, I learned, a newspaper district in our city outside Fleet Street. Two floors of an ancient and crumbling building near Saffron Hill, home of the foreign quarter, sheltered a string of journals belonging to one concern, with a steam-press in the basement that ran day and night, turning out the news of the day in Italian, French, Spanish, German, and several of the Scandinavian dialects, each journal having its own staff fluent in the language of its particular subscribers.

The workers were not paid as well as their colleagues to the west; an easy deduction, based on the variety of odours belonging to packed-in luncheons representing all the nationalities served by the company. Flaking black paint on pebbled glass identified the door belonging to *La Lengua*, the publication that circulated among the Spanish-speaking residents of London.

Before our visit, Holmes and Carter—who, if anything, had more of the language than the polyglot Holmes ("My tutors were my neighbours in old Mexico, Texas, Los Angeles, and Spanish Harlem," he explained)—had bent their heads over their project for an hour. I here translate the text into English:

DESIRED; Spanish-speaking female companion for La
Dona Cristina, twenty-year-old daughter of the Comte
Arturo de el Algarve, grandee, custodian of 10,000
hectares in southern Spain, during her tour of Britain.

Included was the number of a box in the central post office.

"Who is La Dona Cristina?" I'd asked.

"A phantom," said Carter. "Like the count himself. I came across
him in a dime novel."

"The New World's answer to the yellowback," Holmes furnished
before I could enquire. "The name does resound."

"What if Gloriana read the same book?" I challenged.

Carter shook his head. "That brand of literature is in the stalls about
as long as fresh fruit, and once read is thrown in the trash. There's
never a second printing. It's a small risk. We've only to decide how to
handle the response if there is one."

Holmes placed a comradely hand upon the shoulder of the detective from America. "How is your Latin?"

"Rusty, compared to my Spanish," said he, appearing to understand instantly. "Luckily, I never travel without my *Blackstone*."

XVI.

Oliver Nicholas, Esq.

Directly we left the newspaper office, Carter asked Holmes if he had
personal acquaintance with the proprietor of a print shop. "I could
look one up in a directory, but I doubt a stranger could get him to
press fewer than a hundred cards in one lot."

"I know several who are in my debt," said Holmes. "One in particular provides the best engraving, on stock worthy of a representative
of foreign nobility. You know him, Watson."

"I even have a title," said I, "when you let me publish it. 'The Adventure of the Printer's Devil.'"

A four-wheeler deposited us before an address near the Embankment, connected with an investigation whose particulars I have yet to share with the world. The building's location, near the Houses of Parliament and the offices of most of the leading firms of solicitors in the city, gave me an inkling at last of the masquerade that Carter was planning.

Inside, amid the fearsome chattering of Linotype machines and the clunkety-clunk of a platen press, Holmes accepted the hearty handshake of Leopold Szadny, a man of dignified mien whose crisp white hair, full beard, and gold rimmed spectacles might have marked him as a member of the House of Lords but for his ink-smeared leather apron and bizarre paper hat, fashioned by folding a sheet of broadside.

"How good to see you, my friend," said he, in his heavy Hungarian accent. "I have been for some time meaning to bring you a pail of Mrs. Szadny's goulash, the finest this side of Budapest."

"I look forward to it. This isn't a social visit, I'm afraid. You know Dr. Watson. Allow me to present Mr. Nicholas Carter, a newcomer to our shores."

Szadny seized my hand in his powerful typesetter's grip, then turned to Carter, whose own grasp, I could see from the printer's reaction, was formidable despite his slender hand. "New *this* visit," he added. "I've stuffed my belly with *borju rolada* at the Laughing Gypsy more times than I'll count."

The printer fairly squeaked with pleasure. "I celebrate my birthday there every year."

Whereupon the pair conversed for two minutes in what I assumed to be Szadny's native tongue. I began to suspect Carter of possessing supernatural powers.

Holmes broke up the exchange, raising his voice above the din of machinery. "Is there a quiet place we can talk?"

"This I can arrange." Szadny reached inside the bib of his apron, drew out a brass cab-whistle suspended from a ribbon round his neck, and blew an ear-splitting blast. Instantly the press and Linotype went silent. "Tea, gentlemen," said he to his subordinates, then led us through a door into a small office containing an oaken desk and chairs.

When Carter explained what he required, the printer beamed, opened a deep drawer, and hoisted a heavy-looking object onto his blotter. It was identical to the hand-operated press in the shop, down to the treadle, brake lever, platen, table, and flywheel with its gracefully curving spokes, all fashioned from iron; except it was only a fraction of the other's size. It was scarcely larger than a bread tin.

"It was manufactured in Chicago, in the same building as the one outside. The American pedlar carried it round to demonstrate how the machine worked. I persuaded him to include it as part of the purchase."

We watched as he assembled the necessary type and locked it in place. From another drawer he took a flat deal box and showed us the contents. "Swiss linen," he said. "The finest in Europe."

The sheet also in place, he pumped the machine's treadle with his thumb, setting all the parts into whirling, clacking motion. When he'd finished printing, he cut the stiff sheet into ten rectangles, using a guillotine-like device, and passed one over to Carter for inspection. It read:

Oliver Nicholas, Esq.
Solicitor
Villa do Bisto, Spain

XVII.

A Thorn by Any Other Name

"It's a good idea to work my own name into an alias," said Carter, as our cab rolled away from the printer's. "That way there's no suspicious delay when someone I know calls it out unexpectedly."

Holmes said, "That is wisdom. Wherefore Oliver?"

"A tribute to Oliver Wendell Holmes, a famous jurist in my country. I don't suppose he's a relative."

"I've been asked before, but I know rather more about my French roots than any other."

Carter tapped the pocket containing the leather case into which he'd placed all ten cards. "Best to have extras, just in case. Say, that was decent of him not to charge me a cent. What was it you did for him?"

"I prevented him from innocently reproducing a harmless-looking document that would have landed him in Reading Gaol."

"When can I look forward to reading about it, John?"

I winced still at the American's habit of making free with my given name. "That's up to fate. I promised Holmes I wouldn't send it off until ten years after a certain party is deceased."

At Holmes's instruction, we stopped before Claridge's, that magnificent edifice on Brook Street that had brought French splendour to London hotel life nearly a century before.

"I think it best to establish residency immediately, in a place commensurate with the quality of your stationery," Holmes said. "It's dear, I'm afraid. I trust Sir James isn't niggardly when it comes to financing his menials."

"He says I can write my own ticket. Will you send my bags round from Charing Cross station?" He pressed the necessary ransom into Holmes's hand.

"We'll bring them personally. We still have a strategy to map out."

"Even better. There's a trunk and a valise, both crocodile."

"Dear me. You must specialise in well-to-do clients."

"I'm not the snob you think. I shot the rascals myself in the Florida Everglades."

"Everglades," I echoed. "It sounds a placid retreat."

"Does it? I must have you join me sometime for a visit."

On that amiable note we parted. As we made our way to Charing Cross, Holmes lit his pipe. "Interesting fellow; but then, so are most Yankees. He puts me in mind both of the cattle herders of Texas and of that Pinkerton chap, Birdy Edwards."

"He's rather familiar for my taste, but I like him well enough, up to a point."

"Identify the point."

"'How much of what this fellow says he can do can he do,' indeed. I might ask the same of him. It wouldn't surprise me if those bags of his turned out to have been shot in a shop in Philadelphia, with dollars for bullets."

"He's the genuine coin, and no mistake. I may be no hand at stalking ferocious reptiles, but I can sniff out a charlatan with the wind at my back."

At the station we redeemed the trunk and valise, striking in their scaly exteriors, and when we returned to the hotel were directed by the clerk to an upper-storey suite with a balcony overlooking most of Westminster. The linens were impeccable, and the rugs Persian. Holmes inspected the view, then pushed his way back inside through the heavy velvet curtains. "An inspired choice."

"Thanks." Nick Carter had begun to unpack. "Let's hope the lady doesn't insist on taking the air."

I witnessed the transfer of item after item from bags to drawers: a crossbow, a set of tails, several pistols and revolvers, Chinese pyjamas, a knife as big as a hand axe, a collapsible silk hat, a cosh, various cravats, and a twin-barrelled fowling piece no longer than a man's forearm. "Great Scott! Are you going on safari?"

"I was, in a way." He worked his fingers into a brass device that turned his fist into a bludgeon. "Sir James's cable caught up with me in Peru, just as I was set to go down the Amazon. It was blind luck I'd brushed up on both my Spanish and my Portuguese. Fate's a funny old girl." He flexed his fingers, then slid the contraption off his hand. "Cannibals. They say you never see them till they're right on top of you."

"I should keep it within reach," I said, "especially if Osbert is in the picture. He looks meek enough, but my wife is no frail creature, and his arms held her as fast as iron bands."

"So it is with any man who works with his hands." Carter crushed the oval of heavy brass all out of shape in one fist. "I brought along two sets, if you're interested," he said to Holmes.

Smiling grimly, Holmes held out a palm, accepted the mangled weapon, and, using both hands for leverage, prised it back into its former configuration.

Carter whistled, then looked at me. "John?"

I took my revolver from my pocket and showed it to him. "I need my fingers to stitch up cuts and tie bandages."

"It seems we're loaded for all manner of bear," said the American.

Holmes said, "Two talented writers are the best weapons in our arsenal. Should we flush our game, we'll need a description of La Dona Cristina that no white slaver could resist."

"Who needs words?" Carter took a cloth-wrapped parcel from a pocket of the trunk and undid the string.

Holmes and I admired the framed likeness of a comely young woman with black hair and lashes so long they cast shadows on her dusky cheeks. "Christine's uncle was a famous Jewish sculptor. That's where she got her colouring. Wherever I go, she goes with me."

"I see now how you arrived so quickly at a Spanish lady," said Holmes. "Would she not object to being used in such an enterprise?"

"Unfortunately, she's dead. She committed suicide when her uncle objected to her courtship by a Gentile."

I felt a rush of sympathy. "My dear fellow!"

"Water under the bridge. Had we married, I'd never have become a detective. She wanted me to enter the bar."

"That explains the Blackstone." Holmes consulted his watch. "The editor at *La Lengua* promised our advertisement would appear before the afternoon post, which has run by now. Watson, would you do the honours?"

I agreed to go to the post office, although none of us expected results so soon. Holmes and Carter were surprised, then, when I returned bearing an envelope with a City postmark.

Carter examined the envelope. "A woman's hand. I've never known a man who could forge it convincingly." He gave it to Holmes.

"I've known two. One is deceased, the other transported to Australia." After a cursory glance, Holmes slit it open with his clasp knife. He translated the letter aloud:

> Kind sir or madam,
> This letter is in response to your notice seeking a female companion. I am an experienced social secretary conversant in both Spanish and English, and should like to meet with you to discuss an arrangement.
> (signed)
> Celeste Flores

Holmes clucked his tongue. "She's gone back to her earlier alias."

"Perhaps she thinks enough time has passed," I suggested.

"Either that, or she's run out of Spanish synonyms for the firmament," said Carter.

"Well, a thorn by any other name is just as treacherous." Holmes looked at the return address. "The sly thing took a box in the same post office we did. You might even have passed her in the foyer, Watson."

"I passed no woman inside or outside the building."

"Even so, we'll ask Oliver Nicholas to post our reply. Anyone might be expected to walk into so busy a public facility, but criminals are wary by nature, and prone to take flight upon encountering a face connected with an unpleasant memory."

"Any more Spanish and I may have to ask for my fee in pesetas." Nick Carter drew a chair up to the writing desk and dipped a pen.

XVIII.
We Flush Our Game

"Hadn't we better suggest a meeting in the restaurant?" I asked. "She is less likely than most women to agree to an assignation with a strange man in his suite."

"And twice more likely to dodge our net, with only one man to stop her," said Holmes. "There is no place for you and me to conceal ourselves in such an open place."

We were silent for a moment. Then our partner spoke up. "We'll take the bull straight by the horns and invite her to bring a male escort."

"Capital," said Holmes. "We may ensnare her accomplice as well. Dona Cristina, of course, prefers that her representative discuss the delicate negotiations in private."

"We're a fine trio of liars." Carter wrote, placed one of Oliver Nicholas's cards in the envelope, and dashed off to catch the last post.

That night, rather than return to our own respective quarters, Holmes and I made ourselves comfortable in the sitting room. He gallantly offered me the relative comfort of the settee. "Twaddle," said he when I protested. "We shan't have your old wound impeding our success." Whereupon he fashioned himself a bed using two chairs.

In the morning we breakfasted in the suite, then smoked on the balcony to avoid offending our expected guest with the lingering odour of tobacco. We had an excellent view of Hyde Park, with its strollers in light summer clothes carrying parasols and swinging sticks, and Carter regaled us with comparisons to the Central Park in New York City, where he'd once "nabbed a mug," in his colourful parlance.

A knock came to the door just as the mantel clock struck the hour suggested for the meeting. Carter slipped a Norfolk jacket on over his waistcoat and went inside to answer it, carefully closing the curtains behind him and concealing us both. He had no weapons concealed on his person, lest a suspicious bulge tell the tale. Holmes and I took turns peeping through a crack between the curtains as our drama unfolded.

The housemaid I had known as Gloriana bore small resemblance to the glamorous creature who stepped in from the corridor, wearing an emerald-green frock becoming to her slender waist and a fashionable hat with a short black veil pinned to it. Under normal circumstances, I might not have recognised her had we passed on the street. Carter, visibly impressed, held the door for her as she entered, followed closely by a man whose face I would have known anywhere.

"Holmes!" I whispered hoarsely.

Gloriana/Celeste's escort wore the clothing of a boulevardier: grey bowler, patterned jacket and waistcoat, elk's-tooth fob, grey flannels and all, gripping a bamboo cane; but these things could not dissemble his true identity. Holmes and I had met him as Osbert, the ice-cream parlour proprietor. My Mary had known him as the loathsome cab-man Snipe.

XIX.

Lady Judas

He had, to a degree, taken other steps to alter his appearance. A monocle clung to one eye, its ribbon attached to a lapel, he'd dyed his fair hair dark brown, and a mole I had not noticed before drew one's attention away from the rest of his features towards his left cheek. The unnatural ruddiness which Holmes had attributed to an allergic reaction to greasepaint (encountered in his role as Snipe) was absent, but I had no doubt as to his identity. In his present role he looked like a cross between a circus barker and a racetrack tout; and, as the three made small talk, it developed that he had adopted the pose of Celeste's somewhat inglorious uncle. Hinkel was the name he gave.

In preparation, we had ordered an extra pot of tea with our breakfast and two additional cups and saucers. "Mr. Nicholas" bade them sit and poured for all.

"I'd hoped La Dona Cristina would be present," said "Hinkel," in a tone of mild disappointment.

"I wanted to conduct the interview myself and report," Carter replied. "Her most recent travelling companion proved to be unsuitable, a fact that cast a shadow on her judgment."

"You are American, are you not?" Celeste's accent was more pronounced than when I'd known her as Gloriana.

"I am, miss. I studied law in Philadelphia and finished at Oxford." This was the story he and Holmes had collaborated upon to explain Carter's unorthodox British inflection.

"What sort is the lady?" asked the man who called himself Hinkel.

"The very best. She attended the finest finishing school in Barcelona at a young age. She's learning English, and plays the harp like an angel." Carter's smile was disarming. "She almost hired Miss Flores sight unseen when she found out she spoke the language. Any objection to adding 'tutor' to your other responsibilities?"

"I should be glad to assist in her education."

"Let's not put the cart before the horse," said her escort. "I should like to visit my niece from time to time, and I don't mind telling you I'd rather spend the day with two good-looking women. There's a deal of humpbacks and warts among these inbred continental nobles." The leer he wore during this confession seemed worthy of Snipe. *O, what a studied villain is this*, thought I.

Carter affected not to disapprove. "I can settle your worries on that score." From an inside breast pocket he drew the photograph of the late lamented Christine, removed from its frame.

It was my turn at watch. A spark of naked greed flew from "Celeste's" face to Osbert's as the picture passed between them.

Osbert returned it. "Well, sir, I'm satisfied. One doesn't want one's prize foal trotting about with a donkey."

I couldn't decide whom I despised more, this crude Herod or his Lady Judas, who betrayed members of her own gender to her foul profession.

My impatience was growing. I wanted to lay hands on them both, and let the devil take the hindmost as to my position regarding the fair sex. But as Carter took command of the conversation, drawing one genteel lie after another from Celeste about her background and education, I realised that he and Holmes had charted out this very course, to lull our "victims" into laying aside their highly developed sense of suspicion.

Although I had missed this particular conference, I recalled with clarity the signal they had worked out to draw Holmes and me from hiding. Carter had surreptitiously locked the door to the outside corridor after letting them in. The only other exit was by way of the balcony, four storeys above the street, and we would stand before it.

". . . La Dona is quite keen to visit Jersey," said Carter.

Directly he said "Jersey," Holmes and I jerked open the curtains and stepped out between them, revolvers in hand.

XX.

Flight

We had misjudged our foes' reflexes. Recognising us instantly, Celeste Flores pounced, pantherlike, from her seat, ignoring my weapon, and sank her teeth deep into my wrist. In the same instant, Osbert launched himself, rugby fashion, into Nick Carter where he sat, carrying man and chair over backwards onto the floor with a smash. Momentum built, the white slaver charged at Holmes, swinging his cane and striking his gun hand. The revolver fell to the floor.

I had only the barest sense of these actions. In my pain and rage, I struck Celeste a smart blow on the top of her head with my revolver; but her hat, a thing of wire and stiff felt, absorbed most of it, though the impact forced her to release my wrist from her jaws and drove her to her knees.

Osbert neither slowed nor stopped. Shouldering Holmes aside in the same movement with the swinging of the cane, he raced across the balcony, leapt onto the railing, and dropped from sight.

Holmes and I darted to the railing. Down on the street, a buzzing crowd had begun to form round a broken thing lying on the cobblestones like a shattered doll.

We have spent many an hour reliving that moment: Whether the villain intended suicide or hoped to attain the neighbouring rooftop—a good twenty feet away—remains a point of contention. As a practising Christian, I lean towards the former motive, in expiation for Osbert's sins in this life by way of damnation in the next.

Such was not an issue upon the instant. We spun to assist Carter; but were too late.

When Celeste fell to her knees, Holmes's fallen revolver was within her reach. Now she stood with her back to the door to the corridor, closing us all inside firing range.

I retained my weapon, but it was at my side. As I raised it, she fired a shot that screamed past my head.

"Let go of it!" she shrieked. "*Gauchos* taught me to shoot straight!"

My finger tightened on the trigger.

Holmes grasped my wrist, paralysing the tendon. "No, Watson! You may strike an artery, and then we shall never know what became of Jane Chilton."

For a full ten seconds I retained my pressure upon the trigger. Finally I nodded, an almost infinitesimal movement of my head. He released his grip. I let the weapon fall.

Celeste Flores laughed shrilly, a peal of pure madness. It choked off when she reached behind her and discovered the door was locked. She motioned toward Carter. "The key! Throw it!"

The canny American detective took the key from his waistcoat and threw it low; but Lady Judas had the instincts of a cat. She dipped a knee, caught it with her free hand, and fumbled it into the keyhole awkwardly. At length the tumblers turned.

"*Puercos!*" she spat. "It would have made no difference if you killed me. You may find me eventually, but not in time. The Chilton wench will be dead in an hour!"

We stood, arms away from our sides, and watched her open the door behind her and step one foot backwards into the corridor.

Abruptly, something in the shape of a grappling hook closed round the wrist of her gun arm and jerked it downwards. A bullet pierced the Persian rug at her feet and buried itself in the floor.

Carter stooped swiftly, grasped the rug, and jerked it from under her, throwing her onto her back. Her revolver went flying, to be caught by Carter one-handed. Only when we both had her pinned down in our crossfire did I feel it safe to regard our rescuer. Mary

Watson stood in the doorway, resting the crook of her parasol at shoulder arms.

XXI.

A Race with Death

"However did you find us?" I asked her.

We had been joined by a constable, there to enquire after Osbert's fatal leap and the subsequent gunfire. Upon confirming our identities and hearing Holmes's rapid explanation, he had manacled Celeste Flores to the arm of a chair, where she sat seething between Holmes and Carter, both men now armed; the American with his blunt, wicked-looking fowling piece. Having underestimated her once, they were leaving nothing to chance.

"I won't be put off by secrecy," my wife replied. "I went round to Baker Street and spoke to Mrs. Hudson. She is a woman, and we are bound by our gender. She told me you were here. The clerk at the desk gave me the number of the suite. I heard the first shot from the stairwell, but reached the door only as Gloriana was backing out."

"Intuition." Holmes shook his head. "It is the X factor in every equation where a woman is involved. No man has cracked it as yet."

"Call it what you will. When I recognised her voice, I knew what was to be done."

Our captive sent her a look of raw hatred. She spat a torrent of Spanish too rapid for even Holmes and Carter to follow. They looked at each other and shrugged.

"Best not to know," said the American. "Well, Miss Celeste-Gloriana-Paraiso-Estrella, what's this business about Jane Chilton having only an hour to live?"

The rage that had distended her features gave way to a smile of palpable evil.

"She will die gasping. Her last prayer will be for air, and you will be impotent to grant it."

We pressed her for details, but she had fallen silent, and would not be drawn out by threats or pleas to her humanity or promises to speak to the magistrate upon her behalf. When it was clear to us all that we were wasting precious time, Holmes asked the constable to take her away. In seconds she was manacled to his wrist, instructed as to her rights under English law, and removed from our sight; but not before she turned her head at the door and closed her free hand round her throat in the unmistakable gesture of strangulation.

"My God!" said I, in a shuddering whisper. "Can it be she shares the same gender with the Blessed Virgin?"

Mary, the Blessed Virgin's namesake, was less naive. "Let us not forget Jezebel."

"What do you make of it?" rapped Holmes.

"It seems clear to me," I said. "Another accomplice has her in a sort of noose, with instructions to choke her to death if she and Osbert fail to return in the time allotted."

Mary's hand stole to her throat.

Carter spoke up. "I can't agree. I've witnessed hangings. There's not much gasping at the end of a rope—no room in the trachea for it—just a desperate struggle followed by insensibility, and certainly no time for prayer."

"Suffocation, then," said Holmes.

"I'd bet a fiver on it."

"What monsters!" I exclaimed. "They've buried her alive."

Carter shook his head. "If she's got an hour of oxygen—on top of the time these mugs spent with us, not counting coming and going—the burial vault would be the size of this room. Criminals are lazy, by and large, or they'd work for their living. I've never met one who'd invest the time and labour digging a hole that size."

Mary said, "If they came here by cab, the driver would know where he picked them up. Scotland Yard—"

"—is methodical, beyond doubt," finished Holmes. "They might even locate the man by tomorrow morning."

He and Carter exchanged a glance heavy with meaning. Both men nodded. They went for their hats.

"Come, Watsons," Holmes barked. "There isn't time to lose."

"Where are we going?" I asked.

"Did you not hear what I just said?"

"Watsons?" Mary lifted her brows. "I am to accompany you?"

Carter traded the cumbersome shotgun for a revolver that fit his small sinewy hand. His smile glittered. "Well, sure. We need as many weapons as we can muster."

He indicated the parasol she was still holding.

We took the Underground. As noon approached, the streets were clogged with hansoms, growlers, dray-wagons, and pedestrians, and at such times the relative discomfort of the subterranean railway is worth twice its price in terms of speed.

The detectives' expressions were tense. Holmes said, "We mustn't place too much faith in *Señorita* Flores's assessment. The experts themselves seldom agree on matters involving the human lung and cubic feet of air. Not everyone breathes at the same pace."

"Or at his own, under pressure," said Carter. "You don't draw it mild when you're shut up in a box."

Mary's hand gripped mine tightly enough to stop circulation.

The train stopped with maddening regularity, jettisoning and acquiring passengers at station after station. I felt almost like a victim of abduction myself, not knowing our destination and wondering if each name called out by the conductor was our terminus. I expected the detectives to spring to their feet every time we slowed to a halt; but they kept their seats, perched on the edges like cats poised to pounce. Observing their pale, drawn faces, I deemed it inadvisable to ask.

When at last they shot upright, Mary and I exchanged a glance. Instinctively, we knew from the announcement where we were headed.

Holmes and Carter sprinted ahead down the street. We struggled to keep them in sight, Mary on my arm. If we were mistaken, we might have been left inexorably behind, so intent were the detectives upon their race with death.

We did, as a matter of fact, misplace them at one corner, but caught up with them where we'd expected to, before the shuttered ice-cream parlour formerly owned by the late Osbert. But my heart sank when we drew within sight of the front door. The padlock placed upon it by the police was still intact.

Holmes, however, did not hesitate. He grasped the lock and rattled it fiercely, releasing a thin shower of pewter-colored dust: The hasp had been sawn through and plaster and paint applied to make it appear that it still held fast.

"They took no chances," rapped Carter. "Any passerby might have wandered in out of curiosity and freed their hostage."

They swung open the door and bolted inside, Mary and I close behind. The store was empty, stripped of its fixtures and furniture, and we were alone in it. But Holmes and Carter went directly to a door at the back, adjacent to the storage room entrance and built of what appeared to be double-reinforced oak, painted so thoroughly in shining white enamel that no space showed between the planks. Oddly, it had a homely familiarity I could not quite place.

Holmes ran his fingers along one edge. "A rubber gasket. It's the cold room, where the ice cream was stored."

I knew then what the door had struck in my memory. It resembled the hatch of an icebox. The realisation nearly stopped my heart. If cold could not escape, oxygen could not enter. The room beyond was Lady Jane Chilton's death-cell.

It, too, was padlocked, this time securely. Holmes clawed from a pocket the small leather case he was never without, containing an assortment of picks and skeleton keys for any occasion.

Carter, less patient, seized a great chunk of hickory that had been leaning against the wall, evidently intended to prop the door open when someone was inside, and swung it with all his might, striking the lock with such force the door jumped in its gasket. Once, twice it banged against the lock. Then Carter planted his feet apart solidly, brought the piece of timber back as far over his right shoulder as he could, took a deep breath, and swung with biblical force, his muscles splitting his Norfolk wide from collar to hem. The lock shattered.

I nearly cheered; but what would we find inside, a lady or a corpse?

XXII.

We Retire the Spoon

"Watson! Quick!"

Holmes's tone left no room for dispute, even had I wanted to offer any. As Mary and I hurried inside, he and Carter were already bent over something in a far corner of the tiny room, blocking our view of anything but the empty shelves on the walls.

I crossed the floor in a stride, parting the pair roughly, and knelt beside the woman who lay at their feet, a young, slender creature with her strawberry curls in disarray and her fashionable dress soiled for want of a change. Her eyes were closed and she appeared not to be breathing.

I was prepared for the worst—I carried no instruments or restoratives—but as I placed my hand behind her head to lift it and raised my other hand in an attempt to slap colour into her pale cheeks, she arched her back suddenly, took air into her lungs, and expelled it in a fit of bitter coughing. Immediately I lifted her into a sitting position and forced her head between her knees. She coughed and gasped for two minutes at least, then her breathing settled into a rhythm, rapid but regular. I helped her sit up in the normal fashion. Her blue eyes darted from one face to another, like a frightened bird's.

"Calm yourself," I said gently. "I am a doctor. You're among friends. You're safe from the villains who mistreated you. Can you tell me your name?" I was still unsure whether her respiratory ordeal had affected the function of her brain.

"My name is"—she hesitated, then—"Jane. Jane Chilton. My father is Sir James Chilton, of Middlesex."

I sighed in relief, noticing only then that I'd been holding my own breath. I looked up at the others and smiled.

"Who—who are you?" asked the lady.

"Friends," Holmes said. "There is time enough to get acquainted later. For now, I'm sure Dr. Watson will want to admit you to hospital to make certain of your health before your father comes to take you home."

"Home!" she said, with a lovely inflection that warms my heart still.

The coda to our adventure was a happy one for Lady Jane Chilton. Six months after her complete recovery and safe return to her father's arms, her betrothal to Lord Wadsworth, the popular and eligible heir to a fortune equal to Sir James's, was announced. By all accounts, the handsome young peer was delighted with his choice, of whom Her Majesty had approved when she was presented at court.

At this writing, "Celeste Flores" is a bone of contention between Great Britain and her native Argentina. The Crown wishes to try her for complicity in the abduction of seven young women since rescued from bondage, whilst the government in Buenos Aires is eager to reunite her with her old burglary ring behind bars. During this contretemps it came out, interestingly enough, that she was born in a tiny fishing village under the distinctly earthbound name of Inez Sobraco. Holmes informed me that the surname is the Spanish for "armpit."

Scotland Yard—prodded by the newspapers and popular outrage—pledged to apply all due pressure to eradicate the pernicious white slave trade in England, and the Home Secretary declared to do the same in all its possessions. The Foreign Secretary demanded cooperation from those countries that depended upon the goodwill of Great Britain. The Russian Czar and the King of Egypt promised their cooperation. Not to be outdone, the American President vouchsafed to put his Attorney General upon the case, making special mention of Sherlock Holmes in an address to the public.

"He's a politician, after all," said Holmes, when I congratulated him. "Thanks to you and Carter, I'm fodder for his re-election."

Notwithstanding this disclaimer, the flesh pedlars are now reported to be in full rout across the globe, peaching upon their fellows in order to save their own necks from the gallows. Some of the names mentioned in connection with the foul trade locally have rocked the Empire to its foundation; but that foundation is built upon solid rock, and will survive because of its conviction to human decency.

Sherlock Holmes's last conversation with Nick Carter, whilst awaiting the latter's boat train to Southampton, centred, of all things, upon a spoon. Holmes thought it worthy of inclusion in his personal Black Museum of grotesque mementos, whilst Carter made an earnest case in favour of remanding it to the Pinkerton Detective Agency for its edification in persecuting the white slave trade in America. They agreed to break the impasse by appealing to my own judgement in the matter.

"I know you for a just man by your deed as well as your word," Carter said, "and I'm confident you won't be swayed by your friendship with Sherlock."

Holmes, who had come to terms more than I with the American's free use of Christian names, smiled sardonically. "Neither will he be moved by flattery. Well, Watson?" He handed me the utensil, as a bailiff would deliver an item of evidence to a magistrate.

I put the spoon in my pocket, surprising them both.

"I declare Mary Watson to be the rightful owner," said I. "She can throw it in with the everyday silver until it becomes nothing more sinister than an instrument for dining."

THE END